LOST IN LOCKDOWN

(MAY MOURNING)

The 2nd in the Kenny Hughes
Memorial Trilogy

JUDY FORD

Bernie Fazakerley Publications

COPYRIGHT

Lost in Lockdown

(May Mourning)

The 2nd in the Kenny Hughes Memorial Trilogy

Published by Bernie Fazakerley Publications

Copyright © 2021 Judy Ford.

ISBN: 978-1-911083-74-0

DEDICATION

Dedicated to

Care for the Family

Care for the Family is a national charity which aims to
promote strong family life and to help those who face
family difficulties.

CONTENTS

MAP OF OXFORD

© Openstreetmap Contributors. This map was produced using data available under the Open Database License.

1. OUT ON BAIL

'As the number of coronavirus cases in prisons increases, the Ministry of Justice has taken further steps to reduce overcrowding. Last night they confirmed that this included the release on bail of Shane Butler, the man accused of murdering PC Kenneth Hughes in Oxfordshire shortly before Christmas.'

Gavin froze in the act of buttering his second slice of toast. He stared at the teddy bear in police uniform that sat on top of the radio, listening as the news headlines continued, but there were no details. What bail conditions had been imposed? What about Butler's brother and his other accomplices? The bulletin ended and Zoe Ball's familiar voice introduced the next record. The music washed over him as he turned over this unexpected news in his mind.

'Gav!' His contemplation was interrupted by his wife, Chrissie, calling down the stairs. 'Can you get that?'

With a jolt, Gavin realised that the landline telephone was ringing. He stumbled out into the hall to answer it. It was only as he fumbled to pick up the handset that he realised he was still holding the toast in one hand and the knife in the other. He put them both down on the small shelf beneath the telephone and picked up the receiver, smearing it with butter in the process.

'Yes?'

'Mr Hughes? This is Arabella McInnis from Binns Barnard Solicitors?'

'Yes?' Gavin repeated, struggling to get his sluggish brain into gear. The name was familiar, as was the tendency to make almost every sentence sound like a question, but ... 'Oh yes! Of course! I'm sorry, I was miles away.'

'I'm sorry to ring you so early,' his solicitor went on, 'but I was hoping to speak to you before the news broke? I'm sorry to have to tell you that your son's killers are being released on bail.'

'I just heard,' Gavin told her. 'It was on the radio just now.'

'That's what I was afraid of.' Ms McInnis sounded apologetic. 'They only notified me last night. I thought I could leave it until this morning and then, when I got up, there it was on the Breakfast show! So I was trying to ring you before you heard it too.'

'So they're all out?'

'Yes, I'm afraid so.' She paused briefly, then, 'but the court didn't have much choice really. It's all to do with the rules about how long defendants can be kept in custody before being brought to trial. It's looking as if it could be months before jury trials will be back to normal, and then there'll be a big backlog to get through. This is just a sort of insurance, in case ...'

'So not just trying to get people out of jail because of coronavirus?'

'No. That may have been another factor, but basically it's better this way. As a police officer yourself, I imagine you know that if the custody time limit expires while a defendant is remanded in custody then they're entitled to be released without any bail conditions. This way, the court is able to impose conditions on their release.'

'And what *are* the conditions?' Gavin asked anxiously.

'I don't know yet, I'm afraid. I'm going to try to find out about that today. That's something else I wanted to talk to you about. Is there anything in particular you'd like me to ask for? Restrictions on their movements, for example?'

'I'd just like to be sure Chrissie won't bump into any of them in the street. Where will they be living?'

'I don't know. Of course, for the time being nobody's supposed to be bumping into anyone in the street, but I get what you mean. I'll see if I can get a court order keeping them away from your neighbourhood. Anything else?'

'No. I don't think so.'

'OK. I'm sorry about how it's turned out. If it hadn't been for this coronavirus business, the trial would have been over by now and they'd have all been convicted, but we are where we are. I just thought you ought to know. I'll send you over a letter with all the details, and if anything changes I'll be in touch again.'

'Yes. OK. Thanks.' Gavin replaced the telephone receiver and stood silently staring at the wall, trying to work out how he felt about the news. Then he turned and headed upstairs to tell Chrissie.

He found her on the landing with Craig, their lodger, walking admiringly round him and brushing invisible flecks of dandruff from his collar.

'Craig looks very smart in Kenny's suit, doesn't he?' she greeted her husband without looking round. 'And I like his hair better the way it's grown since Lockdown. I've been telling him: he'll knock them all dead at the interview.' Then, turning round, she saw Gavin's anxious expression. 'What is it? Was that phone call bad news?'

'I'm not sure. It was the solicitor. She says they've let the Butler brothers out on bail while the crown courts are closed because of COVID.'

'That's ridiculous!' Craig exploded. 'The bastard confessed for fu-.' He stopped abruptly and looked guiltily towards Chrissie, 'for goodness sake! I thought murderers were supposed to get life!'

'He's admitted to being responsible for Kenny's death, but he's claiming it was an accident,' Gavin reminded him. 'There has to be a trial – unless the prosecution decides to accept his plea and not even *try* for murder. He'll be hoping to get away with manslaughter or even death by dangerous driving. And there are the other two as well. They helped to cover it up and …,' his voice trailed off as another thought struck him.

'What's that got to do with it?' Craig remained unconvinced. 'He killed a policeman. He admitted it. So he ought to be in jail. It's a simple as that!'

He pulled away from Chrissie's ministrations and clumped noisily downstairs. Chrissie looked enquiringly up at Gavin.

'I was just thinking,' he muttered. 'What about the Whittles? Someone ought to tell them too.'

'I could ring Yvonne,' Chrissie offered. 'I'd be glad of an excuse. We haven't had a chance to talk since Lockdown started.'

'Maybe later,' Gavin shook his head. 'I'll call in later this morning and tell them face to face.'

'Yes. I suppose you're right. It isn't the sort of thing you want to hear over the phone.' Chrissie started downstairs. 'Come on! We'd better get on with breakfast or Stella'll be here before you've finished.'

The music coming from the radio was a cheerful song aimed at helping listeners to beat the Lockdown blues. Craig clicked it off irritably before sitting down and pouring himself a cup of tea from the stainless steel teapot in the middle of the table. He sat staring into it, contemplating the day ahead. He wished that he had never mentioned to Gavin and Chrissie that the warehouse in which he had been working for the last six weeks was looking for a new supervisor. He wished that he hadn't listened to Chrissie when she had urged him to apply. He wished that he had not been selected for interview. And he wished above all that Chrissie had not insisted on lending him this suit belonging to her dead son.

He was grateful to them for taking him in off the streets – really grateful – but sometimes he wished … Gavin always said they owed him, because he'd helped to find the guys who'd killed Kenny, but … He hadn't done anything really, and now he had this big burden of gratitude. He had to make something of himself to show them they'd made a difference. And Chrissie was convinced that he'd get the job. She'd be so disappointed when …

'Toast, Chrissie? – Craig?'

He looked up to see Gavin holding out two slices of fresh toast. He shook his head. 'I'm not hungry. I'll just finish this tea and then I'd better get off.'

'Nonsense!' Chrissie took both pieces of toast and put them on separate plates. Then she set one of the plates down in front of Craig and pushed the butter dish towards him. 'You can't go to an important interview on an empty stomach. It's been scientifically proven that the brain functions better all day if you start off with a good breakfast. That's why we run a breakfast club at school. The kids can't settle to learn if they're not well-fed.'

Craig bit back his reflex retort: that he was not a child at her school; that he was used to marching for days on army rations or even, when required to do so, on what he could forage for himself; that if she'd seen the children he'd come across in Basra she wouldn't be worrying about kids coming to school without having had a bowl of cereal and a round of toast! Chrissie could be incredibly patronising at times, but she meant well, and the last thing he wanted was to upset her after the news she'd just had.

How could it have happened? How could a man like Shane Butler have been allowed out on bail? A man who admitted to having run down a police officer, smashed his body against a brick wall, and then driven off with no thought for the devastation he had wrought! How was it justice that he was going to be sent home to the bosom of his family, with no sign that he was going to be tried for his crimes any time soon?

He jabbed his knife into the butter, imagining that it was a bayonet and he was stabbing it into Butler's stomach, as he had learned to do during his army training. In his mind, he could hear the frenzied shouts of his fellow-recruits as they ran at a line of targets with their weapons gripped in trembling hands, fearful of being found wanting in the ability, or the desire, to kill. Butler had better keep away from Gavin and Chrissie or he'd have Craig to answer to! And unlike Butler, he'd been trained to slaughter his enemies – and not from the comfort of the driving seat of a powerful car but hand-to-hand. Compared to the Iraqi soldiers that he'd encountered during the Gulf War or the Taliban fighters that he'd faced on his tour of duty in Afghanistan, Butler would be easy prey.

He watched Gavin pouring a second cup of tea for himself and then topping up the teapot with water from the kettle. The big policeman seemed calm enough, but something about the way in which he kept glancing towards his wife suggested that the news from the solicitor had been unsettling even for his placid nature. His hands shook slightly as he brought a pan of porridge over from the hob and poured it into his bowl.

Chrissie waited while he wandered over to the sink, filled the pan with cold water and left it there to soak. Then, when he returned to the table, she handed him the milk jug and he poured some into the bowl so that the porridge became an island in a small white lake. Refusing her offer of the sugar bowl, he went over to one of the wall cupboards and took out a tin of syrup. Now, Craig knew that he was rattled: as Chrissie had explained on a previous occasion, syrup was what Gavin's mother had put on his porridge when we was a child, and it was what he reverted to in times of stress.

Craig bit viciously into his toast, tearing off mouthful after mouthful as he discovered that he was hungry after all. Chrissie smiled across the table at him and pushed a cereal bowl in his direction. 'Is it cornflakes or Weetabix today? Or how about living dangerously and trying some of my sugar-free muesli?'

Craig poured a helping of cornflakes into his bowl, patted them down with his spoon and added milk from the jug, which Chrissie placed near his right hand.

'Don't worry about the interview. You're bound to be nervous, but all the other candidates will be too. Just don't let it get to you.'

'I'll try,' Craig promised through a mouthful of cereal, 'but I'm really not sure I'm the sort of person they're looking for. I don't have the experience.'

'You were a corporal, weren't you?' Chrissie argued. 'You had men under you. You've been a leader. And you've performed under pressure. Tell them about that.'

'It's not the same!'

'No, but there are parallels. How many of the other candidates will have had to make split-second decisions while they were under fire?'

'How many of them throw themselves to the floor every time someone drops a crate in the next aisle?' muttered Craig, remembering an incident from a few days earlier. 'The guys all think I'm a nutter. How would I ever have any authority if they *did* make me supervisor?'

'It's just a matter of believing in yourself. You tell him, Gav: so long as you don't let them know how terrified you are inside, people will respect you.'

'That's right,' Gavin agreed dutifully. 'I remember the first day I went out on foot patrol on my own. I wasn't even turned twenty then and I felt everyone was staring at me and wondering what a kid like me was doing all dressed up in a police uniform; but then a tourist stopped me to ask the way, and I got a call to sort out a couple of youngsters who'd been sniffing glue round the back of some flats and I discovered that the uniform made them all believe in me even though I didn't!'

'That's right,' Chrissie agreed. 'It was the same when I started teaching. The kids used to run rings round me while I was a student, but after I qualified and I stood up in front of *my class* on my first day in my real job, they all accepted that I was in charge.'

'I suppose so.' Craig tried to force some sincerity into his voice while remaining unconvinced. If he did get the supervisor's job – which of course he wouldn't – he would be in charge of men that he'd been working alongside for the last six weeks, most of whom had been there a lot longer than he had. They'd seen him mess up orders; they'd watched him struggling to understand the system; and worst of all, they'd seen how jumpy he was whenever there was a loud noise or a sudden movement. There was no way they'd knuckle down under his authority. And why should they? He wasn't leadership material. If he had been, four men would be alive now instead of having been blown apart by an IED[1].

He finished his cereal and gulped down his tea. Looking down at his watch and pretending to be surprised at the time that it showed him, he got to his feet.

'I'd better get off: it won't make a good impression if I'm late.'

'Just stand still for a moment and let me give you a final once over,' Chrissie insisted, standing up and walking round him. She flicked a few toast crumbs from his jacket and straightened his tie before standing back and declaring him "ready for anything".

Craig headed for freedom. As he reached the door, he turned and gave a brief nod in Chrissie's direction, then he raised his hand towards Gavin in a semi-salute before escaping into the back garden. He walked briskly over to the

---

[1] Improvised Explosive Device: a "homemade" bomb, typically used by terrorist groups or non-government fighting forces.

garage and got out his bike – or rather Kenny's bike: Chrissie had pressed him into accepting it when he landed the warehouse job and needed transport to get into work.

He put on his helmet – Chrissie had insisted on buying one for him – and pushed the bicycle down the side of the house and out on to the drive. Just as he reached the front gate, another cyclist drew up in the road outside. He recognised the slim figure, dark-skinned face and short, tight curls of trainee police constable Stella Gilbert.

'Hi Craig,' she greeted him. 'You're looking extra smart this morning. I can see my face in those shoes of yours!'

'You mean the old spit and polish?' Craig smiled. 'That's one thing that never leaves you after you've been in the forces.'

'Going somewhere special?'

'A job interview. Chrissie persuaded me to put in for the new supervisor job.'

'Good luck – although I'm sure you won't need it!'

'Thanks. Well, I suppose I'd better be off – don't want to be late!'

He stepped forward and was about to push his bike out into the road when a car sped round the corner and nearly clipped the front wheel. Craig stopped dead and stared in amazement as it hurtled on down the road and round another bend. There was a gasp and a clattering sound from behind him. He stood for several seconds gazing after the vehicle, silently cursing himself for not having caught its number.

Then he turned round and saw Stella cowering down against the low wall that separated the front garden from the pavement. Her bicycle lay beside her. He looked down at her and she looked up at him. He wondered whether he ought to say something. Should he tell her that he recognised the rush of adrenaline, the pounding heart, the sticky palms and racing brain? Should he tell her that he understood about flashbacks that set you reeling physically and mentally? Should he tell her …? But no, what good could he do by sharing the fact that four years on, he could still be spooked by a sudden noise or kept awake by recurring thoughts that refused to be suppressed?

Stella looked up at him with the embarrassed smile and nervous laugh that he understood so well. 'My! That was fast! It gave me quite a shock.'

'Yes,' Craig agreed. 'He should lose his licence, going at that speed in a residential area.'

He did not tell her that he knew what she had seen just then, and that it was not a silver Skoda speeding recklessly along a quiet backstreet, but a red BMW heading straight towards her with murderous intent and deadly consequences.

'Fine police officer *I'm* going to make,' Stella went on with another little laugh. 'I didn't even get his number!'

'Neither did I – and I was standing right here watching him go.' Craig bent down and picked up Stella's bike with his left hand while still holding his own machine in his right.

Stella scrambled to her feet and took it from him. 'Thanks.'

Craig nodded. 'Well, I'd better get off. Gavin won't be long. He's just finishing his breakfast.'

Stella stood on the pavement holding her bicycle and watching Craig's muscular figure as it disappeared round the corner. She concentrated hard on breathing: *deep, slow breaths in and out* the counsellor had said, and *look round and ground yourself in your present surroundings*. She looked down at her hands, gripped tightly round the handlebars, and forced herself to relax the muscles so that the nails of her forefingers were no longer digging into the base of her thumbs. Her heart was slowing down now and no longer felt as if it was hammering against the side of her chest.

She walked slowly up the drive, still breathing deeply and concentrating on taking in her surroundings, here and now. The herbaceous border that separated the drive from the small front lawn was bright with many different colours of aquilegia: deep maroony-red, purple that was almost blue, creamy white, and soft pink. What was it her grandmother called them? Granny bonnets – that's right! An early-rising bumble bee pushed its way into one of the flowers; there would be plenty more of those as the day grew warmer. It looked as if it was going to be another scorcher.

'Put your bike in the garage,' Gavin greeted her as she approached the kitchen door. 'We'll do a walk-round of the roads near here this morning. There've been a few reports of teenagers congregating on street corners: we'll do a bit of engaging, explaining, -'

'- educating and enforcing,' Stella finished for him. This was the mantra that they had been taught as the correct way of dealing with anyone who appeared to be in contravention of *The Health Protection (Coronavirus, Restrictions) (England) Regulations 2020*.

'And there's a family I could do with calling in on, just round the corner,' Gavin added. 'I'll tell you about it as we go.'

In many ways, the new world of Lockdown suited Gavin's style of policing. Walking a familiar beat in the fresh air, providing the reassuring sight of the familiar uniform to law-abiding residents fearful of antisocial behaviour, was much more to his liking than being stuck in the confines of a stuffy patrol car, unapproachable and largely ignored. Let others race through traffic, siren blaring to be first on the scene at the report of a crime, Gavin was more concerned with building a rapport with those members of the public who might be tempted to stray across the line from legality to lawlessness through disaffection, discontent or even boredom.

For many years, single-crewing of police patrol cars had been a cause of discontent among officers; now the idea of spending a 10-hour shift in the confines of a small vehicle with a colleague who might perhaps be an asymptomatic carrier of COVID-19 made lone-working suddenly a more attractive proposition. There had been no difficulty in allocating all the available patrol cars to officers for whom the risk of approaching violent criminals with nobody to watch their back now felt less serious than the chances of contracting the disease by too much close-contact. Gavin's sergeant had been only too pleased that Gavin was content to continue his mentoring of probationer PC Gilbert on foot or bicycle, and he was happy to leave the exact location of his activity very much to his discretion. Gavin's arrest-rate was always well below average, but Sergeant Appleton had a sneaking conviction that this was at least in part because of his skill in diverting potential offenders away from crime (even if that did sometimes involve ignoring minor misdemeanours). And young Stella Gilbert could do with more time to settle to her work following that horrendous experience back in December. A few months with the staid and steady Gavin would give her time to recover from her trauma and to see that there was more to policing than violence and danger.

Gavin neither knew nor cared about his sergeant's assessment of his character; he was more concerned with bringing Stella up to speed with the latest developments regarding the man whom she had witnessed smashing her previous mentor's body against a brick wall.

'Shane Butler was on the news this morning,' he began cautiously as they set off down the road, maintaining some distance between them and avoiding turning towards one another to speak. 'Did you hear it?'

'No? What's he done now?'

'His lawyers have got him out on bail: him and the other two.'

'But why?' Stella's heart began to beat faster and she forced herself to breathe slowly and deliberately.

'According to our solicitor, it's because of the trial being delayed. There are rules about how long someone can be held on remand.'

'But a murderer? And he admitted he'd done it.'

'But the law says he has to have a chance to prove he didn't intend to kill anyone,' Gavin explained patiently, trying to convince himself as much as Stella that this did not represent a serious failure of the justice system. 'You wouldn't want an innocent person to be kept in jail for years just because there wasn't a slot in court for their trial, would you?'

'No-o … but he's bound to be found guilty of at least manslaughter, so why can't he be kept in prison because of that?'

'I suppose he hasn't been sentenced, so nobody knows how long that ought to be. He might have mitigation that he'll ask to have taken into account. And apparently it's part of this drive to get prisoners out of jail to stop the virus spreading there. Anyway, that's what the court has decided so we just have to live with it.'

'I guess so.' Stella did not sound convinced. 'How does Chrissie feel about it?'

'I don't know,' Gavin sighed. 'She wasn't really listening when I told her about it. She was too busy getting Craig ready for this interview he's got this morning.'

'Yes. He told me about it. Do you think he'll get the job?'

'I don't know. I don't see any reason why he wouldn't be able to do the job, but who knows what the interview panel will think of someone who's been living on the streets for three years.'

'Does he have to tell them? He's got a proper address now. Why do they need to know?'

'They'll want to know what he's been doing between leaving the army and getting the warehouse job. It's a long time to be out of work. They'll want to know why, and if Craig doesn't tell them honestly they'll probably just assume the worst anyway. I've seen it all before.'

'But he's been working for them for six weeks: surely they'll know he's a good worker?'

'I hope he is: he never seems that sure of it himself!' Gavin sighed again. 'But, getting back to Shane Butler and co., I'm worried about how Harry Whittle's family will take it when they hear about them being let out. It's worse for them: Harry was killed in their house!'

'You mean: the gang knows where they live? But surely they wouldn't dare to come anywhere near?'

'I've told our solicitor to make sure they aren't allowed to, but I don't suppose that'll be much of a reassurance to Trev Whittle and his wife – not to mention young Leo!'

'So we're going round there now to tell them not to worry?'

'I wouldn't go so far as that: I just want to see how they all are and to let them know they aren't on their own. I *hope* they won't have heard the news yet and I can break it to them gently, but … Well, we'll just have to see: they're not particularly fond of the police at the best of times.'

They walked on down the unnaturally quiet street – together, and yet not together – keeping as far apart as the width of the pavement would allow, looking ahead when they spoke instead of turning to look at on another, conscious all the time that one of them might be harbouring the virus and might be capable of passing it on.

Stella pondered on Harry Whittle: the other victim of the Butler brothers and their heavy man, Stuart Hatton. He had been there too: in fact it may well have been Harry at whom Shane Butler had directed the car that crushed Kenny against the wall. Not yet turned seventeen, he was just a tiny cog in the vast machinery of the Butlers' illegal drugs business. It may even have been true what he told them when they questioned him at the police station: perhaps he really didn't know what the plants were that he was tending in that empty house in Kidlington.

Stella found her heart speeding up and her breathing becoming shallower as she pictured the scene. She was standing behind Harry, fumbling to fit the handcuffs on his wrists – her very first arrest! And then came the roar of a fast car, a shout from Kenny and suddenly he was pushing them aside … and then everything seemed to slow down as the vehicle struck Kenny and pinned him to the wall.

She forced herself back to the present, studying each house as they passed, counting off the numbers in her head, noting which had cars on the drive and what colours and ages they were, observing the well-trimmed hedges and lawns that bore witness to the extra time that some of the residents had for gardening now that they were no longer travelling to work every day.

'Do you see much of the Whittles?' she asked, trying to make normal conversation and prevent Gavin from noticing her agitation. 'With you living so close, I mean?'

'Not really. I try to bump into the younger boy every so often, just to check he's OK, but, like I said, they're none of them all that keen on the police. Chrissie's quite friendly with Yvonne Whittle – or she tries to be.'

They turned into the next street. Stella focused her mind on the sign attached to the wall of the end house: Chichester Road. This was where the late Harry Whittle's parents and younger brother lived. More deep breathing and she was ready to face them, but she was glad that Gavin would be the one to inform them that their son's killers were about to be set free.

2. BLACK LIVES MATTER

Trevor Whittle emptied the last of the milk from the carton into his coffee and went to the fridge for more. Usually there was a line of cartons in the rack on the door, but this morning it was empty. He got down on his knees and peered in. The shelves were uncharacteristically empty too: only a box of eggs, a tub of margarine and a few shrivelled carrots. He slammed the door closed again and went across to the cupboard where they kept the bread: just two crusts left from a sliced loaf. The shelf above was empty too; he couldn't remember what Yvonne usually kept there, but it must have been food of some sort.

He tipped the crusts out of the bag, scattering crumbs across the worktop, and then jammed them both into the toaster. He would have to go to the supermarket later, he supposed. There was no point waiting for Yvonne to do it: the lazy bitch wasn't even out of bed yet. Just because she was furloughed from her morning cleaning job, there was no need for her to lie around all day leaving him to do everything.

He went back to the fridge and opened the egg box: it was empty! What idiot puts an empty egg box back in the fridge? He hurled it across the room, then went after it, picked it up and stepped outside to cram it into the overflowing blue recycling bin. As he closed the door after coming back in, the toast popped up. He snatched the two black-edged crusts out of the toaster, burning his fingers as he did so, smeared them with margarine from the almost empty tub and carried toast and tea out of the kitchen and into the front room.

The television set was already on and *Good Morning Britain* was in full flow. He sat down and bit into his toast.

'In a surprise announcement it was revealed last night that many remand prisoners are to be freed on bail to relieve the pressure on prisons due to coronavirus outbreaks there,' the presenter read from her script. 'Among those to be released later today are the killers of PC Kenneth Hughes of Thames Valley Police, who was crushed to death by a vehicle during a raid on a cannabis farm in Oxfordshire shortly before Christmas. We invited the Ministry of Justice to come on the programme today to explain this decision, but they were unable to provide a spokesperson.'

Trevor stared at the screen waiting for more details: when exactly would they be released? Where would they go when they came out of jail? How long would it be before they were brought to trial? But the presenter had moved on to an item about the growth in pet ownership during Lockdown and was interviewing an animal psychologist on the best way to settle a dog into a new home.

'What about Harry?' He shouted at the screen. 'They killed him too, you know!'

Leaving the toast on the low table in front of the settee, he got to his feet and started pacing the room. His head felt as if it were going to explode with anger. Why was this happening? And why did nobody seem to care? Why was the man who strung Harry up from their own bannister rail going to be free to walk the streets instead of being jailed for life? It was an open-and-shut case, for God's sake! The trial should have been over by now – it should have been held before Lockdown. What was the big delay all about? Expensive white lawyers arguing with white judges about points of law, and white prosecutors going along with it all because, at the end of the day, it was only a black kid who'd been killed – and what did that matter?

And why was he the only one in this house that was up to hear the news? What was Yvonne doing, still lying in bed sleeping off the gin that he'd caught her adding to her water glass as she set the table last night? Why wasn't she down here, keeping the house clean and making breakfast for her husband and son? And what about Leo? Just because there was no school, that was no excuse for him to laze away the day in his room!

He stormed upstairs, calling out to his son as he went.

'Leo! Leo!' He opened the door of the room that Leo had shared with his older brother and glared round. The lower bunk was occupied and his son was pretending to be still asleep. He strode across the carpet and seized Leo by the shoulder. 'Up – now! Have you seen the time?'

'Sorry Dad,' Leo mumbled, turning over and yawning. 'I'll be down in a minute.'

'No, not *in a minute* – now!' Trevor barked. 'I'm not having you lying here all day, wasting your life. You've got homework to do from school and there's plenty of jobs you can do around the house. Make yourself useful for a change!'

'I've done all the work they sent me from school,' Leo protested. 'I finished it yesterday.'

'Then you can go over it again and make sure you've got it all right. You must've rushed it if you've done it already.'

'OK Dad.'

The boy threw back the duvet, rolled out of bed and started scrabbling around on the floor for his clothes. Trevor watched with mounting frustration as he pulled on a grubby tee-shirt and retrieved crumpled jeans from under the bed.

'Don't you ever hang anything up?' he growled at last. 'If you folded your clothes properly when you went to bed you'd be able to find them in the morning, and they wouldn't be in this state! You can't wear those! Look at the mud all over the front of that shirt! It looks like you've been walking all over it in football boots. And those jeans ain't fit to be seen! Get 'em all off and go and have a shower. I'll find you some clean things to put on.'

He turned round and flung open the wardrobe. A basketball rolled out from the top shelf and hit him on the head. The hanging space contained a heavy fleece-lined parka, two white school shirts, a blazer and an assortment of garments belonging to the dead Harry. What were they doing still there? Yvonne was supposed to have got rid of them all. And where were Leo's clothes? The shelves to the right of the hanging space were virtually empty: just a pair of football socks and a baseball cap. He slammed the wardrobe shut and started attacking the small chest of drawers that stood next to it, pulling out drawers at random. The top drawer contained a jumble of Lego parts, chargers for electronic gadgets and unidentifiable pieces of moulded plastic. Further down, he found a single pair of underpants, three odd socks and a tee-shirt even dirtier than the one that his son was currently wearing.

'Where've all your clothes got to?'

Leo shrugged. 'In the wash?'

'Well, go and have that shower and then I suppose you'll have to put your pyjamas back on while I sort something out.'

Leo escaped to the bathroom while his father gathered up all the garments that he could find from the bedroom floor and carried them downstairs to the kitchen. He wrenched open the door of the washing machine and was surprised to see a sock and a bra fall to the floor. The lazy bitch must have forgotten to take the clothes out after the washing cycle had finished!

He left Leo's clothes in a pile near the back door and searched under the sink for the washing basket. It was already full of damp towels and underwear. She must have hidden the basket away there, out of sight, instead of hanging them up to dry. How long had they been there? He sniffed suspiciously. They smelled a little musty to him, but too late to worry about that now.

He sighed. If Yvonne was incapable of getting herself out of bed and doing her chores he would just have to do them himself – as if he didn't have enough to worry about right now, what with no work and no money coming in, and a son who didn't care about doing his schoolwork, and now those murdering bastards being let out of jail. He didn't know why he bothered, he really didn't!

It took him nearly half an hour to hang up all the damp laundry on the rotary airer in the garden. Then he put Leo's clothes in the washing machine and went upstairs to check the linen basket in the bathroom. As he had suspected, it was full to over-flowing with discarded garments. He carried the basket down to the kitchen, filled the washing machine and set it going. He looked at his watch: half the morning gone, and nothing to show for it! And where had Leo got to? What was taking him so long?

He found his son standing by the bedroom window staring out into the road. Music was blaring out of the headphones that he was wearing, loud enough for Trevor almost to be able to make out the lyrics. Why did kids these days have this passion for deafening themselves with this constant cacophony? To prevent their parents from talking to them, he supposed.

'Leo!' The boy jumped at the sound of his father's voice, and turned to face him. 'Take them things off of your head and listen to me.'

Leo obediently removed the headphones and switched off the music.

'That's better. Now get your school books and go down to the kitchen where I can keep an eye on you.'

Leo disconnected the headphones and tossed them up on to the empty top bunk. Then he dived under the small computer desk in the corner of the room and retrieved his school bag. He pulled out a maths textbook and half a dozen pieces of squared paper. He put them down on the desk, pushing the dilapidated laptop towards the wall.

'I can concentrate better in here,' he insisted, sitting down and opening the text book.

Trevor stood watching as his son bent over the book, studying a page of algebra exercises and then picked up a pen and started writing on the top sheet of paper. Satisfied, he turned and walked out of the room and down the stairs.

Just as Trevor reached the ground floor, the doorbell rang. Leo got up and pushed the bedroom door closed, grateful to the visitor, whoever it might be, for providing a distraction that might keep his father off his back for a while.

Trevor gazed towards the front door. Through the frosted glass, he could see a bulky figure looming. Coming closer, he could make out the distinctive shape of a police helmet. What could *they* want now? He pulled open the door and stared belligerently out.

Gavin smiled apologetically. 'Good morning Mr Whittle. I'm afraid I have some news about the men who were responsible for your son's death, which may be rather distressing for you.'

'I've already heard!' Trevor barked.

He made to close the door, but Gavin put out his hand to prevent it. 'I wanted to explain-'

'Explain? Explain!' Trevor retorted. 'You don't have to explain! It's all plain enough, isn't it? Nobody's interested in what happens to a black kid like Harry. You all think you're better off without him! If you want to do some explaining, why don't you try explaining how you lot allowed three murderers to break into our house in broad daylight and string him up when you *knew* he was the only witness who could have told you their names? Or you could explain why it took three months before they even gave us a date for the trial! Except that I know what the answer is already – it's all because he's only a black kid and he don't matter to any of you!'

Stella stepped forward, briefly emboldened by indignation on behalf of Gavin, whose intention she knew was only to alleviate the Whittles' inevitable distress at the news of the Butler gang's release.

'Mr Whittle, sir, that isn't fair,' she said earnestly. 'The delays in the system affect everyone. And I know the SIO was gutted when your Harry was killed after he let him go home instead of keeping him in custody overnight.'

Trevor gave her a look of utmost contempt. Then he turned back to Gavin. 'So, you've brought along your token black policewoman,' he sneered, 'to prove to me that Harry's colour don't have anything to do with why *he's* dead and those damn butchers are walking the streets, scot free! Well, you don't fool me!'

Stella felt her cheeks burning and her eyes prickling. She turned away to hide the hot tears that were welling up and starting to run down her cheeks. Behind her, she could hear Gavin's calm voice continuing to offer sympathy and reassurance. Then the door slammed shut. A moment later she felt Gavin's hand on her shoulder.

'Better get a move on. Can't stand around here all day!'

'Is that all I am?' Stella asked. 'A token black officer? Is that the only reason I was selected by the panel?'

'No, of course not!' Gavin's reply was just a bit too quick to be reassuring. 'You got your place on merit. Everyone agrees you're going to make a really good officer.'

'Everyone keeps saying the force needs more officers like me,' Stella's voice was desultory, 'but what they mean is more black women.'

'Well, I suppose that's true,' Gavin admitted, 'but that doesn't mean you're not good enough in your own right. It just means … It just means … It's like … It's like being a superhero,' he said at last. 'They all have some sort of special power: yours is your colour. However much I try, I'll never be someone that the likes of Trevor Whittle will really trust, but with you … well it's different, isn't it?'

'He didn't seem very impressed by me just now.'

'He's upset. He didn't mean half the things he said.'

As they squeezed past Trevor's taxi, which almost filled the narrow drive, Stella glanced back at the house. Gazing anxiously down at them from the window of the front bedroom was a face.

'I guess that must be the other Whittle boy,' she murmured. 'He doesn't look very happy. Do you think he's OK?'

'I hope so.' Gavin turned to wave at Leo, who seemed to be about to wave back then changed his mind and disappeared abruptly from view. 'It must be difficult for them, being stuck in the house together all day. Mrs Whittle in particular was finding it hard-going after Harry died.'

'I heard she hit the bottle after she found him hanging there in their hall.'

'She does tend to self-medicate with alcohol,' Gavin answered guardedly, 'but she'd got herself together again pretty well once Christmas was over. She and Chrissie got quite pally – women are better at talking about things like losing a son, and Chrissie was interested in all the West Indian recipes that Yvonne's mother taught her.' He sighed, 'but, of course, they haven't been able to meet up since Lockdown started, and I don't think they've even spoken on the phone for a while now.'

'So, do you think …?'

'I don't know. Yvonne Whittle isn't a bad mother, but … I'm probably making a mountain out of a molehill, but it was a bad sign that Trevor answered the door not Yvonne. Usually she'd see that as her job – along with making sure the house was presentable if she invited anyone in.'

'Maybe she was just busy doing something – hands covered in flour or something like that,' suggested Stella.

'Yes, you're probably right. I just wish I'd seen her, that's all.'

They walked on in silence. The streets were deserted. Everyone seemed to have taken to heart the rule of three: Stay at Home; Protect the NHS; Save Lives.

'Will I have to give evidence at the trial when it happens?' Stella asked.

'That depends on the prosecutor, but I should think you will. After all, you're the only eye-witness left, now that Harry Whittle's ...'

'But I didn't see his face properly,' Stella argued. 'I can't identify him. And anyway, he admits he was driving; he just says it was all an accident.'

'Still, you can tell the court that he drove straight at you and Kenny, can't you? And that it didn't look like an accident.'

'I suppose so,' Stella said dubiously, 'but what if I mess it up? When you see people being cross-examined on the telly, the lawyers always seem ever so frightening.'

'But those are only TV dramas. They have to make them look like that. Don't worry: the judge will soon stop them if the defence barrister tries to intimidate you. And you'll have training before you go in the witness box for the first time. I can help you too, if you like.'

'Would you? If I could just have a practice first, maybe it won't be quite so bad.'

That's the spirit! Now, it's not far off lunchtime: where do you fancy taking our sandwiches today?'

3. SAVING LIVES

Crystal Johns put down her tray on the plastic-topped table in the hospital canteen and slumped into her chair. Only halfway through her shift and already she was exhausted! She pulled the bowl of soup towards her and then picked up the bread roll that accompanied it and broke it in two. She dipped it into the warm cream-coloured liquid and then sucked it off into her parched mouth. She could do with some water, but she didn't have the energy to get up and make the circuitous journey following the one-way system round the room to fill a plastic cup from the fountain at the side of the room. She would make do with the soup for now and try to snatch time for a glass of water or a cup of tea when she was back on the ward.

'Hi Crystal!' Beatrice, another of the Jamaican nurses called softly from the next table – safely distanced by at least 2 metres as specified in the catering manager's COVID-19 risk assessment. She put down the newspaper that she had been reading and smiled across at Crystal. 'How're you doing?'

'Hello,' Crystal smiled back. 'I'm doing fine, except for being a little tired after reorganising the ward. We had a patient test positive and we've had to isolate everyone who's been in close contact with them; and, of course, that means all the staff have been working in full PPE[2], which is so hot and tiring! I'm just glad I was off-duty yesterday and the day before, so I haven't been working since he came on to the ward. I'm really scared about getting it.'

'Me too,' Beatrice nodded. 'They keep saying black people are more at risk. But you're young! It's the middle-aged people like me who need to worry.'

'Still …'

'Yes, I know.' Beatrice sighed and picked up her paper again. 'D'you remember that young policeman who was killed in Kidlington just before Christmas?'

'Certainly I do: my father-in-law knows his family. He used to work with the young man's father.'

'It says here they're letting the man who did it out of jail.'

'Surely not! But why?'

'Too many COVID cases, so it says: *All remand prisoners will be assessed and only those that pose a serious threat to the public will continue to be held in custody.*'

'But a murderer?'

'I know! But here it is in black and white.' Beatrice held up the newspaper and pointed at the headline over a smiling photograph of a young police constable in uniform. 'Shane Butler, self-confessed killer of PC Kenneth Hughes, will walk free pending his trial for murdering the young police officer, assisting in another murder and a wide range of drugs offences! It really beggars belief, doesn't it?'

'Yes, it does.' Crystal put down her spoon and fished in her pocket for her phone. 'Now, you'll have to excuse me,

---

[2] Personal Protective Equipment, a term that became suddenly familiar as the COVID-19 pandemic advanced and hospitals were unable to provide it to all of their staff who were working with highly infectious patients.

I need to ring my husband to check he's doing OK with the kids. It's a struggle for him keeping them entertained as well as getting his work done.'

'I'd better be going now anyway.' Beatrice got to her feet. 'No rest for the wicked, eh?'

Crystal selected her husband's entry from her list of contacts and sat with her phone to her ear while continuing to consume spoonfuls of soup, mindful of the need to be back on the ward in only a few minutes' time. Soon the ringing tone clicked off and Eddie's familiar voice came through.

'Hi Crystal! You've managed a lunch break this time then?'

'Yes. Mind you, I certainly needed it! I was dead on my feet by the time we'd finished re-organising the ward. A patient who came in the day before yesterday developed COVID symptoms and now he's tested positive; so it was all hands to the pumps moving things around. Goodness know how it happened: he shouldn't have been allowed on the ward without testing negative before he was transferred. How's your day been?'

'We tried taking our exercise early today. I thought we'd be less likely to meet people then and maybe it'd tire the kids out and they'd give me some peace afterwards, but nothing seems to do anything to repress Ricky's energy. He's been bouncing off the walls since about ten. You can probably hear him now: he's found that tambourine that Bernie gave him and he's teaching Abbie all the songs he ever learned in nursery. If I have to listen to *The Wheels on the Bus* one more time, I think I may go mad!'

'It makes you wonder how your dad manages to cope with them all day normally, doesn't it?' Crystal smiled. 'Now, speaking of Peter, there's something I've just heard that he'd be interested to know. Have you seen in the papers about them releasing remand prisoners?'

'I think I caught something on the radio about them wanting to reduce over-crowding to stop the spread of coronavirus in prisons. But what has that got to do with Dad?'

'Apparently, one of the prisoners they're letting out is the man who killed that friend of his, just before Christmas.'

'Kenny Hughes?'

'That's it. I thought he'd want to know.'

'You're right; I'm sure he will. He was saying only the other day how upsetting it must be for Kenny's parents not knowing when the trial was ever going to happen. This'll only make things worse – if it's true. I'd better check that the papers have got it right first before I ring him. There must be some sort of official announcement that I can find if I search online – if it *is* true, but surely they wouldn't release a murderer, would they?'

'That's exactly what I said to Beatrice when she showed me the piece in the paper, but it looked very clear – there was a photo of the officer and everything. Now, I'm sorry, but I'll have to go. I promised to get back on the ward as soon as I could.'

'Bye then – and do take care!'

'Bye Eddie. Give my love to the kids.'

Edward Johns turned back to the laptop computer that he had been using for his job in the design department of a small IT company in Bicester. It nestled among his wife's combs and face creams on the dressing table in the main bedroom of their tiny flat, which was the only place where he could escape from their two lively children. He opened a web browser to search for news of Kenny Hughes and his killers and leaned forward from his uncomfortable perch on the edge of the bed to see the screen more clearly. It did not take long to find reports in the local press denouncing the decision to release "these vicious gangsters" on bail. The national tabloids also had angry headlines with words such as "scandalous", "outrageous" and "shameful" playing a part. The more measured tones of the BBC explained the need to reduce the numbers of prisoners held on remand and the rigorous vetting procedure that was taken to ensure that those released would not pose a danger to the public. It looked as if it must be true then.

'Hello Ed!' his father answered the call with the forced cheerfulness that betrays an underlying concern. 'Is everything OK?'

'Yes, Dad: we're fine,' Eddie hastened to assure him. 'Well, apart from the kids driving me up the wall with their noise,' he added with a laugh. 'You can probably hear them. They've got that tambourine of Bernie's, and Ricky's entertaining Abbie with a medley of songs. We're on *Miss Polly had a Dolly* at the moment. What I was ringing about was: have you seen the reports about them releasing the guy who killed Kenny Hughes? Apparently they're clearing as many remand prisoners out of the jails as they can because of the pandemic.'

'Yes,' Peter replied, 'we heard about it on the *Today* programme this morning. 'Bernie was all for ringing Gavin right away, but in the end we decided to wait until this evening. They're always in a rush in the mornings. It must have been a shock for them both – just what they don't need on top of everything else!'

'Can they really do that? Release a murderer on bail? It doesn't make sense to me.'

'The law says you're innocent until you're proved guilty, which means that you should only be kept in prison if there's a danger you'll commit another crime or else abscond – or if you might try to intimidate any witnesses. I suppose they must've decided that Shane Butler and the others weren't going to do any of those things.'

'I thought you said they killed one of the witnesses to Kenny's murder. Doesn't that suggest they might be a danger to other witnesses?'

'I suppose … look, Ed, it isn't my call. The people who made the decision must have thought it wasn't a big enough risk to worry about. And they won't have just opened the prison door and said, "Off you go!" There'll have been bail conditions they have to keep to: things like staying in one place and reporting to the police regularly.'

'It still seems … oh well! I'd better go. It's sounding ominously quiet in the living room all of a sudden. I don't know whether to go in and see what they're up to or to hope for the best and get on with some work while I can hear myself think!'

'Well, if you'd like me to read them a story or something by Skype later, just give me a ring.'

Peter put the phone down on the kitchen table and turned back to the pan of carrot and courgette soup that he was making for their lunch, using the last bag of frozen courgettes from last year's bumper harvest and the last few, rather limp, carrots from the box beneath the lowest shelf in their cool under-stairs larder. Thanks to the unusually warm spring weather, this year's plants were already starting to poke their heads through the soil in the raised bed that their friend Jonah had instigated two years ago. Thanks to him, they were almost self-sufficient in fruit and vegetables – something that had felt very fortunate during the panic-buying of March and April when seemingly random items suddenly disappeared from supermarket shelves. Things appeared to have settled down now, but apparently the supermarkets had been forced to draw on the stocks that they had built up in preparation for Brexit chaos next January, so who knew what might be still to come in the way of shortages in the shops?

The timer on his phone went off, bringing Peter out of his reverie. He silenced it with a smart tap on the screen and went over to the oven to get out the fresh bread rolls that he was baking. He turned them out and tapped them on the bottom to check that they were done before spreading them out on a wire rack to cool. He looked at his watch. Bernie should be back soon – in fact it was strange that she wasn't here already. There must have been a queue at the supermarket. There were always queues these days, and then it was difficult to find what you wanted because the one-way system meant that if you missed something you couldn't go back.

He turned down the gas under the pan of soup and started laying the table. The Beryl Ware[3] soup bowls were odd ones that Bernie had picked up at a church sale. There were only three, but that was enough for them – especially now that her daughter Lucy was away at university. He went to the fridge to get out the butter. Would she be allowed to come home when term ended? If she did, would she have to be quarantined from them to avoid spreading the virus between households?

There was the car now! Bernie was back. He put down the butter dish on the table and headed out to the hall. When he got there, he saw Jonah coming out of his study, also on his way to meet Bernie – or was he seeking news of lunch?

The front door opened, making the hall suddenly much lighter. Bernie entered carrying a large cake tin.

'Sylvia's been baking,' she explained. 'I keep telling her she doesn't need to, but I think it makes her feel better to be able to give us something in exchange for doing their shopping for them. It looks like an enormous cake for just the three of us, but she insists that it isn't bad for us because it's got so much fruit and nuts in it.'

'Give it here and I'll put it away,' Peter reached out for the tin, 'while you go and wash your hands for twenty seconds like a good girl. The lunch is all ready.'

Bernie handed over the tin and headed upstairs to the bathroom.

A few minutes later they were all three gathered round the big kitchen table with steaming bowls of soup in front of Peter and Bernie, and a plastic cup with a straw on the special attachment on the side of Jonah's electric

---

[3] Beryl Ware, a distinctive green design of crockery manufactured for many years by Wood & Sons of Stoke-on-Trent, was once almost universal in church halls and school dining rooms.

wheelchair. Paralysed from the shoulders down by a bullet more than a decade earlier, DCI Jonah Porter nevertheless managed to lead a full and active life with the help of his two friends. Soup was one of the few foods that he could eat independently, provided that Peter made sure that it was liquid enough to be sucked up through the wide straw of Jonah's special feeding mug.

'How are Stan and Sylvia?' asked Peter.

'Pretty fed-up with this shielding malarkey,' Bernie answered as she broke off a piece of bread from the thick slice that Peter had cut for her. 'Stan's itching to get over here to see to his pigeons. I told him we were following his instructions to the letter, but it was a case of *except I shall see in his hands the print of the nails* ... And then Sylvia's feeling useless because she can't get out doing things for people the way she's used to. She's been making face masks, but her real forte is distributing cake and kindness to all the "old dears" who are living on their own – and are mostly no older than she is!'

Stan and Sylvia Corbridge were two of Bernie's oldest and dearest friends. They had left their home in Newcastle when Stan retired from his job in the shipyards there, in order to help Bernie to care for her daughter, Lucy, after Lucy's father had been killed in a tragic accident in the course of his job as a police officer. Stan's small flock of racing pigeons had come with them, and their descendants lived in a loft at the bottom of Bernie's extensive garden.

'I told them about Shane Butler being let out on bail,' she went on. 'I've never seen Sylvia so angry and upset. She was on the phone to Chrissie while I was still there on the doorstep, but she wasn't in. Is her school open?'

'It is for the kids of key workers,' Jonah told her. With an unusual amount of time on his hands since he was debarred from working in mid-March, he had spent long hours web-browsing, with the result that he was now a mine of useful – and not-so-useful – information on almost every subject you could imagine. 'And with it being a special needs school, probably a good percentage of them qualify as needing to go to school for their own well-being.'

'Last time I spoke to Gavin, I got the impression that Chrissie was going in some days and teaching online from home on other days,' Peter chipped in. 'It sounded like horrendously hard work to me, but Gavin says she likes to keep busy. It helps to keep her mind off … other things.'

'This bail nonsense won't exactly have helped in that regard,' Bernie declared forthrightly. 'Did they even bother to tell the family first?'

'They certainly should have done!' Jonah agreed. 'They should have been given the opportunity to raise objections before the decision was made. And not just Gavin and Chrissie – the Whittles should have been consulted too. In fact, it's worse for them because it wasn't a case of Harry being in the wrong place at the wrong time the way it was with Kenny: they deliberately targeted him and they came right into the family home and killed him there. We slipped up badly letting that happen, and the Whittles have no reason to believe that we'll be able to protect them any better this time.'

'You're not seriously suggesting that the gang might be a danger to them, are you?' Peter asked in astonishment. 'What could they possibly hope to achieve by that?'

'It was the younger brother – Leo – who put us on to Terry Butler, wasn't it?' Jonah had been the Senior Investigating Officer in the investigation into Kenny's – and later also Harry Whittle's – death. 'They might have a go at intimidating him – or even silencing him for good the way they did with Harry.'

'Surely they wouldn't try anything like that when they're on bail?' Bernie protested. 'Won't they be being watched 24/7?'

'Have you any idea how much round-the-clock surveillance costs?' retorted Jonah scornfully. 'No. The best the Whittles can hope for is bail conditions that restrict their movements – not that any of us are supposed to be going anywhere at the moment! – and a uniformed officer patrolling past their house a couple of times a day to check there's nothing untoward going on.'

'I'm sure Gavin will keep an eye on them,' Peter put in, 'and I think Chrissie has been keeping in touch with Harry's mother.'

'It must be pretty grim for the Whittles,' Bernie nodded. 'Even without having lost a son, with no sign of his murderers being brought to trial, and now this bail business, I wouldn't want to be locked down in a small house with a teenager! Staying at home is all fine and dandy if you're a Tory MP with a country residence and acres of land. It's not so easy if you've got a few kids battened down with you in a tiny terraced house!'

4. HOMEWORK

Across the city in the suburb of Rose Hill, her young friend Wayne Major would have agreed heartily with this sentiment. He and his husband, Dean O'Brien, had adopted two lively young boys the previous year. Carl, aged nearly nine, and his younger brother, Harry, were remarkably well-behaved in normal times, but being deprived of the sport that they enjoyed so much and prevented from meeting friends of their own age was taking its toll on their patience and good nature.

When the government ordered everyone to "Stay at Home; Protect the NHS; Save Lives" both Wayne and Dean had done their best to manage their small engineering company from home. This meant setting up the dining room as an office, from which Wayne co-ordinated the moving of other staff – administrators and the small design team – into similar home offices in locations across the city of Oxford and beyond, while Dean carried out risk assessments of the manufacturing plant – just a large warehouse really – housing the machine tools necessary for hand-building a wide range of largely custom-made gadgets designed to improve the independence of their disabled customers.

Fortunately, this was located in a unit on the Oxford Science Park adjacent to the, now deserted, design office, which could now be pressed into service as additional manufacturing space. That meant that it would be possible to continue working at the pre-COVID rate and nobody would have to be laid off or furloughed. The biggest problem was that they could not go out to visit customers in their own homes to assess their needs and propose solutions to their problems. There were enough orders in the pipeline for the time being, but how would they get more business while most of their potential new clients were shielding themselves from all human contact?

Somehow the orders continued to come in. Existing customers passed round recommendations on social media. While there were fewer people wanting the high-end purchases – tailor-made electric wheelchairs, for example – there was a constant stream of enquiries about the many gadgets that made everyday tasks easier if your fine motor skills are impaired or if you dare not get down to pick up something from the floor for fear of not being able to get up again. That prompted the start of a mail-order arm to the business, which provided another challenge. Wayne designed a new website to take online orders, while Dean made a sortie to the Science Park to work out how to make space for packing and shipping.

From that point onwards, it became clear that one of them would have to be physically present on-site for at least part of every day. That was how it was that Wayne was now struggling to help Harry with the work that his teacher had sent home for him to complete, while Carl (who claimed to have finished all his school work) flicked rapidly through the television channels, pausing to watch short clips and then moving on in a vain search for something that caught his interest. The volume was turned up far too high and Wayne was finding it hard to concentrate, but he knew that Carl had got to the stage where the slightest parental remonstration was liable to send him storming off up to the room that he shared with his brother. The subsequent devastation to the décor and to any number of his and Harry's possessions was not to be contemplated; so Wayne strove to comprehend the instructions at the top of a page of English exercises while mentally blotting out the blaring sounds from the television set.

'Underline all the **nouns** in these sentences,' he read out slowly. 'Then draw a box round the **proper nouns**. OK Harry, can you tell me what a noun is?'

Harry shook his head. Then he twisted round to gaze at the TV screen as Carl hit upon CBeebies and the familiar tone of Bing, the animated rabbit, announced that his friend Coco was very good at skipping. A moment later the bright cartoon colours vanished and the soft voices were replaced by the authoritative delivery of the News Channel.

'There has been a storm of protest on Twitter at the release on bail of the men accused of murdering PC Kenneth Hughes in Oxfordshire last year.'

Wayne raised his head and stared at the screen. The face of a smiling young police officer met his eyes. The Hughes family lived just a few streets away. Wayne didn't know Kenny personally, but he had passed the time of day with Gavin more than once. They had taken a keen interest in the investigation into Kenny's death and Dean had joined the throng of well-wishers at the funeral. What was all this about? He leapt up and snatched the remote control out of Carl's hand.

'What d'you want to do that for?' the boy screamed, flinging himself on Wayne and knocking him off his feet. They collapsed together into Wayne's chair as the newsreader continued to explain the background to the case and the reasons for the decision to release more remand prisoners.

'It's alright, Carl. You can have it back now. I just wanted to listen to the news for a moment, that's all.'

Wayne handed over the remote and Carl retreated back to the sofa with a sulky look on his face. The TV picture changed abruptly and the newsreader was cut off in mid-sentence.

'That policeman – who is he?' asked Harry. 'He's been on before, hasn't he?'

'His name's PC Kenny Hughes. He used to live near here: in Arundel Road. His parents still do.'

'But he's dead now?'

'Yes. He was killed just before Christmas.'

'And now they're letting the men who did it out of jail?'

'Only for a bit. There has to be a trial first – to make sure they really did do it.'

'Why hasn't that happened yet? Christmas was ages ago!'

'These things take time,' Wayne sighed, 'and this coronavirus business has meant they've had to close the courts and stop doing trials.'

'I think they ought to keep them locked up,' Harry declared. 'What if they kill someone else?'

'I'm sure that won't happen,' Wayne tried to reassure him. He knew that both boys were inclined to worry and to allow their imaginations to conjure up all sorts of hypothetical scenarios to worry about. 'The police will be keeping an eye on them.'

'I still think people who kill someone ought to be kept locked up,' Harry insisted.

'Aren't we all locked up now?' demanded Carl unexpectedly without moving his eyes from the television screen. 'We can't go swimming; we can't go to football training; I can't go round to Ollie's house. We might as well be in prison!'

He jabbed viciously at the keys on the remote. Music blared again and the opening credits of *Millie Inbetween* appeared. Apparently satisfied at last, he lay back with his legs stretched out above him and his feet resting on the back of the sofa.

'Why don't we go in the kitchen?' suggested Wayne to Harry. 'I bet we'll get this done in no time there, and then you can help me make chocolate pudding for when Daddy Dean gets home.'

His younger son nodded absently, but did not move. His eyes drifted across to the television screen.

'Go on then,' urged Wayne, giving him a gentle prod on the shoulder. 'The sooner you get started the sooner you'll be finished.'

Harry picked up the worksheet and his pencil, and made his way out of the door at a snail's pace, his eyes still fixed on the screen, which seemed to have a magnetic attraction. Wayne hauled himself to his feet and followed him haltingly out, leaning on his stick. It was nearly two years now since the road traffic accident that had left him with one-sided weakness in his limbs. His walking was much better now, but when he was tired or under stress, every type of exertion became more difficult. Roll on the day when the schools were open again and he could take a rest during the day to re-charge his batteries!

The dishwasher beeped at them as they entered the kitchen. Wayne opened it a crack to allow the steam out. Harry climbed up on to a high stool and put his homework down on the breakfast bar.

'A noun,' Wayne told him, 'is a *naming* word. It tells you what something is – like *stool*,' he added, pointing, 'or *door*.'

Harry looked down as the sentences in the work book, 'The monkey ate a banana,' he read aloud. 'Is *monkey* a noun?'

'Yes, that's right,' Wayne encouraged. 'So underline it.' He watched as Harry laboriously drew a line under the word with his pencil. 'And there's another noun in that sentence as well.'

'Banana?' queried Harry.

'That's right. Well done! See! You know how to do this, don't you? Have a go with the other sentences and then I'll have a look at with you when you've finished.'

Harry nodded, smiling with satisfaction at the praise. He leaned forward over the worksheet and began reading the next sentence slowly to himself. Wayne sighed with relief and turned to empty the dishwasher.

Within half an hour, they had disposed of nouns and adjectives, and Wayne was able to send Harry upstairs to put away the worksheet in his school bag. He clattered back down to help with making the promised chocolate pudding, calling out as he did so, 'Daddy Dean's back! I saw the car from the landing window.'

'Go and open the door for him then,' Wayne smiled back, anticipating a welcome respite from childcare. 'He must've knocked off early today.'

'Me and Daddy Wayne are making chocolate pudding!' Harry greeted his other father, holding the door wide for Dean to enter, carrying a laptop in one hand and a folder of papers in the other.

'That's nice,' Dean replied smiling down at his son. 'I hope you and Carl have been good for him while I've been out.'

'Of course we have!' Harry declared confidently. 'We're *always* good!'

'Well, you always try hard,' Dean conceded, 'and that's what matters. Now you'd better get back to Daddy Wayne and help him with that pudding, hadn't you?'

He pushed open the dining room door with his elbow and dumped the laptop and papers on the table before heading for the kitchen himself. Wayne was sitting on one of the bar stools supervising Harry in weighing out sugar and margarine and mixing them together in a bowl. Dean came over and put his arm round his husband's shoulders. He kissed him gently on the cheek.

'It's been two steps forward one step back today,' he sighed. 'I'm knackered! Mail-order is a whole lot more difficult than I thought it would be. The staff are all doing their best, but it's all new to them. We could do with someone who knows something about logistics to give them a bit of direction.'

'Well, at least you've managed to get home early today,' Wayne responded, returning the kiss. 'D'you think you could look in on Carl and see if he'll show you his maths homework? He claims he's done it all, but he won't let me see it and he was only working on it for about ten minutes, which make me suspicious. Perhaps you could take him for a kick-about outside to work off some of his energy, and then he'll probably be more willing to co-operate.'

'It'll have to wait, I'm afraid,' Dean apologised. 'I came home because I didn't seem to be getting anywhere, but I've brought a mountain of stuff that needs doing. And I've got a Teams meeting booked with Nick in five minutes. Sorry!'

He turned to go, giving his son a brief pat on the shoulder as he did so. 'You're doing a great job there, Harry! I'm really looking forward to that pudding.'

Wayne watched him out of the room. It was all very well for Dean! If *he* was tired, how did he think Wayne felt after seven hours non-stop trying to keep the boys occupied? However difficult the staff may have been, it was a safe bet that Dean hadn't had to pull any of them apart physically to prevent a squabble turning into a serious fight. And the chances were he'd spent most of his day sitting at a desk, not chasing up and down stairs or mopping up spillages on the kitchen floor.

'Daddy Wayne!' Harry's piercing young voice interrupted his thoughts and brought him back to the present with a jolt. 'I've finished mixing. What goes in next?'

5. HAPPY FAMILIES

'But it's Saturday!' protested Carl. 'There's no school on Saturday. 'You said you'd give me a piano lesson. You promised!'

'That was before I discovered you hadn't even started the worksheet Mrs Gibbons gave you on Monday,' Dean argued. 'And there'll be plenty of time after you've done it. Come on! The sooner you get started, the sooner you'll have finished.'

'You aren't making Harry do homework,' Carl complained. 'It's not fair!'

'That's because he's finished all his,' Dean countered, keeping his voice level with a great effort. 'You lied to Daddy Wayne and now you've been found out. Perhaps next time you'll be more sensible and do your homework when you're supposed to.'

'I *did* do it!' Carl insisted. 'I looked at *all* the questions. I just couldn't work out the answers. It's fractions. I can never do fractions.'

'Then let me help you with it.' Dean sat down next to Carl and pointed to the first question on the worksheet. 'This one looks easy: three eighths plus five eighths. What do you think that might come to?'

'I don't know,' Carl answered sulkily. 'I told you: I can't do fractions.'

'Come on, Daddy Dean!' Harry pulled at Dean's arm. 'You said you'd play football with me. You promised!'

'Did I?' Dean looked round and smiled at his younger son. 'I'm sorry. I'm helping Carl just now. Maybe later. Or,' he added, seeing Harry's crestfallen face, 'Wayne? Do you think you could help Carl with his maths homework while I take Harry out in the garden for a kick-about?'

Wayne looked up from the magazine that he was reading. 'No! It's your turn. I've been helping the kids with their homework all week – *and* cooking all the meals and cleaning the house – while you've been off out to the Science Park, meeting people and – and –'

'For work!' Dean cut in. 'I was working, remember? Keeping *our* business going. One of us had to be there to get this mail-order thing up and running.'

'*One* of us,' Wayne echoed. 'But it was bound to be you, wasn't it?'

'Only because you haven't got your driving licence back yet. You're welcome to have a go at organising a socially-distanced packing station in a room designed to be an open-plan drawing office! I'd much rather be spending time at home with the boys, but we agreed it had to be me that went into the office, because you can't get there on your own.'

'Of course! It's all because I'm a bloody cripple! That's why Harry wants you to play football with him too, isn't it? You might as well say it: I'm bloody useless, aren't I?'

'No! It's not like that at all!' Dean protested. 'It's just a matter of playing to our strengths. You're a great dad. Harry was telling me earlier about the wormery you helped them to make, and he's been showing me how his bean in a jar is growing. And it's thanks to you that he's finished all his schoolwork.'

'And thanks to me that we didn't realise Carl hadn't done his,' muttered Wayne, apparently determined not to be placated. 'Oh alright! Go on! You go out and play footie with Harry and I'll have a look at those fractions.'

'No,' Dean said at once. 'I've started, so I'll finish. I'm sure you won't mind waiting for a bit, will you Harry?'

Harry stood clutching the ball tightly against his stomach. He appeared to be staring at a patch of carpet a few feet away from him. His lower lip wobbled, making Dean's heart give a lurch as it crossed his mind that the boy might be about to burst into tears. He knew that seeing adults arguing always made him anxious.

Then the little boy turned abruptly away and ran out of the room. A few seconds later the back door slammed shut. Wayne hauled himself to his feet and shuffled towards the door. 'I'd better go to him.'

'No. You sit down and read your mag. He's got to learn to wait for things. Give him a few minutes to cool down and then I'll give him a game while Carl finishes his worksheet. Speaking of which,' he continued turning back to the older boy, 'have you had any thoughts on that sum we were looking at?'

Carl shook his head. 'It's fractions. I told you I can't do them.'

'OK.' Dean thought fast. It was a long time since his own Primary School days and he found it difficult to comprehend where Carl's difficulty lay. He looked down at the worksheet again. This first question was so simple! He took a deep breath and had a go. 'Well, let's suppose it isn't fractions. Let's suppose, instead of eighths it was … let's see … bananas! What would three bananas plus five bananas be?'

'Eight bananas!' Carl replied promptly. 'That's baby stuff!'

'OK. And if it was three apples plus five apples?'

'Eight apples.' Carl's face took on an expression of deep concentration.

'So-o-o …?' prompted Dean

'So, is three eighths plus five eighths, eight eighths?'

'Yes. That's right. Well done! Write that down on the sheet.'

Carl picked up his pencil and carefully wrote "8" then a line underneath and another "8". 'Is that it?'

'Well, not quite. I mean, that's the right answer, but we don't usually talk about eight eighths because there's an easier way of thinking about it. Can you tell me what an eighth is?'

'No. I can't do fractions. I told you.'

'Think about it this way.' Wayne put down his magazine. 'Suppose you've got a cake and you want to share it with eight people. If you cut it into eight equal pieces then each piece is one eighth of the cake. Does that make sense?'

'I suppose so,' Carl agreed reluctantly.

'And then if all eight of you put your pieces back together again, how much of the cake have you got?'

'All of it.'

'Good,' Wayne smiled. 'So if you have eight eighths of a cake and you put them all together you've got one cake, haven't you?'

'Ye-es,' Carl admitted suspiciously.

'So eight eighths of a cake is the same as one cake,' Wayne persisted gently. 'Does that help you to think of an easier way of saying "eight eighths"?'

'One?' suggested Carl hesitantly.

'That's right!' both of his fathers chorused together. 'Well done!'

The boy carefully wrote "=1" on the worksheet next to his previous answer. 'Is that because there's an eight on the top and an eight on the bottom?'

'Yes,' Wayne confirmed. 'It's called cancelling. Let me show you. Give me the pencil – and have you got some more paper?'

'I'll get some.' Dean hurried out of the room, returning a few moments later with an A4 pad.

Wayne laid it on the low table, at which Carl was kneeling, and began drawing diagrams. 'This is the whole cake,' he explained, 'and now, if we draw a line down the middle of it, we've made it into two halves. A half is one over two. The line between the one and the two is like the knife cutting the cake. The one tells us that we've taken *one* cake, and the two tells us that we've cut it into *two* equal pieces. If we put two of those pieces back together again, we've got the whole cake. Now let's cut the cake into more pieces. How many would you like?'

'Three!'

'OK.' Wayne drew another circle and began adding lines to divide it into three slices.

Dean got silently to his feet and crept out. He felt guilty about leaving Wayne to cope with the recalcitrant Carl, but he did seem to be managing to get through to the boy in a way that Dean despaired of doing. He would make it up to him somehow. He had been too much taken up with the business and had taken Wayne's home-making role for granted. He ought to have remembered how exhausting it was keeping the boys entertained at home – and how easily Wayne got tired since his accident.

He wandered out into the garden and found Harry aimlessly kicking his football against the wall beneath the kitchen window. He looked up momentarily as Dean approached and then gave the ball another mighty thwack with his right foot. It struck the wall with a loud thud and bounced off into a clump of lavender.

'Would you like me to be the goalie so that you can practice taking penalties?'

'If you like,' Harry shrugged. 'Or you can go back and do Carl's homework for him. I don't care!'

'Oh Harry!' Dean sighed, 'Don't be like that. Being shut up at home like this is hard for everyone. We've just got to all try our best to get along together. And it's specially hard for Daddy Wayne, because of his head having been hurt. So you boys need to be good and not-'

'I *am* good!' Harry protested indignantly. 'I did all *my* homework. *And* I helped to clean the bath! It was Carl who had his music up so loud it gave Daddy Wayne a headache, and Carl who got mud on the carpet and – and – and -'

As he stumbled to a halt, Dean saw that the boy's lip was trembling again. He strode across the garden and kneeled down so that he could put his arm around him. Harry pulled away and then gave in, burying his face in Dean's shoulder as he hugged him close.

'I know you've been good,' Dean murmured. 'We're all trying our best – you especially. I'm sorry I can't make this horrid virus go away so we can go back to normal, but that's just how it is. If I could do anything to make things better for you and Carl, I would – you know that, don't you?'

Harry nodded and sniffled.

'Now, I'm all yours for the moment; what would you like us to do while Carl's finishing his homework?'

Harry pressed his face harder against Dean's body, and clung on more tightly. Dean rested his cheek against the top of the boy's head and waited. He could feel the movement of Harry's chest as his breaths came jerkily like silent sobs. Was it Harry's heart or his own that was beating with such urgency and rapidity?

At last Harry's breathing slowed and became more regular. His grip around Dean's chest slackened and he moved his head to look up into his father's face. 'Would you read me a story?'

'Yes, of course. Shall we go up to your room and you can choose a book.'

They walked upstairs hand-in-hand. As they passed the open door to the lounge, they heard Carl shouting out triumphantly, 'That makes two sixths, which is the same as … one third!'

Dean could imagine him punching the air in his excitement. Wayne had certainly worked some sort of magic there! Perhaps they would all get through this somehow, after all.

As they rounded the head of the stairs, he heard Wayne's voice, a little weary, but somehow joyful with it. 'That's right! Well done! Who says you can't do fractions?'

* * *

A few streets away, another boy was keeping out of the way of the adults by bouncing a ball around outside. Leo Whittle had picked up his basketball and walked out when his mother slumped down next to him on the sofa with a glass of vodka in her hand. He could hear his father clattering around in the kitchen doing some household chore that he considered to be his wife's sole responsibility as noisily as he could, hoping to make her feel guilty. It was only a matter of time before he came looking for her to berate her for her slovenliness and demand that she rouse herself to do her duty.

Leo preferred to be elsewhere when this happened. He hated to see his normally kind-hearted father roused to anger, shouting in his frustration at the silent and withdrawn woman that his mother had become. She hardly seemed to notice either of them anymore. After spending most of the morning in bed, she would wander down in pyjamas and dressing gown, find herself a bottle of gin or vodka and then dream the day away watching – or pretending to watch – soap operas and game shows or whatever other programmes were on offer to numb her mind and shut out the outside world.

She had been like this when Harry was killed. But at least then she still had her jobs to go to: a daily routine that kept her from the booze until their evening meal. She had to be up early for her first job – cleaning offices before the workers got in to start their own day – then back home for a quick breakfast before going out again to her main occupation, cleaning students' rooms in one of the colleges.

Now, the office workers were all working from home and the students had not returned to Oxford after their Easter break; so Yvonne Whittle's days had no structure, and she had nothing to keep her from numbing her grief and anxiety with alcohol.

Leo did not blame his father for shouting at her when she was like this. Sometimes he wished that he could follow Trevor's example and seize her by the shoulders, shaking her to try to make her take notice. But then, one day he had walked in on his mother when she was getting dressed. (It must have been one of her better days, because she often didn't bother changing out of her pyjamas at all.) She was sitting in front of the mirror in a sleeveless dress, doing something with her hair. As she reached forward to pick up something from the dressing table his eye was drawn to her upper arms. The bright sunlight slanting in through the window showed up some darker patches on the brown skin. His heart gave a lurch as he recognised them as bruises. And they matched the size of his father's hands! He suddenly felt very small and frightened. What if Dad really lost his temper with Mum – as he had seen him do once with Harry when he was alive?

He took aim and threw the ball towards the hoop that was attached to the front of the house, high up between the front door and the shared archway that led through the terrace to the back gardens of the two adjacent houses. It bounced off the backboard, struck the edge of the hoop, teetered on the brink and then dropped through. Smiling with satisfaction at his achievement, Leo allowed it to bounce on the concrete driveway before stepping in and dribbling it round the large silver car that was parked there in a lap of honour.

He lobbed the ball towards the wall, jumping to catch it as it bounced back, pretending that it had been passed to him by an imaginary team mate. He allowed his hands to swing down and up again in a smooth rhythmical movement and then leapt high before releasing the ball, which bounced awkwardly off the rim of the net and came back in a wide arc heading towards his father's taxi. Leo darted forward and only just managed to bat it away with his hand to prevent it landing on the bonnet of the car.

It bounced off the drive and across the next-door lawn. Leo hurried to retrieve it before it could roll into the bed of peonies, which he knew were Mrs Prentice's pride and joy. As soon as he was back on the drive, he started bouncing the ball again, dribbling it expertly between the car and the house and then turning to take aim at the net again.

'What the devil do you think you're doing?'

His father's angry voice ripped through the silence of the deserted street. Leo's hands faltered as he released the ball. It hit the wall short of the net and bounced away out of his reach, landing on the roof of the taxi, bouncing again and then rolling down the windscreen on to the bonnet and finally down to the ground and out into the road.

Leo stood for a moment staring at his father who, also apparently transfixed by the incident, stood at the corner of the house with a bucket of water in one hand and a large sponge in the other. Then Trevor put down the bucket and advanced towards his son. Leo ran out into the road in pursuit of the ball. There it was, in the gutter, gathering speed as it rolled downhill. Leo ran after it.

He caught up with it a few houses down, where the road curved to the right and became less steep. He picked it up and started making his way back, walking slowly, unsure what to expect when he got home. He hadn't meant to damage the car. He was being careful not to allow the ball to touch it. If Dad hadn't shouted at him it would all have been OK! What harm could the ball have done to it anyway? Probably nothing! A bit of a dent on the roof at the very most.

'Hey! You there!'

He turned his head and saw an elderly man with a pair of garden shears in his hand standing behind the privet hedge that divided the front gardens from the pavement. It was Mr Thomas, a retired bus driver. Mum said he was over ninety and he'd lived here ever since the houses were built.

'Yes, you! What do you think you're doing, playing in the road? You ought to be inside. Stay at home. Protect the NHS. Save lives.'

Leo felt his heart pounding in his chest. His cheeks felt as if they were burning. Tears pricked at the back of his eyes. He quickened his pace; then he broke into a run. By the time he turned in at his own drive, he was panting with the effort of racing uphill.

Trevor was waiting for him. He gave him a quick cuff to the side of his head – not hard enough to hurt much, but powerful to humiliate. Leo tried to make a dash for it through the passageway into the back garden, but his father side-stepped to block his way.

'Now you listen to me young man: see this car here?' He made a wide gesture with his arm. 'This is what puts clothes on your back and food on your plate. No taxi, no money: do you understand?'

Leo nodded, not daring to speak.

'And I've told you before: you do not use that basketball hoop when the taxi's on the drive. I thought we had an agreement about that.'

Leo nodded again. He would have liked to point out that since March the taxi had hardly been off the drive; that he'd practised shooting every day since then and this was the first time that the ball had struck the car; and that it was Trevor's sudden shout that had caused the accident on this occasion. But he knew that such protestations would only have infuriated his father. Silent submission was the only safe course.

'OK. Now give me that ball. I'll give it back to you next Saturday, *if* you behave yourself until then.' Trevor took the ball from Leo and handed him the sponge. 'Now, to show you're sorry, you can wash the car. Be sure and make a good job of it or I may change my mind about letting you have that basketball back!'

* * *

High up in a small flat on one of the upper floors of a tower block in East Oxford another father-son relationship was under strain. Weekends count for very little with the nursing staff of a busy hospital – especially during a pandemic – and Crystal Johns was working another "long day", which meant a shift that lasted from seven in the morning to seven at night. That left her husband with the monumental task of keeping Ricky, aged four, and Abigail, shortly to turn three, amused. They had barely reached the middle of the afternoon and already it felt to Eddie that he had had a very long day indeed!

The morning had appeared to start well. The two children helped their father to clear the table after breakfast and then went obediently to their room to play while he washed the dishes. He dried them and made some preliminary preparations for lunch before noticing that the flat had become ominously quiet. Sure enough, when he went to check that all was well, he found the children's bedroom deserted. The only evidence of what they had been doing was a row of dolls and soft toys lying on their backs in the centre of the floor and a toy stethoscope hanging from the end of Ricky's bed.

A giggle from the next room gave away their secret. Eddie hurried in pursuit of the sound. Sure enough, there they were! Ricky was standing at the dressing table busily rummaging in his mother's makeup drawer, while Abigail sat on the edge of the bed, leaning forward to admire her reflection in the mirror. Her face was covered with a thick layer of moisturising cream, which extended into her thick red hair and down her neck to the collar of her dress. Her smiling face turned suddenly sober as she caught her father's eye in the mirror.

'What do you two think you're doing in here?' Eddie demanded, doing his best to sound jocular rather than accusing.

'Face painting!' Ricky replied promptly.

'We've got some proper face paints for you to use. Why didn't you ask me to get them down for you instead of taking Mummy's things?'

'You were busy. We didn't want to bother you.'

Was Ricky being cheeky in his reply, or had he really been acting in a misguided desire not to make demands on his father? Eddie decided that at this stage of the day it would be better to give his son the benefit of the doubt. He led both children firmly out of the bedroom and closed the door. He banished Ricky to the children's room with orders to tidy the toys off the floor. Then he took Abigail into the bathroom and began the slow and messy process of cleaning her face and hair.

That episode set the tone for the day. Eddie tried to stay calm and not to think that Ricky was deliberately going out of his way to exasperate him, but it wasn't easy!

Take their morning walk, for example. Eddie had selected a route for their daily permitted exercise which included a park where the two children could expend some of their, apparently boundless, energy running round on the grass. That was all fine in theory, but Abigail wanted to play on the slide and she started to wail when Eddie told her that the children's play area was out of bounds. She flung herself against the locked gate and kicked her feet against the ground in frustration. Ricky, taking on the role of the know-all older brother, then treated her to a lecture on not touching anything outside the house and keeping two metres away from anyone apart from their family.

Time to head for home, thought Eddie. He removed Abigail's hands from the gate, forcibly uncurling each finger and gripping them firmly to prevent her clinging on again. Then he carried her over to her pushchair. 'Come along, Ricky! We need to go back now.'

But Ricky had spotted a group of teenage boys sitting on the swings, smoking cigarettes. With all the fervour of a Southern Baptist preacher berating backsliding members of his flock, he advanced upon them and started explaining the social-distancing rules in a voice so loud that Eddie was convinced the words must carry across the whole park and probably into some of the surrounding houses. He ran after his son and grabbed his hand, grateful that they were separated from the youths by the railings that surrounded the play area.

'Come along, Ricky. Time to go back. If you're a good boy, we'll do baking after lunch.'

Ricky pulled away, but Eddie held fast to his hand and dragged him back to where Abigail was sitting in her push chair. She had recovered from her tearful outburst and now, with green eyes smiling and red hair shimmering in the bright sunshine, had the appearance of a cherub.

Their departure from the park was accompanied by Ricky declaring to the world his opinion that the police should be called to arrest the offenders.

Eddie felt hot and sweaty just thinking about the incident. Where had Ricky got this forthright determination to set everyone right? He would never have had the courage to approach perfect strangers to admonish them in such a way himself, and he certainly could not imagine Crystal doing so! Perhaps it was spending so much time with his grandfather that did it. Being a retired police officer, Peter did have the ability to assert calm authority when the need arose. Perhaps he would have felt obliged to speak to the youths and ask them to go home. But then he wasn't four years old and a mere three foot four tall – and he didn't have brown skin and frizzy black hair! Eddie didn't want his son to think that he owed white people any sort of deference because of their race, but was it time that he learned that his colour was liable to make that sort of insolent behaviour all the more unacceptable to certain people than if it had come from, say, his white, red-haired sister?

He was still pondering on this question when they arrived back at their block of flats. Ricky proudly held open the glass doors of the foyer to allow his father through with the pushchair. Then he turned and started marching across towards the lift. Eddie called him back.

'No Ricky! Come back over here! We've got to wait our turn.'

The middle-aged woman who was waiting for the lift to descend turned and smiled at them. She waved at the children, and Abigail waved enthusiastically back. Ricky recited solemnly the words printed on the notice on the wall next to the lift doors: *Only one household at a time in the lift.*

The doors opened and the woman got in. Then they closed again and the family crossed the foyer to wait their turn. Abigail clamoured to be lifted up to press the button to summon the lift, but Ricky was there first. He grinned round triumphantly as the light came on signifying that his request had been noted.

'Not fair! Not fair!' his sister wailed. 'My turn!'

'That was naughty, Ricky,' Eddie agreed. 'You pressed the button on the way down. You should have let Abbie do it this time.'

'She did it both ways yesterday,' Ricky argued.

'No, she didn't. You did it on the way back. Don't you remember? You were still eating your ice cream and I had to hold it for you.'

'I didn't mean *then*!' Ricky retorted. 'I meant afterwards, when Mummy was back and you and Abbie went to get more milk 'cos we'd run out.'

'But you didn't come then,' Eddie protested. 'You stayed at home with Mummy.'

'So I can't have pressed the button!' Ricky smiled smugly up at his father, confident that he had made a compelling point in support of his case. Perhaps, after all, his vocation was to become a barrister in later life, rather than a police officer.

'Not fair! Not fair!' Abbie repeated, kicking her feet against the frame of the pushchair. Her shrill voice echoed around the bare walls of the foyer.

Eddie kneeled down and put his face close to hers, speaking softly in an effort to comfort her, while keeping an eye on the illuminated numbers displayed next to the lift doors. It was still on its way up. What a pity that Mrs Cartwright lived on the top floor! Abigail continued to scream. She was tired after her time in the park and hungry for her lunch – and, despite the undoubted logic of Ricky's reasoning, Eddie had every sympathy with her assessment of the lift button situation as unfair on her.

A mother and two children emerged from behind the double doors that separated the stair well from the foyer. They were lucky enough to have a flat on the second floor. The two little girls stared at Abbie as they passed. Ricky smiled at them in a superior way and informed them sagely that *two-year-olds are always throwing tantrums*.

At that moment, Eddie was unsure whether he most desired to smother his daughter or to throttle his son. What he was certain about was that he fervently wished that the lift would come back down soon and that nobody else would enter the foyer in the interim.

'Hi Eddie!' the young mother greeted him with a sympathetic grin. 'I can see it's one of those days!'

Eddie smiled and shrugged. 'You could say that!'

The lift gave a beep, signifying that it had arrived at the ground floor. The doors opened and Ricky raced in. He stood beneath the control panel eager to be lifted up to press the "8" button that would send them speeding – if that was the right word; the ageing lift often seemed to travel painfully slowly – up to their flat.

'No Ricky,' Eddie told him, as he carefully manoeuvred the pushchair inside. 'It's Abbie's turn now.'

'But she did it on the way down!' Ricky protested.

'And you pressed the button outside, just now; so now it's her turn again.'

Eddie picked up Abbie and held her so that she could reach the button marked "8". She pressed it, grinning as it lit up to show that the lift had noted her request and would stop at that floor. An electronic voice announced, 'Doors closing! Lift going up.'

Angry at what he perceived as a monstrous injustice, Ricky reached up and pressed all the buttons that he could reach: 1, 2, 3. He stretched as high as he could, but the others were beyond the tips of his fingers. Eddie put Abigail down and pulled Ricky away from the control panel.

'Ricky! That's naughty.'

The lift doors opened; they had reached the first floor. Eddie hastily pressed the door-close button. The disembodied voice declared once more, 'Doors closing! Lift going up.'

The same happened on the second floor. Then, at floor three, the doors opened and an older couple first stepped forward and then drew back. They retreated down the passage to allow space for the lift passengers to emerge.

'Sorry!' Eddie called out in deep embarrassment. 'Wrong floor!'

'Doors closing! Lift going up.'

He turned to see his son grinning broadly. Ricky had managed to reach the door-close button. Fortunately, Abigail seemed not to have noticed her brother stealing a march on her in the button-pressing stakes. She was more interested in watching the lights changing on the display that indicated which floor they were currently on.

'Six … seven … eight!' she announced.

'That's right, Abbie,' Eddie agreed. 'Eight. Out we get!'

He steered the pushchair out on to the landing, turning to check that both children had followed him out of the lift. Ricky pushed past and headed off in the direction of their flat. Abigail started off after him, then hesitated and took hold of the side of the pushchair instead.

'Ricky was naughty, wasn't he?' she commented as she walked sedately along beside her father. '*I'm* a good girl, aren't I?'

'Well, most of the time,' Eddie conceded, fumbling in his pocket for the key to open the front door.

'I rang the bell!' Ricky declared proudly. 'I've grown! I can reach it now.'

Eddie sighed. 'If you're big enough to reach the doorbell,' he told Ricky, 'you're big enough to know that you mustn't ring it. What's the point, anyway? There's nobody to answer it: we're all out here!'

Lunch was uneventful and Eddie began to hope that his son had exhausted his propensity for mischief and that they might survive the remainder of the day, until Crystal returned from her shift, without any more tears or tantrums. However, Ricky was not about to allow him to get off that lightly! As soon as the plates were cleared from the table, he reminded his father that he had promised to do baking with them that afternoon. Eddie could not argue with this, although, what had seemed like a harmless bribe to persuade his son to stop making an exhibition of himself in the park, now appeared like an extremely rash move, and he was filled with foreboding that this was not going to turn out well.

He flicked through the loose-leaf binder where Crystal kept her recipes, looking for something simple. Remembering the cookies that the children had brought back with them from their grandfather's house on several occasions, he homed in on a recipe for rice biscuits, which you rolled out and cut into shapes. He remembered that Bernie had given them some fancy cutters for Christmas. They would be perfect! The children would enjoy making biscuits in the shapes of different animals, and with any luck, they would be sufficiently absorbed in the task to allow him a few precious minutes in which to check his emails.

Making the dough proved more difficult than he had anticipated. He soon made the discovery that "rubbing in" is not a method that young children find easy or mess-free – especially when they were expected to take turns with the mixing bowl. Their small hands did not lend themselves to manipulating the margarine, flour and sugar with their fingertips in the approved fashion, and soon their palms were coated with a dough that was rapidly taking on an unpleasant greyish hue. The addition of a spoonful of syrup only served to make everything – and everyone – stickier.

Eventually the dough was mixed and Eddie turned it out on to the floured table to roll out. Ricky insisted on going first, causing Abigail to start grizzling. It was only then that Eddie remembered that she still often took a nap after lunch. The exertions of the morning had most likely tired her out and now the least aggravation was liable to provoke uncontrollable sobs – or else angry screams and stamping of her small feet. Never mind – too late now!

He divided the dough into two pieces and hastily cleaned off the rolling pin that belonged with the children's play dough. Now they could both roll and cut at the same time – except that there was only one of each shape of cutter. Predictably, as soon as Abigail selected the teddy bear shape, that became the only one that Ricky wanted to use. Eddie's appeals to him to be grown up and give way to his little sister only made him all the more determined to have his own way. Abigail responded by pulling off pieces of dough and throwing them round the room.

In the end, Eddie marched them both out of the kitchen and sat them down on the settee in the living room. He rang his father, who immediately agreed to hold an impromptu Zoom meeting with them, in the hope of keeping them occupied while Eddie cleaned up the mess in the kitchen and tried to rescue some of the biscuits. For perhaps ten minutes, peace reigned as Ricky gave Granddad a detailed account of their expedition to the park (including his opinion that a major crime had been committed by the boys on the swings) and Peter in his turn showed them the radishes and lettuces that he had harvested that afternoon from their large garden.

Eddie hurriedly rolled the remaining dough and cut it out, hoping all the while that he had not been rash in leaving the children alone with his work laptop. He put the biscuits in the oven and hurried back to the living room just in time to hear Ricky boasting about being tall enough to reach the doorbell. He hastily intervened before the wider subject of button-pressing and the fair allocation of button-pressing duties could be aired. Tact and diplomacy were not Ricky's strong points and neither was Abigail known for her willingness to set aside past wrongs.

'Why don't you show Granddad the paintings you did yesterday?' he suggested, changing the subject with the first thing that came into his head. 'Or better still,' he added when he saw Ricky clambering up on to the back of the sofa to pull down the paint-daubed pieces of sugar paper that his father had attached to the wall, 'I'll turn the computer round so he can see them where they are.'

He walked round the room showing off his children's artistic masterpieces while Peter made suitably admiring remarks about them across the airwaves. The children themselves soon became bored with the proceedings. Abigail fell asleep with her head resting on the arm of the settee. Ricky, deprived of his partner in crime, settled down on the floor with his box of Lego bricks and started building a Fire Station.

Still holding the computer, Eddie wandered back to the kitchen to get the biscuits out of the oven. They were rather uneven in thickness and some had gone a bit too dark at the edges but, on the whole, they did not look as much of a disaster as he had feared. The kids would enjoy eating them at any rate, and that was the main thing. He slumped down in a chair at the kitchen table with the laptop open in front of him.

'How are you all?' Peter asked. 'I mean, apart from the kids doing their best to break up the happy home?'

'We're all fine. Well you can see how full of beans the kids are. I just hope it stays that way. At least Crystal isn't on a COVID ward … but,' he added remembering the incident earlier in the week, 'they do sometimes get patients who turn out to have got it. And however careful everyone is, she must be more at risk than the general public. I do worry that she could bring it home with her – or worse, what if she accidentally contaminates the lift or the door handles in the foyer? She could start an outbreak in the block, and there are lots of older people living here – people who've been here since the flats were built.'

'It *is* a worry,' Peter agreed. 'And it's also not satisfactory having the kids shut up all day in that tiny flat. Why don't you let us lend you the money to get a house with a garden – once Lockdown is over I mean, and you can think about moving?'

'We'd rather wait until we can afford to do it by ourselves,' Eddie insisted. This was a subject that recurred frequently, even in normal times. 'You shouldn't have to subsidise us, and it wouldn't be fair on Hannah.'

'But the money from selling the Divinity Road house is just sitting in the building society doing nothing. It might as well be giving you a leg-up on to the housing ladder.'

'But still …,' Eddie continued to hesitate, although the prospect of having their own front door that led straight into the outside world and a back garden where the children could safely be left to play on their own had recently become extremely alluring.'

'Well, do at least think about it,' Peter urged. 'If you don't like the idea of a loan, how about me buying a house with you and Crystal. You could pay me the interest on my half as rent, if you like, and I'll get the benefit if house prices rise.'

Eddie did not reply, so he went on, 'or the other thing Bernie and I were thinking about was converting our attic into a proper self-contained flat. It wouldn't take much to put in a kitchen and bathroom up there, so you didn't need to share with us. It would probably be a bit smaller than what you've got at the moment, but at least there'd be a garden for the kids.'

'OK Dad, I'll talk to Crystal about it; but really it's not so bad as all that. It's really just Crystal having to work such long hours at the moment, and me trying to work from home as well. At least with all the overtime she's doing we'll soon be able to afford the deposit on a house without you needing to chip in! Anyway, I'd better go. It's always ominous when Ricky hasn't been making any noise for a while.'

Peter sat staring at the blank screen for several seconds after his son's face disappeared. It was now more than a month since he had relinquished the daily care of his grandchildren, but it still felt strange only to see them as images on a computer screen or else standing in the road, in a brief pause during their daily exercise, while he waved to them from his front doorstep. When would things begin to get back to normal? What would this "new normal" that people kept talking about now actually be like?

A month since Lockdown started? That must mean it was … He looked down at his watch to check the date. How strange that he had missed the anniversary of Angie's death. Eddie didn't mention it either. Had he forgotten too? Normally (that word again!) they would have gone together to her grave in Headington Cemetery and put flowers on it: sweet peas from the garden or perhaps wild flowers that the children had picked. Was visiting graves allowed under the Lockdown regulations? Perhaps, if it was part of daily exercise? Or would the cemetery be closed to all but funeral parties?

In any case, he wouldn't want to take the risk. He and Bernie were being especially careful about going outside as little as possible, because it was likely – although nobody really knew – that Jonah was at increased risk of serious complications were he to contract COVID-19. Their awareness of the seriousness of the virus had been heightened all the more by the death of Bernie's Aunty Dot only last week. It had been her funeral three days ago. That must have been what made him forget about Angie. Too many deaths and anniversaries of deaths! And in years to come there would be many more people for whom April was a sad month of remembrance instead of a time of looking forward as the days lengthened and nature blossomed into new life.

He folded down the lid of Bernie's laptop and went upstairs to return it to her study. As he went, he caught sight of the old framed photograph on the wall of her first husband, Richard Paige, as a young police constable. The uniform and youthful face reminded him of Kenny Hughes. Gavin and Chrissie had opted to bury his ashes beneath a new tree that they had planted on Shotover Hill. They must miss being able to drive over there to visit the spot, which they had chosen because Kenny had been happy there. Peter sighed. So many people must be missing the old routines that had provided comfort for their sorrows and some relief from their grief!

6. HOLDING IT TOGETHER

Chrissie tore the headphones from her ears and flung them down on the table in front of her. The voiceover that she had so carefully recorded to accompany the slideshow of images for her lesson on climate change was mysteriously silent when she attempted to play it back. What was wrong? *What had gone wrong?* **What the **** was ****-ing wrong!**

She pressed *record* again and had another go: *testing, testing!* Playing it back produced more obstinate silence. It had worked yesterday. Why wouldn't it-? Her eyes fell on the trailing cable that stretched from the microphone, across the table and ... down to the floor! She bent down to follow its course and realised with a gasp of exasperation that the end was dangling free in mid-air. She had forgotten to plug it into the computer!

It took another two hours to complete the recording to her satisfaction. Now that the microphone was live, her voice seemed singularly uncooperative. She stumbled over simple phrases; her mouth went dry and the words sounded forced and strange; a coughing fit interrupted an otherwise perfect section. Then the neighbour started up his lawn mower and she had to get up to close the window and shut out the background noise.

At last the slideshow and commentary were complete and she was ready to upload it to the *cloud* (wherever that might be), from which, her head teacher had assured her, the children in her class would be able to download and watch it at times that suited their own home routines. She watched hopefully as the progress of the upload was reported on her screen: 20%, 40%, 50%, 75% … and then it seemed to get stuck. Had her computer crashed? Was this *cloud* too full for the whole of her video to fit?

Gavin wandered into the kitchen. It was a rest day for him and, with it being Saturday, he had been hoping that they might have spent some time together. Chrissie, however, was determined to provide the same quality of teaching to those members of her class who were forced to stay at home as to those who would be physically present in school next week. And that meant double lesson preparation and mastering technology that she had never imagined she would ever need.

'Would you like a cuppa?' he asked mildly.

'OK. Thanks,' his wife answered absently without taking her eyes off the screen. A small blue circle was rotating in the centre of it, which, she believed, indicated that the computer was thinking about something. Whatever it was seemed to be taking it a long time – like Alfie, a little boy in her class who always sat with his eyes closed for about five minutes before answering her questions. The final outcome of his cogitation was highly variable: sometimes it was so absurd that she hardly knew where to begin in explaining what the error was in his reasoning; but on other occasions his response was so deep that she wondered if she were in the presence of some sort of philosophical genius. Let's hope the computer was emulating Alfie on one of his good days!

Gavin busied himself with kettle and mugs. While the tea was brewing, he went to the cupboard and got out the biscuit barrel. Then he fished out the tea bags from the mugs and added milk before carrying them across to the table.

'No! Not there!' Chrissie shouted as he set down one of the mugs near her right hand. Put it further along where I can't knock it over.'

Gavin obediently moved the mug and sat down next to his wife, taking care to keep far enough away that he would not obstruct her arm as she moved the computer mouse.

'I think something's gone wrong,' she muttered. 'It's taking forever to upload.'

'Kenny always used to complain that our internet connection was slow,' Gavin pointed out.

'But it got up to seventy-five percent quite quickly and then got stuck,' Chrissie argued. 'Why would it do that?'

'Maybe the computer's doing too many other things. I remember being told that having too many different applications running all at once could slow them down.' Gavin reached over and peered at the screen. 'How about closing some of these windows?'

Chrissie relinquished the mouse and Gavin started going methodically through the tabs at the bottom of the screen, selecting each and closing it down. Eventually, only the file upload window was left and, to his immense satisfaction, the counter had increased to 90%. A few seconds later it announced that the slide show had been successfully saved in the mysterious *cloud*.

'Thanks,' Chrissie smiled. 'Now I can get back to editing this week's learning plan for the parents. And then, once that's done I'll be all set up for Monday.'

'Have a biscuit first,' Gavin urged, holding out the barrel, 'and give yourself a breather. You've been at this all day; it must be time for a break.'

'OK.' Chrissie picked out one of her own home-made chocolate chip cookies and bit into it. 'I suppose you're right. I just want to get everything done so that the parents will have everything ready for next week. Their kids have been coming on with leaps and bounds since Christmas, and I don't want them to lose all the momentum they've built up. Take Rakiya, for example, she was practically non-verbal when she moved into my class in September, and now … And then there's Ryan: he could be in school, seeing as he's registered with Social Services, but his mum's shielding his gran and won't let him out of the house. I thought I'd ring her tomorrow and talk her through what she needs to do with him to stop him falling behind again. We're supposed to be getting some laptops to give to kids who don't have a computer, and Ryan's going to be top of my list to get one.' She sighed. 'But who knows when they'll arrive!'

Chrissie finished her tea and turned back to the computer. Gavin looked on as she clicked the mouse and moved things around on the screen. After a few minutes, he began to sense that there was something wrong, but he remained silent, not wishing to disturb her concentration.

'It's gone!' his wife exclaimed at last. 'Where is it? I can't find it!' She turned and looked accusingly towards Gavin. 'My learning plan isn't there anymore. You must've deleted it when you closed all those windows.'

'I didn't delete anything,' Gavin protested. 'All I did was to close down all those applications you had running.'

'But one of them was where I was editing the learning plan. It must've not saved it. It always asks if you want to save it when you try to close it down. Why didn't you click *yes*?'

'If it asked, I'm sure I will have done,' Gavin insisted, 'but I don't remember it asking.'

'Well, it's gone now. It must be something you did.'

'Have you looked in the recycle bin? If it was deleted it'd have gone there.'

'So you admit you *did* delete things!' Chrissie seized upon this apparent admission of guilt.

'No!' Gavin raised his voice for the first time and then hastily moderated his tones. 'No,' he repeated in the unnaturally calm voice of someone who is struggling to keep his temper under considerable provocation, 'I didn't delete anything, I just meant: if either of us did accidentally delete your file, that's where it'd be.'

'Are you saying *I* deleted it without even knowing? That's ridiculous!'

'No more ridiculous than saying *I* did. And at least you've got your video uploaded now!'

'It'd probably have been OK just leaving it to finish. What did you want to interfere for?'

'I'm sorry. I was only trying to help.'

'Well don't! Just go away and let me get on. I've got to start writing that Learning Plan all over again now.'

'OK, if that's what you want.' Gavin put his mug in the sink and returned the biscuit barrel to the cupboard. 'I'm going for a walk.'

He opened the back door and almost collided with Craig, who was on his way in.

'Hi there! I'd forgotten you were working an early shift today. I was just on my way out for a walk. Care to come too? Chrissie's up to her eyes in lesson preparation, so I thought I'd get out from under her feet.'

'No thanks,' Craig sighed. 'I think I'll go up to my room, if it's all the same to you. I've been on my feet all day.'

'Sorry. Yes, of course.' Gavin looked more closely at the younger man's tired face. 'Is everything OK? You look all-in.'

'Sure, I'm fine.' Craig advanced into the kitchen. 'Hi Chrissie. D'you mind if I just get myself a drink of water, and then I'll get off upstairs out of your way.'

'Nonsense!' Pushing her lost Learning Plan to the back of her mind, Chrissie forced herself to smile cheerfully. 'The kettle's just boiled. You sit down here and have a cup of tea. How did things go today? Have they decided who's getting the supervisor's job, yet?'

'Yes,' Craig mumbled morosely. 'Yes, they have.'

'And?' Chrissie continued to smile, although it was clear from his demeanour that the news had not been welcome.

'They've given it to Declan. Declan! What does he know about anything? He only left uni last summer! But that's why they picked him. He's got a degree, and the idiots on the panel think that makes him a cut above the rest of us. But if he was any good he'd have got a proper job wouldn't he? Instead of lugging stuff around in a warehouse, and packing boxes!'

'Oh well!' Chrissie tried to be reassuring. 'At least you got an interview. That's good experience for the future. And next time-'

'Next time, I'll know better than to bother applying,' Craig growled, still heading towards the stairs. 'I *knew* they weren't looking for someone like me!'

'Oh! I expect you were just nervous at the interview and didn't do yourself justice.' Chrissie, got up and stood barring his way. 'Now just sit down and Gav will get you some tea – we've both just had some – and there's still some of that chocolate cinnamon cake left, that you said you liked. I'll get some plates and we can all have a slice.'

'That's your answer to everything!' Craig retorted, pushing Chrissie roughly out of his way. 'Have a drink and something nice to eat and that'll make everything right again! I'm not one of your retarded kids that just needs a pat on the head and they'll stop crying. I'm-'

'Just cut that out!' Gavin shouted, cutting across this outburst. 'Chrissie's only trying to help. And if you think she's treating you like a child, maybe it's because you're behaving like one.'

'And you shouldn't talk about the children like that,' Chrissie put in. '*Retarded* isn't acceptable language now. They have Special Educational Needs. And they all have their own talents – they're just different from what most people expect.'

'Whatever!' Craig shrugged.

He took another step towards the door, but Gavin grasped his shoulder and held him back.

'Look here,' he said, planting his bulk firmly in front of Craig and looking him directly in the eye. 'Chrissie's been working on these lesson plans all day. She's just as tired as you are. She doesn't deserve to have you coming in here talking like that. I reckon you owe her an apology, don't you?'

Craig maintained a sulky silence. He knew that Gavin was right, but he was still sore at the result of the interview – not so much because he had been passed over for promotion, which was only what he had expected – but at the thought that anyone had considered the hapless Declan to be the better candidate, and he could not help laying some of the blame for his humiliation at Chrissie's door. If she hadn't badgered him to apply, he would never have known how much his boss didn't rate him.

'Come on, I'm waiting.'

Craig glared back at Gavin. 'Now you're doing it too! I am *not* a child; I don't need cake; and I don't need you to teach me how to behave!' He forced his way past and out of the door, calling back as he slammed it shut behind him, 'I'm off to put myself on the naughty step, OK?'

'Oh Gav!' Chrissie sighed. 'Now look what you've done!'

Gavin opened his mouth to protest, then changed his mind and strode across to the back door in silence. He wrenched it open and marched out, at first leaving it swinging and then coming back to pull it closed, not slamming it but making sure that there was enough sound created to mark his departure.

Chrissie watched him go, fighting back the tears that were starting to well up. What had happened to them all? They didn't usually fight like this over nothing at all!

She blinked her eyes and tried to concentrate on the screen in front of her, but the words all appeared out of focus. She wiped her hand across her face, but it made no difference. What was wrong with her? She just *had* to get this Learning Plan sorted! She got up and walked across the room to get a tissue from the box on the windowsill. Sitting on top of it was a teddy bear wearing a police uniform. It had been left by a well-wisher among the flowers that had accumulated at the site of Kenny's killing. There had been no name, just a line or two expressing regret at his passing. Such a nice gesture – but so sad!

She stared at it thoughtfully before picking it up and pulling out a tissue from beneath it. She wiped her eyes and then returned to her seat carrying the bear in one hand. She put it down on the table next to the computer and addressed it solemnly.

'*I* know what I can give the class for this week's English project,' she told him seriously. 'You need a name. We can't go on calling you "the bear" forever! I'll ask the children to research names and find a good one for a police bear. And then I'll get them each to give a little talk explaining why the name they've chosen is the best! There can be a little prize for the best idea, and … I know! *I* won't choose the winner; we'll get a real police officer to do it. Gav would, I'm sure, but maybe … I wonder if DCI Porter would be the judge? And he could present the prize too – well it would have to be a virtual ceremony, but … Yes! I'll get Gav to ask him. He's such a good role model for the children.'

She settled down happily and opened *Word* with the intention of producing some written instructions to explain the teddy bear naming task. Immediately a message appeared: *Word has recovered files that you might want to keep*. Beneath that was an icon and the words: *Show Recovered Files*. Of course! Somehow, Gavin must have crashed the word processor instead of closing it down properly, but it had kept a copy of the files that she was working on at the time. She clicked on the link and was presented with a list of files, including the missing Learning Plan.

She looked towards the door, hoping that her husband would be back soon so that she could tell him that all was well. And what about Craig? Should she go up and apologise to him and explain that she wasn't thinking straight because of worrying about the Learning Plan? No, probably better to give him time to cool down. She would finish her work and then take him up a cup of tea and see if she couldn't raise his spirits a bit. It must have been a blow not getting the promotion that he so clearly deserved.

7. CABIN FEVER

Chrissie was not the only one experiencing computer problems that Saturday afternoon. In a small Victorian terraced house in another part of the city, Stan and Sylvia Corbridge were struggling to get to grips with an old laptop that Bernie had given them. She had delivered it two days earlier, along with their groceries, leaving them on the doorstep and then standing well back while they took everything inside. There had followed a short exchange of greetings and then they had closed the door, leaving Sylvia's cake tin (containing her cake and a cheque to pay for the shopping) outside for Bernie to pick up and take home.

Was all that really necessary, Stan wondered. He and Sylvia never went out anymore, and Bernie was staying at home with only Peter and Jonah; so how could any of them have coronavirus? But, of course, Bernie hadn't been at home all the time: she'd been to the supermarket every week to get their shopping. She could have been infected there, but not be showing any symptoms. That was why she insisted on keeping the statutory two metres away from them when she visited, and wouldn't come inside at all.

That was the problem. Usually when Bernie introduced them to a new bit of kit – the mobile phones that they took with them whenever they went out, or the alarm pendant that she had insisted they wore, in case one of them were to have a fall when they were alone in the house – she sat down with them and showed them how it worked. This time, she had assured them that it was "all set up", but that did not take into account their ignorance of the technology. She had talked them through what to plug in where, over the phone, but that was only the beginning!

Take the mouse, for example: Stan could see that when he moved it across the table a pointer moved across the screen, but what should he do when his hand hit the wall but the pointer still had some way to go before it reached the position he was aiming at? And it was all very well for Bernie to tell him to "click on the Zoom icon", but whenever he tried to click the mouse button, the pointer moved so that it was longer pointing at the right place on the screen!

'It's no good!' he declared eventually. 'I give up! You can't teach an old dog new tricks. And what do we need a computer for, anyway? I've managed for eighty years without one.'

'Let me have a go,' Sylvia said, coming up behind him and leaning over the back of his chair. 'Go on! You go and make us a brew, while I see if I can't get it to do something.'

Stan took hold of his stick, which was leaning up against the side of his chair, and heaved himself into a standing position. Walking stiffly, because he had been sitting awkwardly for the last hour, he made his way from the dining room into the adjacent kitchen, allowing his wife to take his place at the table.

An hour and a half – and three cups of tea – later, she was still sitting there, staring dismally at the screen. It had all seemed so straightforward when Bernie had described what they needed to do, but somehow nothing looked the way she had told them it would!

'I'd give up, if I were you,' Stan advised. 'It's only an old computer that Bernie had lying around doing nothing. She won't mind if we tell her it's not for us.'

'But I want to be able to do things,' Sylvia insisted. 'I want to be able to get our shopping delivered, so Bernie doesn't have to do it for us, and I want to know what these Zoom calls that everyone keeps talking about are like. I'm getting there – I hope! I think I sent Bernie an email just now.'

'You think?'

'Well, the computer said it had sent it, but I can't tell for sure until she replies.'

'I could give her a ring and ask her if she's got it.'

'No. I expect she's busy. I'll have another go at ordering next week's shopping. I think I'm nearly there. I got on the website, but then it said I was in a queue.'

'If you still have to queue, you might as well go to the shop and do it,' Stan grumbled.

'Well, at least in this queue you're sitting down! Oh look! Bernie's got my email. She's sent one back!'

After a few seconds of fumbling with the mouse, Sylvia managed to open Bernie's email: '*That's great*', she read aloud. '*Now let's try a Zoom meeting. Just click on the link below.* What does she mean by a *link*?'

'It must be that blue writing,' Stan told her, pointing at the screen. 'That stuff there, that looks like gibberish.'

Sylvia moved the mouse. At first, she couldn't see the pointer. Then it suddenly appeared at the opposite side of the screen from the blue text. She carefully drew the mouse across the table, watching the pointer intently as it, too, moved. To her surprise, when it reached the blue text the pointer vanished and was replaced by the image of a hand with one finger pointing.

'That's it!' Stan said with unexpected excitement in his voice. 'Click the mouse now!'

Sylvia pressed down the button on top of the mouse. At once the screen seemed to burst into life. Boxes seemed to be appearing and disappearing all over the place. Messages popped up and then vanished again. Then, all of a sudden, Bernie's smiling face appeared, occupying a large rectangle near the centre of the screen.

'Hi there!' came her unmistakeable tones, with that broad Liverpool accent that came across even in those few words of greeting. 'No – hang on a minute! You're on mute. I can un-mute you, because I'm the host of this meeting, but I'll show you how you can do it yourself as well, for if you're doing a Zoom with someone else. … OK. Say something, so we can check the audio's working.'

'Hello?' Sylvia ventured uncertainly. 'Is this alright? Can you hear me?'

'You're coming across loud and clear!' Bernie confirmed. 'Now let's sort it so that I can see you as well. Can you see somewhere on your screen a black rectangle? It's probably at the top. It should say "Stan and Sylvia" in white writing inside it.'

'I'm not sure … oh yes! There it is.'

'OK. That's where you'll be able to see yourself once we get the video working properly. Now if you hover your mouse down near the bottom of the Zoom window, some buttons ought to pop up.'

Sylvia moved the mouse pointer down towards the bottom of the screen. For what seemed like a long time nothing happened, then some strange pictures appeared near where the pointer was positioned.

'Can you see them?' Bernie asked.

'I can see something,' Sylvia answered doubtfully.

'Can you see an icon that looks like a TV camera?'

'Yes, I think so. It's second from the left.'

'That sounds right. Try clicking on that.'

Sylvia tried to follow Bernie's instructions. She carefully manoeuvred the pointer along the line of icons and clicked the mouse button. For several moments nothing happened. Sylvia and Stan sat looking hopefully at the screen, where Bernie's face also registered concentration.

'Hang on!' Bernie called out at last. 'You must've hit the *mute* button by mistake. Can you see? There's a red line through it now. Click on it again, so I can hear you again; and then have another go at turning the video on.'

It seemed like forever, but in reality it was only a few minutes later that they had got everything sorted out and Sylvia could see both a large image of Bernie in the centre of her screen and a smaller one of herself (with Stan sitting beside her) above it.

'That's better,' Bernie declared with satisfaction. 'Now, if we had more people on the call, they'd each have their own window, like the one you can see me in, and the person who's speaking at any given time would be the one who appears largest.'

'I see,' Sylvia said, hoping that she did.

'It all seems like a lot of faffing about, when we could just give you a ring,' Stan grumbled.

'Except that you can only speak to one person at a time on the phone,' Bernie pointed out. 'Now you've got a computer, you'll be able to join in virtual church on Sundays, with all your friends.'

'And I'm going to start ordering things online,' Sylvia added. 'Then we won't need Bernie to do all our shopping for us.'

'Not that I mind doing it,' Bernie said hastily. 'That isn't why I gave you the laptop.'

'But I'd rather you didn't have to,' Sylvia insisted. 'The trouble is, I haven't managed to get through to them yet. It says I'm in a queue.'

'Why not have another go, while I'm here to help,' Bernie suggested. 'I set up accounts for you with three separate supermarkets. You could try a different one. And you can do that at the same time as carrying on this conversation with me. Just go back to the browser and click on one of the bookmarks I made for you. The computer will remember the password I set up, so it all ought to happen pretty much automatically.'

"Pretty much automatically" seemed to involve a lot more effort from Sylvia than the words suggested, but eventually she did manage to get logged in on the site of another major supermarket. She peered at the screen, trying to work out what to do next.

'It says "select delivery slot",' she told Bernie. 'Should I click on that?'

'Yes.'

'It says "Sorry no slots available".'

'Oh! I suppose they're busy with so many more people wanting food delivered. You could try again another day.'

None of the shops that Bernie had chosen for them was able to deliver next week's groceries to Sylvia.

'Never mind,' Bernie said cheerfully. 'I'm perfectly happy to get it for you. I have to go out for ours in any case, and it's nice to see you each week, even if I can't come in for a chat. The main thing is that it'll be easier for us to keep in touch now.'

'We're very grateful,' Stan assured her, 'but to be honest, this all seems to be a lot of palaver when we already have the telephone.'

'Yes,' agreed Sylvia. 'It was really just the shopping I wanted.'

'And anyway,' Stan continued, 'they said on the radio last night that we've passed the peak and infections are on the way down. Things could be back to normal before we've got the hang of all this stuff!'

'I'm afraid infections are only down because we're *not* letting things get back to normal,' Bernie said, with as much patience as she could muster. 'As soon as people start mixing again, the rate will start to climb again; so we really do all need to work out how to live with the restrictions.

And, Sylvia,' she went on, 'I expect you *will* be able to use it for shopping when supermarkets have had time to get geared up for more online customers, but really that isn't the main reason I gave you the laptop. Now you'll be able to watch the Sunday service and join in with the discussion afterwards. And – and I'll be able to show Stan that his pigeons are doing OK,' she added, desperately trying to think of something that would make persevering with the new technology appealing to him.

'Alright, lass,' he growled back. 'I've got the message. The old curmudgeon is going to be dragged into the twenty-first century, whether he likes it or not. Don't you worry! Just leave us be for a bit and we'll figure all this out. We're not going to let some stupid machine get the better of us!'

Bernie smiled as she ended the videoconference. Then, as soon as she was sure that Stan and Sylvia could no longer hear her, she sighed. Why couldn't they be more like Aunty Dot! She had been twenty years older than they were, and yet she had embraced new technology eagerly. It must have been five years ago – no, more than that – that she had obtained an iPad and started browsing the internet. She had been an avid user of Twitter and Facebook too – much more so than her niece who had so much else to occupy her time! When Lockdown came, Dot had taken Zoom meetings in her stride – unlike her nephew, Bernie's cousin Joey, who had only ventured into the world of videoconferencing when it became the only way of checking on his elderly aunt in her Care Home.

Joey! She really ought to ring him to see how he was after the funeral. It was good of them to make a video of it so that the whole family could feel that they had been given the opportunity to say goodbye, even though only six were allowed in the crematorium chapel. Father Nat's eulogy had been spot-on. He obviously knew Our Dot very well. Poor Lucy, having to be there on her own – well, not quite because her younger cousins were with her.

Bernie reached across the desk and pulled a tissue out of the box that lay hidden away behind the computer screen. She dabbed her eyes and blew her nose. She ought to have spent more time with her aunt when she was alive. Those thirty years – no, it must be more like thirty-five – when she'd been "too busy" to make the journey to Liverpool to visit her relatives, were the years when she could really have got to know her as adults together. As it was, her memories were split between those of the strict aunty, helping her mother to bring up a recalcitrant teenager, and the old lady crippled with arthritis confined to a Care Home. All those years! Years when they could have been walking together in the park or taking the ferry to New Brighton or …

'Pull yourself together, Bernadette!'

Bernie froze in the act of reaching for another tissue. The voice sounded so real. It was Aunty Dot's voice: not the wheezy voice of an old woman struggling for breath as she slowly dies from COVID-19, or the weak, cracked voice of a centenarian, but the vigorous voice that so often used to call Bernie into line when she was a child.

'No point crying over spilt milk,' the voice continued. 'Too late to start worrying about that now. And what makes you think I was pining for you all those years? What so special about you, young lady?'

Bernie smiled through her tears. Yes, that was Aunty Dot alright; she never liked to be pitied – like Bernie, herself. Still, she shouldn't have had to die alone. Well, not really alone: Jonathan had been there, holding her hand as she wheezed her last. Jonathan, her favourite member of staff at the Care Home, the nurse who had seen her through years of decreasing mobility and increasing pain. He couldn't have been kinder or more compassionate, but still …

Dot had always been the one who was there for people: the dutiful daughter, the older sister, the maiden aunt. She must have presided at any number of death beds – like a sort of midwife in reverse! She had seen Bernie's mother out of the world all those years ago. And she had insisted that seventeen-year-old Bernie was allowed to be there too. She had understood that sometimes it was worse to be left to imagine the horror that the grown-ups were shielding you from than to experience the reality.

'But your mam didn't have a highly contagious virus, did she?' There was that voice again. 'They couldn't allow you to be there. I was a nurse for more than forty years. I know about infection control. I only hope Jonathan doesn't get it.'

'He's been alright so far,' Bernie murmured back. 'Don't you remember? He was at the funeral.'

This was ridiculous! She had actually been having a conversation with her dead aunt! What on earth would Aunty Dot have had to say about that? Something scathing, certainly – and probably more injunctions to pull herself together. That had been a favourite phrase of hers, usually aimed at members of the younger generation, whom she believed were all considerably lacking in backbone.

Yes, Aunty Dot was never afraid to speak her mind. She had soon put a stop to Bernie's ideas of giving up her place at Oxford in order to stay at home to look after her father after her mother died.

'What ever put that idea into your mind, Bernadette? Don't you think Our Kid has enough on his plate with his wife hardly cold in her grave, without you threatening to keep hanging round the place like a November fog? And it would have broken your mam's heart to think of you throwing up your chances just because she's not here to give you a good kicking in the you-know-what! It isn't every mam who can say her daughter's got a scholarship to Oxford! You get off down there and show them soft southerners that a good Catholic girl from Liverpool can run rings round the lot of them!'

Our Kid! Dad must have been nearly fifty then, but he was the youngest of the thirteen Fazakerley siblings and hence forever "Our Kid". The youngest, but one of the first to follow "Our Elspeth" into the grave. Even with Dot's best efforts, Bernie had only *just* made it to that death bed.

There were no mobile phones in those days – at least not any that ordinary people had – and it had taken several hours for Dot to get the message through that Gerard Fazakerley had been admitted to the Royal Liverpool Hospital with a major stroke. Then more hours as the train made its tediously slow progress north.

And Aunty Dot had been there on the concourse at Lime Street station, waiting for her; still in her nurse's uniform, because she'd come straight from the ward to meet her, to take her to the hospital room where he lay, barely conscious. Had he even recognised her?

Then, after Father Leneghan had administered the last rites and the doctor had confirmed that he had "passed away" – what a silly way of describing it, as if he had somehow slipped out of the room while she wasn't looking – Dot had gone back with her to the little terraced house in Toxteth, where Bernie had lived all her life until she made the momentous journey down to Oxford and a new beginning.

Dot had guided her through the business of arranging a funeral, clearing the house and settling accounts. Years of short-time working and the care of a disabled wife had depleted any savings her father had had. Would he have lived longer if she had made more effort to persuade him to accept financial help once she had secured her fellowship and with it a steady income? Or if she had come back to Liverpool and found a job there, where she could see that he was looking after himself?

'Nonsense! You have a very high opinion of yourself, young lady! Our Kid was already worn out with looking after your mam all those years. Once he'd seen you settled in a good job, he was ready to join her. There's nothing *you* could have done to change it.'

But she could have been more grateful for all the sacrifices he'd made, bringing her up. And she should have been more devastated when he died. She shouldn't have felt relieved that now there would be no reason to return to her childhood haunts. And she should have done more to keep in touch with Aunty Dot and Uncle Michael and Aunty Rose, and all the other uncles and cousins. She'd hardly even exchanged Christmas cards with any of them except Joey!

'You had your own troubles! That half-witted fiancé of yours, topping himself on the eve of your wedding. We all understood.'

Stephen wasn't half-witted! And who knows why he took his own life? Yes. She'd forgotten about that. That was where the rift with Aunty Dot had begun. She always prided herself on "speaking as I find", but in a rare error of judgement, she had gone too far when expressing her contempt for the young man who had won her niece's heart and then, as she saw it, failed her dismally.

'You're better off without him,' she had declared. 'Suicide is an act of cowardice. He'd have let you down in the end; you mark my word.'

Was that why Dot herself had never married? Was she too exacting? Were her expectations of a husband too high? Or had she scared off all her admirers with her straight talking? But that was what Bernie had most admired in her – or was it just that she wanted some justification for her own forthrightness? She might well have said much the same thing if it had been someone else's boyfriend. She thought she'd mellowed over the years, but maybe it was just that she didn't care enough to bother giving her opinion to all and sundry.

No, she did believe that she was more tolerant now – and more tactful. Perhaps it was Richard's influence. He'd certainly suffered enough at her hands, with her pride and self-reliance and resentment of any offer of help! Or could it be motherhood that wrought the change? You had to be gentle with someone who appeared so small and fragile that the least trauma might break them. Peter must have had a hand in it too: poor long-suffering Peter, who'd seen through the upbringing of his own two children and then embarked on the whole parenting business all over again with Lucy, after his first marriage had tragically ended.

'Pull yourself together, girl! You're getting maudlin. Stop feeling sorry for yourself and get on with things. What was it you came up here to do?'

Ordering! She had logged into her computer to order more PPE; and then she'd seen Sylvia's email and everything had snowballed from there. She must get that order in before it was too late to get a delivery next week. They were almost out of disposable gloves and they had already had to resort to re-using supposedly single-use plastic aprons.

She opened a browser and clicked on the bookmark that took her to their usual supplier. A message immediately popped up in a red box, telling her that they still had no stock. Understandably, supplies were being diverted to the NHS and Care Homes. The COVID pandemic had massively increased demand, but what about people whose disabilities and long-term medical conditions meant that they needed these things all the time? How were they going to manage Jonah's daily bowel care routine without any gloves to wear?

Another site, another disappointment: they were taking orders, but delivery was expected to be in four weeks' time. In desperation, she turned to eBay and Amazon. There were plenty of advertisements here, but the prices were sky high. And how could she be sure that the suppliers were reputable? Better put in an order with the two companies that she'd used before, and then, what to do as a backup? Would the local pharmacy have some gloves? She'd better ring them before going out, but they'd be closed soon. Where had all the time gone? Should she go out now and place the order after she got back, or …?

'Peter!' Bernie put her head round the living room door. Her husband was reading in one of the arm chairs near the French windows that overlooked the garden. 'Could you pop down to the chemist to see if they've got any disposable gloves? I'm going to order some, but they're saying three to six weeks delivery time and we've only got enough for a few days.'

'OK.' Peter put an old railway ticket in his book to mark the place and got to his feet. He'd been looking forward to an hour or so relaxing, now that the casserole that he had prepared for their evening meal was in the oven, but Bernie's request obviously must take precedence.

'Oh! And see if you can get some face masks while you're there. I think maybe I ought to start using one when I'm getting close up and personal with Jonah – just in case I were to pick up coronavirus at the supermarket.'

'Right you are!' Peter picked up his cycle clips from the dresser and headed out through the French windows. People kept talking on the radio about how difficult it was to fill the hours during Lockdown, but they all seemed to be busier than ever!

The first two pharmacies that he tried had no gloves or masks, but he did manage to obtain a pack of five plastic aprons. He returned to his bike and set off again, venturing further and further afield in the hope of locating a shop that still had supplies of PPE left. The queue outside a pharmacy on Cowley Road looked promising. They must have something that people needed or there wouldn't be so many of them waiting for their turn to enter.

He locked his bike to a drainpipe and walked over to stand two metres behind the young black woman at the back of the line. She turned to look at him.

'Hello Peter! What brings you all the way over here?'

'I'm on a quest for surgical gloves. How about you?'

'Collecting my gran's repeat prescription.'

'Can't you get it delivered?'

'We did, but this month they missed out one of her pills and she didn't notice, and now she's run out.'

'How is she?'

'Fed up! She's had a letter telling her that she's in the shielding group and mustn't go out at all. With her age and her heart condition and her chest it's only what we expected, but she seems to be taking it personally!'

A woman came out of the shop and the middle-aged man at the head of the queue went in. Everyone shuffled two metres closer to the door.

'And Danny doesn't make things any easier. He's on furlough from work, so he's stuck in the house all day too – or he should be! I have a nasty suspicion he takes more "exercise" than just once a day for the sake of his health!'

'It must be hard for him – a young man, full of energy and always used to being out and about.'

'It sometimes makes me feel guilty about my job,' Stella confessed. 'I'm off out every day, while Gran and Danny are stuck at home watching TV. Gran's always been a busy sort of person and Danny …' She sighed. 'Well, Danny never likes being told what to do.'

'They also serve, who only stand and wait. I mean: staying at home is their way of helping to keep everyone safe.'

'I keep telling them that, but it doesn't make it any less boring for them. To be fair, Gran seems a lot better now she's started sewing scrubs for the hospital. At least she feels she's doing something now.'

Another customer left the shop and they moved up a place. Stella was now first in the queue and a young woman with a baby was waiting behind Peter.

'It's Danny I'm more worried about, if I'm honest. He nearly blew a fuse this afternoon. I was glad of the excuse to get out of the house. I was only trying to cheer him up, but he tore into me like I was …' Stella sighed. 'I guess it's difficult for him having his little sister giving him advice.'

The door opened again.

'Your turn,' Peter pointed out. 'It was nice talking to you. Give my love to Danny and your gran.'

Stella nodded and smiled before turning away and stepping into the shop. There were two assistants serving at the counter – spaced well apart and with a Perspex screen between them and the customers. The one on the right beckoned to her to approach. She gave her grandmother's name and explained about the missing medication. The customer at the other end of the counter paid contactlessly with his credit card, took his receipt and went out.

Peter came in just as the assistant returned with a paper bag containing Celeste Gilbert's prescription. Stella murmured her thanks, nodded goodbye to Peter (who smiled back and raised his hand to her) and escaped back into the fresh air to walk the short distance back home.

On the corner of the street, her way was blocked by a group of white youths. As she approached, she saw a tall fair-haired lad hand a lighted cigarette to one of his companions. So much for social distancing! Should she remind them that they should not be socialising, or pretend that she thought they were members of a single household? Without her uniform, she did not fancy her chances of establishing her authority over them, and things might easily turn nasty if they were to take offence at her presuming to lecture them on their behaviour.

She walked out into the road in an attempt to pass them, but as she did so some of those on the outer edge of the group also stepped off the kerb. Now that she had rounded the corner, she could see that there were more of them than she had realised, perhaps two dozen, maybe more. She crossed over to the opposite pavement, but they continued to spread out so that it was impossible to enter the side street without pushing through the mass of human flesh. Was this a deliberate attempt to block her way?

'Excuse me,' she said, conscious of a slight tremor in her voice which she tried to suppress. 'I need to get through here.'

She immediately felt all their eyes on her. Was it her imagination or did they look as if they were amazed at her audacity in daring to speak to them? Then two of them moved and the sea of bodies parted. Stella walked forward. No chance of keeping apart by two metres, but at least …

An enormously fat lad, bare to the waist, his body covered with tattoos lurched in front of her, belching loudly in her face. Laughter went round the mob as Stella flinched involuntarily and took a step back. The youth took a swig from the two litre bottle of cheap supermarket cider that he was carrying and then held it out towards her.

'Have a drink,' he drawled. 'Go on! 'S on me!'

'No thank you.' Stella tried to maintain her dignity and to speak politely, as she had been trained to do. She could feel her heart beating faster and had to concentrate hard to control her breathing. 'I need to get home right away. My grandmother needs her medication.' She held up the paper bag with the name of the pharmacy on it.

'Did you hear that?' came a voice from behind her. 'She's going home!'

She felt a dig in her ribs and turned to see a brawny young man with greasy black hair flopping over his face. He breathed beer fumes over her as he went on, 'It's a long way to Africa! Be sure and take plenty of bananas for the journey!'

Another wave of raucous laughter spread through the group. Stella could feel her palms becoming sweaty. Her breathing was out of control now and her heart was pounding as if it were trying to break out of her chest.

'Please! I really do need to get home to my gran.'

'What's stopping you?' slurred the young man with the cider bottle. 'I was only offering you a drink.' He turned round to his comrades, holding the bottle high above his head. 'That's right, isn't it? I was only being friendly!'

He turned back to Stella and put his arm round her shoulder. She sensed her muscles tightening as she felt its warmth and weight. 'Come on! Lighten up!' He belched again. 'Have a few drinks with us.'

'Let the bitch go, Mitch.' It was the lad with the greasy black hair. 'Them black tarts ain't nothin' but trouble. She'll be calling the cops next, claiming you assaulted her!'

This remark provoked another round of guffaws. Clearly the idea of a black woman summoning the police was a highly amusing one. Stella braced herself and pushed past "Mitch" who tottered backwards at this unexpected move and collided with a spotty teenager who was in the act of taking a swig from a can of lager.

'Watch it, Mitch!' he shouted as the beer spilled down the front of his tee shirt.

Taking advantage of the confusion, Stella strode forward, trying to remain calm and purposeful. But as she soon as she was sure that she was clear of the crowd, she broke into a run. She could still hear their strident voices and coarse laughter as she turned in at the gate that separated their small front garden from the road, but mercifully none of them had followed her home.

She stood on the doorstep, forcing herself to breathe deeply and slowly for several minutes before putting the key in the lock. Everything was fine. They weren't dangerous. They were just foolish young people who had had too much to drink. And she wasn't a failure for not having attempted to disperse them, or a coward for having run away.

'Hi Gran! I'm back! Sorry it took so long; there was a queue at the chemist.'

8. LOSING IT

'Oh! *You're* back early.' Chrissie hesitated in the doorway of the lounge when she caught sight of Craig slouched on the sofa staring into space. He had the TV remote control in his hand, but the set was turned off. At the sound of her voice he looked up and grunted something indecipherable.

Chrissie put her school bag down on the floor next to her favourite chair. She had been hoping to mark the mathematics exercises that her class had done that afternoon before getting the evening meal, but Craig's demeanour – and his presence here when his shift was not supposed to end for another hour – made her change her plans. Something was up and she would not be able to concentrate until she had found out what it was.

'I'm going to make myself a pot of tea,' she said brightly. 'Shall I make you a cup too?'

'Whatever.'

Yes; there was definitely something wrong. Chrissie went out to the kitchen and filled the kettle. She must be careful. Too much overt solicitousness might make him clam up with accusations that she was treating him like a child. She must remember that he was not her son, although she felt equally protective of him, just as she did for each of the children in her class at school. He was just a friend – a paying guest – a lodger, even.

She put the teapot on a tray, alongside plates, cups and saucers. Now, which would be better – cake or biscuits? He had felt patronised by her offering cake when he was upset the other day; perhaps biscuits – especially shop-bought ones – would be less likely to provoke resentment. She got out the biscuit barrel and added it to the tray. That was definitely the better idea. She would take one herself and leave him to help himself if he wanted, so that it didn't look as if she was pushing them as some sort of therapy for whatever it was that was bugging him.

'I'm sorry!' she called out as she walked down the hall towards the lounge. 'I've got the tray in my hands. Do you think you could open the door for me?'

There was a muffled reply from inside and then a few moments later the door swung wide. As soon as she was in the room, Craig darted back to the sofa and started clearing a space on the coffee table, making a tidy pile of magazines, which he stowed on the shelf beneath it, and moving aside a box of bicycle spare parts that Gavin had been rummaging in the previous evening.

Chrissie put down the tray and poured the tea. Softly, softly, she reminded herself; don't say anything to spook him. It was like stalking a particularly timid species of rare antelope: any sudden movements might send him racing for cover. She bent down and got out the police teddy bear from her bag.

'I introduced him to the children this morning,' she said, trying to pitch her voice so that she might almost be speaking to herself. 'They liked the idea of finding a name for him – but they weren't quite so delighted that I wanted them to write about why they'd chosen it and give a little talk to the rest of the class!'

Craig muttered something unintelligible and reached forward for his tea. Chrissie opened the biscuit barrel and laid the lid down on the table. She selected a Bourbon cream for herself and then pushed the barrel silently along the table towards Craig, who ignored her. He took a silent sip from his teacup and then put cup and saucer back down on the table.

'I wish I knew who left him,' Chrissie went on. 'There was a note with him, but I couldn't read the name.'

'Maybe they wanted to be anonymous.'

Well, at least Craig was talking at last!

'I suppose so, but then you'd think they'd just not sign it at all, wouldn't you?'

'Yeah. Maybe.'

Not very promising, but he was still responding – after a fashion!

'Rakiya wanted to know what the prize would be. I hadn't really thought about it. Do you have any ideas?'

'Chocolates?' Craig reached into the biscuit barrel and fished out a Jammie Dodger. 'Kids always like getting sweets, don't they?'

'Well, we're trying to encourage them to eat more healthily,' Chrissie said cautiously, anxious not to sound critical. 'And we have to be careful about allergies. Maybe some allergy-friendly sweets for the runners-up and something for the winner that they'll be able to keep.'

'You wouldn't let them have the bear?'

'No, whoever left it meant it for Kenny. I was torn whether to put it in the coffin with him, but Gavin said it would be better for whoever it was to see it at the funeral, and now I couldn't possibly part with him.'

'Could you get another one?'

'I suppose perhaps I could … or … I know! I've got a friend who does sewing. Well, it's Sylvia – you know Sylvia, don't you? When she rang the other day, she seemed a bit down because of not getting out and doing things for people. She'd probably enjoy the challenge. I'll give her a ring this evening. That's an excellent idea of yours!'

Craig reddened at the praise and took refuge in his teacup. Chrissie, fearful that she might have overdone her appreciation, remained silent as she poured another cup for herself.

'You must be tired after lugging boxes around all day,' she ventured. 'I always feel dead on my feet by home-time, and all *I* do at work is talk!'

There was a long silence while Chrissie tried to think of something else to say and Craig finished his biscuit.

'I don't suppose I'll need to worry about that much longer,' he said at last. 'Not after today.'

'What do you mean?' Chrissie looked at him anxiously.

'I walked out without finishing my shift. I don't suppose they'll want me back after that.'

'So, what happened?'

'There was this new chap – fresh from school I think. Declan had me showing him the ropes. He was a right cocky so-and-so: thought he knew it all. And then he started dissing the military. I told him to shut his face, but he just kept going on and on, saying the army had committed war crimes in Iraq and …,' he trailed off into silence.

'It must have been very provoking for you.'

'I told him he didn't know what he was talking about. I was there! I've seen my mates blown to pieces, and I've seen skinny kids with no clothes on to speak of running after us begging for food. If anyone committed crimes it was Saddam Hussein letting them kids starve.'

'But this lad wasn't convinced?'

'He just went on about everyone closing ranks and covering up for each other. He wasn't interested in hearing about what it was like out there. He knew it all already! I got hold of him and shook him to try to shake some sense into his thick head and then …'

'Yes?'

'I walked out before I hit him in his stupid face,' Craig muttered, lowering his eyes and staring into his teacup.

'Well done!' Chrissie said approvingly. 'It's always better to walk away than to start a fight.'

'But I didn't finish my shift, and he'll have gone running to Declan, won't he? And Declan'll love having an excuse for getting rid of me.'

'But it won't be just up to Declan, will it? There must be some sort of process to go through before you can be dismissed. You'll be given a chance to put your side of the story, surely?'

'Oh yeah! Very likely!'

'They interviewed you for the supervisor's job, didn't they? They wouldn't have done that if they didn't think you were a good worker.'

'They gave Declan the job, and now they've seen I'm unreliable. There are plenty of people queuing up for jobs. Why would they keep me on?'

'Well, *I* certainly would! Not everyone would have had the strength of character to do what you did. And there must be other people who'll stick up for you. Didn't anyone else see what happened?'

'Dunno,' Craig shrugged. 'Why would they stick their necks out for me?'

'You'd stick up for your mates, wouldn't you? Isn't that what being in the forces is all about?'

'That's different. These guys aren't my mates. I've only been there a couple of weeks.'

'Longer than this new fellow. That must count for something.'

Craig replaced his cup and saucer on the tray with a bang which made Chrissie's delicate bone china clink ominously. In silence, he picked up the TV zapper and switched it on. The twenty-four hour news was reporting on the state of the pandemic across the world. An upturn in cases in Brazil was causing concern, while they had levelled off in the UK and America and were falling across most of mainland Europe.

Chrissie sat looking at Craig, who was staring ahead as if entranced by the graphs and tables on display. It was no good: he wasn't going to listen to her reassurances, and he would probably just get angry if she persisted in trying to bring him out of his low mood. She picked up the tray and carried it out to the kitchen.

No point trying to get that marking done now! She would get the goulash in the oven and then change the sheets. Then she could put the washing on overnight and hang it out before going to school.

As she chivvied onions and peppers around the pan, she pondered on Craig's story. It would be a gross injustice if he were to lose his job for having left work early, but why hadn't he gone to his supervisor to explain what had happened, instead of just walking out like that? And you could understand his employer thinking that he had overreacted or that he was just looking for an excuse to skive off, but surely they would understand if they knew what had really happened. Could she ask Gavin to go and explain Craig's history to them, so that they would recognise why he was touchy on the subject of the army's role in Iraq?

No, he would definitely consider that to be interfering. Maybe it would be better for her to get Gavin to sit down with Craig and help him to be more positive about himself. If he could be persuaded to stop believing that he was a failure and assuming that he'd lost his job and, instead, went back in with an apology for walking out and …

She tipped the vegetables into a casserole dish with the browned steak and beef stock. That warehouse job wasn't really using Craig's potential anyway. Hadn't Gavin talked about how useful he'd be as a PCSO? Was Thames Valley recruiting them at the moment? They could certainly do with some more boots on the ground by all accounts, what with the sickness absences and so many officers self-isolating. And that incident today would be just the sort of thing he could talk about at an interview. It showed how he controlled his own anger and avoided confrontation, so that nobody got hurt. DCI Porter would put in a good word for him, she was sure – which reminded her, she still hadn't asked him about presenting the prize for the Teddy Bear naming competition.

She opened the oven door and slipped the casserole dish inside. At least that was one job done, and it wouldn't matter if Gavin was late home, because it could just stay keeping warm until he got back. Now what was it she was going to do next? Her mind often seemed to be in a fog these days. Everything took longer and she kept forgetting things.

She stood in the middle of the kitchen with her oven gloves in her hands. Sheets first, she decided eventually, and then ring Sylvia to ask if she fancied making a police bear for the winner of the competition.

Craig was still sprawled in the front room, so she went to his bedroom first. It looked very bare and spartan compared with when it had been occupied by their son Kenny. She and Gavin had cleared all his things out before Craig moved in. That was another job that she never seemed to find time for: sorting through all the boxes stacked in the little spare bedroom containing his personal effects.

Four months after his arrival, Craig didn't seem to have personalised the room much. It could easily have been a hotel room that was freshly cleaned, ready for a new guest. No: a hotel would have left things around: a breakfast menu, maybe some leaflets about local attractions, teabags and those little sachets of coffee and maybe a few biscuits wrapped in cellophane. The desk was bare and dust-free, as were the windowsill, the chest of drawers and the little bedside cabinet. Not even an alarm clock by the bed. Every surface was bare and wiped clean.

Of course, after living on the streets, Craig could not be expected to have many possessions. He had been forced to carry all his worldly goods around with him in that old army-style rucksack that he'd brought with him. But it was sad that, after four months, he had still not accumulated any of those little personal things that made a room feel lived-in.

She put down the clean bedlinen on the chest of drawers and advanced on the bed. The single pillow was positioned in the exact centre of the end next to the wall, partially covered by the duvet (laid square-on to the bed and smoothed flat with military precision). She pulled off the duvet and started unbuttoning the cover. Soon she had the sheet, pillowcase and duvet cover lying in a heap near the door and was ready to make up the bed again.

Working methodically, she pulled the fitted sheet over the mattress and smoothed it down carefully. Kenny had always been very sensitive to unevenness in the surface on which he was sleeping – surprising that he had so enjoyed taking his scout troop camping! Without thinking, Chrissie looked up at the wall over the bed. It was bare. The photograph of Kenny in his scout leader's uniform, surrounded by boys and girls attired in the familiar khaki shorts and shirts was gone. Where had they put it? It must be in one of those boxes that she'd meant to go through during the Easter holidays, only she'd been too busy planning how to deliver lessons online as well as in school. They ought to get it out and hang it up somewhere downstairs. Kenny had been proud of that picture, which had been taken at a rally somewhere when his troop had won a competition of some sort. What had it been? Pathfinding? Gadget-making? Maybe there would be a note about it on the back of the picture, if she could find it.

She replaced the pillow on the bed and turned her attention to the duvet. Why didn't someone invent a duvet cover that would go on without getting the duvet folded over inside? Or maybe she just hadn't learned how to do it properly. She took hold of duvet and cover by two corners and shook them vigorously, trying to get the quilt to lie flat. The cover was plain brown: dark on one side and lighter of the other. Which way up should she put it? Not much to choose between them – unlike the Thomas-the-Tankengine cover that had been Kenny's favourite as a child. That had a picture of Thomas on one side and Bertie-the-Bus on the other. Whichever she chose, Kenny would be sure to insist on turning it over when he came to bed!

Craig never talked about his family. Were they dead? Or perhaps they had disowned him after he came out of the army and couldn't cope with civilian life. Had he ever had a family? Maybe he had been brought up in Care. A boy who had lived all his life in an institution might well have seen the army as a source of stability and security. Better not to pry. He would tell her in his own good time, if he wanted her to know.

She spread the duvet over the bed, drawing it up to overlap the pillow and smoothing it down all round. Satisfied with her work, she gathered up the pile of used bedlinen from the floor, ready to carry it downstairs. The sliding door on the wardrobe was slightly open. It looked odd in the context of the almost obsessional tidiness of the rest of the room. She reached out to close it. Then she hesitated and, without knowing why, she slid it open and looked inside.

The first thing she saw was Kenny's best suit lying crumpled up in a corner. She dropped the washing and bent down to retrieve it. There were plenty of empty hangers on the rail. She took one and carefully draped the jacket over it, smoothing out the creases with her fingers before hanging it back up in the wardrobe. Then she turned her attention to the trousers. They needed ironing and there was mud dried on near the bottom of the legs. A clothes brush might get the worst of it off and then the trousers could go in the wash with the sheets.

She was about to pick up the pile of bedclothes again when she noticed more marks on the trousers. There was the familiar oily black imprint of a bicycle chain on the inside of the right-hand leg. As she examined them more carefully, she could make out less distinct smears of oil all over the trousers. Some of them looked like finger marks.

He must have got oil on his hands and then wiped them on his trousers. He must have known the oil was there! Why didn't he do something about cleaning it off instead of throwing the suit higgledy-piggledy into the back of the wardrobe and hoping that nobody would find it?

Leaving the washing lying on the floor, she strode out of the bedroom and ran downstairs. Flinging open the door of the front room, she held the trousers out in front of Craig, who was still slouched on the sofa staring into nowhere. On the television, two journalists were speculating on what the Health minister was likely to say in today's coronavirus briefing.

'Just look at this!' Chrissie stormed. 'See this? Oil! This sort of thing needs cleaning off right away. What do you think you were playing at, hiding Kenny's suit away all scrumpled up on the floor at the back of your wardrobe? When you borrow things, you ought to look after them.'

Craig leaped to his feet. He seemed to tower over Chrissie as he snarled back, 'I didn't borrow it. It was all your idea. You *made* me wear it.'

''I was trying to help you get that job.'

'Which I never wanted to go for in the first place. It was all your idea. I always knew I had no chance!'

'You'd have a better chance if you'd stop being so defeatist,' Chrissie muttered. Then louder, 'but that's all beside the point. The point is, I lent you this suit because I trusted you to look after it and now I find it stuffed away at the back of the wardrobe like a – like a-'

'And what were you doing nosing around in my wardrobe anyway?' Craig demanded.

'I was changing your sheets. The wardrobe door was open.'

'And you just happened to see this suit that I'm supposed to have been hiding there?'

'I only peeped inside in case there was anything else that needed washing. Look, we're getting away from the point here. I just want you to-'

'You just want me to be a replacement for your Kenny,' Craig cut in. Chrissie stood in shocked silence as he continued, 'but I can't do it, OK? I'm not your son and I can't make you proud by getting the job you want me to have. I don't need you to do my washing or tidy my room. I just want you to leave me alone and let me get on with screwing up my life the way I've always done!'

He strode past Chrissie and out into the hall. She heard his angry footsteps on the stairs and then the slamming of a door. She stood motionless, shocked at his words. He'd got it all wrong! She didn't see him as a replacement for Kenny. That was absurd! She'd only been trying to help! But some people just wouldn't let you help them.

She took the trousers out to the kitchen and left them on the working surface over the washing machine for later. Perhaps the oil would still come out if she could find the white spirit to dissolve it. Why couldn't Craig have done that as soon as he got in from the interview? And why did he have to be so negative about that? He could have got that job if he'd really tried! Now where had those sheets got to?

She went back upstairs to get them. Perhaps, now that Craig had had time to calm down and to see the merits of her case, he would be ready to apologise. The door of his room was firmly shut. The pile of bedlinen lay outside on the landing. The message was clear: Keep Out. Chrissie snatched up the washing and stamped her way back downstairs, irrationally indignant at not having been given the opportunity for a further confrontation.

She flung open the door of the washing machine and stuffed the duvet cover inside, followed by the sheet and pillowcase. Then she turned her attention to the trousers. Vigorous brushing, with the scrubbing brush that she usually reserved for the bench that stood in a sunny corner of the back garden, removed the bulk of the mud.

She was searching in one of the wall cupboards for a bottle of white spirit, with which to attack the oil, when Gavin arrived home. Seeing her standing on a chair to reach the top shelf, he came over and offered to help. She explained what she was looking for and then stepped down to wait while he explored the cupboard. Then she noticed the lumps of dried mud that had fallen from the deep tread of his boots as he had walked across the floor, having entered through the back door.

'Oh Gav!' she exclaimed reproachfully. 'Look at the mess you've made! Wherever have you been? And why can't you take your boots off before you come in?'

Abandoning the search of the cupboard, Gavin walked back to the door, leaving a trail of footprints where the mud on the soles of his boots had been moistened by his having trodden in a small puddle of water near the sink, spilt by Chrissie when she had been washing the vegetables for the goulash. He took off his boots and put them down on the path outside the door.

'There was an incident down by the river,' he explained, closing the door and padding across the room in his socks. 'A Chinese student. I had to get down in the mud to pull her out.'

'Suicide?' Chrissie's mind was briefly diverted from her concern about the muddy floor.

'We're not sure. One of her friends said she'd been harassed by people blaming her for coronavirus.'

'Because she's Chinese?'

'Seems like it. Anyway, that's where all this mud came from. Don't worry about it. I'll clean it up.' He handed her the bottle of white spirit. 'You get on with what you were doing.'

While Chrissie began attacking the oil marks with the white spirit, Gavin filled the mop bucket at the sink. Not wanting to disturb Chrissie, who seemed absorbed in her task, he added some washing up liquid rather than asking her where to find the floor cleaner. He started from by the back door and worked methodically across the floor towards the sink. It was more difficult than he had expected to get the floor clean. The red quarry tiles were pitted with age, and the mop only seemed to make the mud settle more firmly into the cracks. Often, rather than picking up the small pieces of dried mud, his efforts merely sent them skittering across the floor.

'Oh Gav!' Chrissie, satisfied that she had removed the oil marks, had added the trousers to the load in the washing machine and was now standing in front of it staring at him with a look of exasperation on her face. 'You're only making it worse!' She strode across, seized the mop from his hand and thrust it into the bucket. 'Just leave that!' she commanded. 'All you're doing is spreading the mud all over the floor. You need to brush up the dry stuff first.'

'OK,' Gavin said meekly. 'I'll get the broom.'

'No. I'll do it. Just get out of the kitchen so I can finish getting the dinner.'

Gavin retreated to the lounge. It wasn't like Chrissie to be so short with him. There must be something else up. Maybe something had gone wrong at school. Best keep out of her way until she was ready to talk about it.

The television was still on. There was the familiar scene of the daily coronavirus briefing: three well-spaced podiums, each bearing the slogan, "Stay at Home; Protect the NHS; Save Lives", against a background of oak panelling. The presentations had just finished and it was time for questions. The camera homed in on the central podium where Matt Hancock was explaining that, for the first time, they would be starting with questions sent in by members of the public. Funny, a few months ago, Gavin wouldn't have known who he was. Government ministers seemed to come and go so frequently these days!

The Health minister leaned forward to see the question on a screen invisible to the viewers. It was from a woman who said that she was missing her grandchildren and wanted to know whether hugging close family would be one of the first steps out of Lockdown. Predictably, he quickly handed this question over to the Chief Medical Officer, who gave a guarded answer hedged around with provisos relating to the age and health of grandparents and their vulnerability to COVID-19.

Mr Hancock had by now had time to formulate a response, and he took over with words designed to demonstrate his empathy with those who were separated from their families, followed by re-iteration that keeping to the Lockdown rules was the best way of hastening the day when they could be relaxed. It all washed over Gavin, whose mind had begun to wander at the first mention of hugs and grandchildren.

Chrissie had always loved children. That was why she had trained as a teacher; and that was why, after her second miscarriage, they had fostered. And then, like a miracle, her third pregnancy lasted to full term – the doctor's had always said that there was no underlying reason why it should not. What an emotional roller coaster that had been! The anxiety that things would go wrong yet again, then the jubilation when Kenny was born, followed so quickly by Chrissie being rushed into the operating theatre for emergency surgery. Gavin had never felt so alone as in that hospital room with his new son, waiting to hear whether they had saved his wife from bleeding to death.

No more children after that, and now no chance of grandchildren. As the tears began to flow, Gavin felt a deep indignation welling up. People who complained at being unable to hug their family didn't know how lucky they were! They just needed to wait for this crisis to be over. Gavin's separation from his son was never going to end, and his grandchildren would never even be born! And Chrissie would never be the same person that he'd married. She'd changed since Kenny's death. She was more driven, never daring to relax and just be. It was as if she were afraid that, if she didn't have something to occupy her mind and her body, one or other of them would collapse into despair or self-pity.

And she never used to let little things get to her the way she did now. The mud on the floor, for example. In the old days – only six months ago – she would never have flown off the handle like that about such a minor transgression on his part; and she would merely have laughed at his inept attempt to put things right.

He pulled a handkerchief out of his pocket and blew his nose, not sure now whether he was crying for the loss of his son or his estrangement from his wife. Kenny's death should have brought them together in shared grief, but instead it seemed to have put up a barrier that he didn't know how to deal with.

He could hear her now, moving about in the kitchen. The mop bucket clanged on the tiled floor. The washing machine began a spin cycle. Gavin turned back to the television screen. The news conference had moved on to questions about testing capacity. Would the government hit its target of 100,000 tests per day by the deadline at the end on the week? The minister was upbeat but seemed to be on the defensive and failed to inspire confidence.

Sighing, Gavin looked round for the remote control to change channels, but when it was not immediately to hand he couldn't summon up the energy to hunt for it. He leaned back and closed his eyes. The minister was comparing UK testing levels favourably with those in South Korea. Was that relevant? Gavin couldn't decide. Was that footsteps he could hear on the stairs? No probably the sound was on the TV. A few seconds later, there was a noise in the hall, it sounded like the front door closing quietly or maybe a package falling through the letterbox. Had Chrissie gone out? Probably just taking some rubbish out to the wheelie bin. No, he could still hear her in the kitchen. Maybe it was Craig coming in, except that he hadn't heard the key in the lock. He usually came in the back way, anyway. Come to think of it, his bike had already been there in the garage, so he must have got home first. He tried to rouse himself to go out into the hall to see what had happened, but somehow it was too much effort. Whatever it was could wait.

9. PARENTING

'Out! Out! Out!' shouted Abigail, banging her tiny fists against the front door of the flat and kicking it with her feet. 'Park! Swings!'

'Sorry Abbie.' Eddie picked her up and carried her back into the lounge, closing the door behind them in an attempt to deter her from further attempts to get out. 'We've been out already today. We're only allowed out once. Come and sit down and we'll do a jig-saw together.'

He put her down beside the low table in the middle of the room and tipped out the first puzzle that came to hand in front of her. She immediately swiped the pieces on to the floor.

'No jig-saw! Go out!'

'Stay at Home; Protect the NHS; Save Lives,' recited Ricky virtuously.

'Yes, thank you Ricky,' Eddie said warningly, aware that a knowing big brother offering advice was not calculated to improve Abigail's mood. Ricky, however, did not take the hint.

'We've got to stay at home to stop all the old people dying of coronavirus,' he continued earnestly. 'If everyone keeps going outside, it'll make the virus spread more and more, and people like Granddad Peter will get ill and die.'

At the mention of her grandfather's name Abbie stopped kicking the leg of the coffee table and stared at her brother with round frightened eyes. Then she turned to look up at their father.

'Granddad Peter? Is he going to die?'

'No, of course not,' Eddie said quickly. 'Ricky's just being silly.'

'Aunty Dot died,' Ricky pointed out, affronted at being contradicted. 'And it said on the television that lots and lots of people have died.'

'Aunty Dot was much older than Granddad Peter,' Eddie told them firmly. 'She was over a hundred. Not many people get to be that old – ever!'

'Will Aunty Bernie die too?' persisted Abigail, 'and Uncle Jonah?'

'No. nobody's going to die.'

'Mrs Scott says old people like Granddad Peter mustn't go outside at all,' Ricky insisted.

'She didn't mean people like Granddad Peter. She meant really old people-'

'Like Uncle Stan and Aunty Sylvia?' suggested Ricky.

'Yes, if you like.' Eddie sighed. Why couldn't Ricky's Nursery School teacher have taken into account his propensity to take everything that adults told him at face value? 'And they *are* staying indoors all the time. Aunty Bernie's doing their shopping for them so they don't have to go out. And Granddad Peter and the others are all being very careful too – just like us. Now, can we give it a rest, please? Let's read a story, shall we? And then after that, we'd better tidy this room before Mummy gets home.'

A few minutes later, as he crawled behind the sofa picking up stray pieces of Lego, Eddie reflected that Ricky had got it all wrong. If any member of their family was at risk of dying from COVID-19, it was Crystal. She was working daily in a building where there were hundreds of seriously ill coronavirus patients. Only the other day, one of the patients on her ward had tested positive. Every day on the News there seemed to be reports of more healthcare workers dying after contracting the virus at work. And black people appeared to be more vulnerable, although nobody had been able to say why.

How would he ever cope without her? These past few weeks had been bad enough, with the kids at home and Crystal working longer hours than normal. What would he do if he were left to manage as a single parent? Perhaps it had been a mistake coming back to England when he lost his job in Jamaica. Crystal's parents were younger than Peter, and she had siblings who could have helped with the kids. If anything were to happen to his father, they really would be up the creek without a paddle!

He closed his eyes and offered up a silent prayer: please, please keep Crystal safe!

Crystal was on her way home. In normal times, she would have taken the bus from the main entrance of the hospital and it would have dropped her outside the flats in under a quarter of an hour. Now, nervous of public transport, she set off to cover the mile and a half back to the tower block on foot. It was a pleasant enough walk down quiet tree-lined residential streets, but she could have done without it on top of another exhausting day on the ward. Bernie had suggested getting a bicycle. That would certainly have been quicker, and with so much less traffic on the roads than normal it should be safe enough, but somehow Crystal did not think that she would be comfortable travelling on two wheels.

'Hi there Crystal!'

She turned at the sound of a voice coming from the other side of the road. A cyclist had stopped and was looking in her direction. He waved, and called out again,

'On your way home? I'd offer you a lift, only there isn't much room on the back!'

'Dean! I'm sorry, I didn't recognise you at first,' she called back across the road. In normal times, she would have crossed over to speak to him, but now the width of the road ensured that they did not accidentally approach within two metres of one another. 'Yes, I'm heading home now. It's been a long day.'

'I bet it has! I don't know how you nurses cope with all the pressure. How're Eddie and the children?'

'Oh they're just fine! At least the kids are fine and Eddie's managing. It's not easy for him, stuck indoors with them all day.'

'Tell me about it!' Dean sympathised. 'Poor Wayne had our two at home all last week and he looked like a limp rag by the weekend. I ought to do more to help him, but someone has to look after the business too.'

'Eddie's supposed to be working at home, but I think most of his work gets done after the kids are in bed or when I'm off.'

'Yeah, we're trying to do more at night too, but it's not easy. Take today, for example, we got a call from a client whose automatic hoist had stopped working. That's where I've been just now. It wouldn't have been any good telling him he had to wait until after the boys' bedtime for someone to come out to have a look at it. That's the thing – it's not just the money, there are our customers to think of as well. Some of them rely on our gadgets to help them do really basic activities of daily living.'

'Yes,' Crystal nodded. 'I can see that, and I suppose there isn't anyone else who could do it?'

'One of the technicians probably could have fixed the hoist,' Dean admitted, 'but this guy's one of our oldest clients and he can be a bit ... well, he's not always as careful as he should be about his own well-being. I was glad of the excuse to call round to make sure he's OK – which he is, thank goodness!'

'Maybe you could look after the boys and Wayne could mind the business for a bit,' Crystal suggested.

'Yes, we're working on that. The trouble is: Wayne's still waiting on the DVLA[4] to approve him getting his driving licence back. The doctor's signed him off as fit, but that was only just before Lockdown started and his application seems to have gone into a black hole somewhere in Swansea. So, for him to go into the office means me driving him there. That's why it seemed simpler for me to supervise the staff and go out to clients, while he works from home and looks after the boys.' Dean sighed. 'But I think it's all been a bit too much for him. We need to work out a better plan somehow.'

'Yes,' agreed Crystal. 'It's hard finding things for kids to do when they can't go out anywhere. I can see Eddie's feeling the strain, but I don't feel I can ask for fewer shifts when the hospital is so short of staff.'

'Oh well!' Dean smiled his understanding of her predicament. 'I suppose we just have to get on with things and hope we all get through this OK in the end.'

He got back on his bike and started off again, heading downhill towards the south. As he passed the end of Wood Farm Road he glanced to the left and caught a glimpse of the tower block where Crystal and her family lived. He and Wayne were lucky! At least they had a garden for the boys to play in, even if it was too small for a proper game of football.

He negotiated the mini-roundabout at the Corner House pub, turning right past the new student flats and on to where twentieth century semi-detached houses gave way to Victorian terraces. The normally busy streets of Cowley

---

[4] Driver and Vehicle Licensing Authority: the government organisation responsible for maintaining records of all UK vehicles and driving licence holders. Its headquarters is in Swansea, South Wales.

were ominously quiet and he experienced no difficulty in crossing the main road to reach Rose Hill.

He pushed his bike round the back of the house and left it in the shed. Entering through the kitchen door, he saw Wayne bending down to look into the oven and Harry sitting up at the breakfast bar with his back to the door idly fiddling with the cutlery.

'Why won't you play?' he whined. 'Just until Daddy Dean gets back –please!'

'Because Daddy Dean *is* back!' Dean called out, stepping forward and planting both hands on his son's shoulders. Harry squealed with delight and twisted round to give Dean a hug.

'What time do you call this?' demanded Wayne. 'I've been keeping the dinner warm in the oven, but it's probably all dried up by now.'

'I'm sorry.' Dean let go of Harry and hurried over to help. 'I couldn't help it. Ray Bentham called and I had to go out to fix his hoist.'

'I see,' Wayne said flatly, as if he were not listening.

'Well, we couldn't leave him stranded, could we?'

'But you *could* leave *me* expecting you back by dinner time. You said you'd try to be early today!'

'I know. I'm sorry. I should have rung. It's just, Ray was on the phone and I didn't realise it would take so long to cycle over there. And then it took longer to fix than I expected and … Look: you sit down and I'll dish up.'

Dean took the oven gloves from Wayne's hands and gently pushed him out of the way. 'I bet you're tired after looking after these two live wires all day! Where *is* Carl. He's usually first down for meals.'

'Sulking in his room. I told him off for using his bed as a trampoline and now he's lying flat out on it refusing to budge.'

'I'll go and tell him dinner's ready,' Harry volunteered, slipping off his stool and heading for the door.

'No, Harry. You stay here,' Dean said quickly, anxious about Carl's reaction to this proposal. It might go well or he might consider it an affront to his dignity to be summoned by his younger brother. 'I'll dish up and then go and find him.'

'You need to wash your hands first,' Harry pointed out, disappointed at having had his offer turned down and determined not to be ignored. 'You've been outside, so you've got to wash them.'

'Thank you, Harry.' Dean put down the oven gloves and went over to the sink to wash his hands. Out of the corner of his eye he watched Wayne making his way slowly across the kitchen to take his place next to Harry. His right foot dragged on the ground – a sure sign that he was tired – and he leaned heavily on the edge of the breakfast bar as he hauled himself up on to his stool. They really must do something to lighten his childcare load.

The dinner comprised sausages, chips and baked beans. Wayne was quite correct in his assessment that they had not benefitted from having been kept warm in the oven for over twenty minutes, but they were not the charred remains that Dean had feared. He distributed the food between four plates, which he carried over and set down in front of Wayne and Harry before heading upstairs to summon his older son.

Carl was sitting cross-legged on his bed, staring into space while moulding and re-moulding a lump of silly putty between his fingers. He gave a little start at the sound of Dean entering the room, but quickly resumed his steady gaze towards a Harry Potter poster on the wall opposite.

'Hi Carl! Dinner's ready. Come down and eat it before it gets cold.'

'I'm not hungry.'

There's chocolate fudge pudding for afters. I saw it in the oven.'

'I said I don't want anything.'

Dean sat down on the bed and put his arm around Carl, who shrugged it off and shuffled further down the bed to get away from the embrace.

'What's wrong? Is it something we've done?'

No answer. Dean debated in his mind whether to pursue the matter further, but in the end contented himself with giving Carl a pat on the shoulder before getting up to go.

'Well I'm off to have my dinner. Come down when you're ready.'

Harry had cleared his plate by the time Dean got back to the kitchen. Seeing his father entering the room alone, he called out hopefully, 'doesn't Carl want his? Can I have it?'

'Don't you want to leave room for your pudding?' Dean smiled back.

'I've got plenty of room!' Harry declared. 'I can eat both.'

'No,' Dean said firmly. 'Carl will probably be down in a minute.' He sat down and started eating. Glancing across the table he noticed that Wayne was struggling to persuade his knife to cut the overdone sausages. Fatigue was certainly affecting his motor skills.

He gave up the battle and speared the sausage with his fork, bringing it up to his mouth to bite off a piece. 'I wouldn't bank on it,' he mumbled as he chewed it. 'He's been sitting up there all afternoon. I don't know what's got into him. He's been in a right mood all day.'

'So, can I have his sausages?' piped up Harry again.

'No!' his two fathers chorused.

'Just wait nicely until we've both finished and then you can have some pudding,' Dean told him between mouthfuls. 'Too much fried food is bad for you.'

Harry got off his stool and ran across to the door. 'I'm going to practise goal kicks,' he called out. 'Tell me when it's time for pudding.'

'No Harry.' Dean got up and frogmarched the boy back to his seat. 'That's not how we do things in this house. If you want pudding, you sit up to table until everyone's finished their first course.'

Harry pulled a face, but consented to get back on the stool. He sat with his elbows on the breakfast bar and his chin in his hands, staring fixedly at Carl's plate. Dean hurried to finish his food as quickly as he could, keeping one eye on his husband who still seemed to be struggling. He slowed down, keeping pace with Wayne so that they would both be ready for the pudding at the same time and neither could be accused of holding up the proceedings. Nobody told you that being a parent required so many diplomatic skills!

As soon as Dean put the last chip in his mouth, Harry was on his feet collecting the plates and carrying them to the dishwasher. Dean got up to follow him, staying close enough to catch the crockery if the boy were to drop it, but far enough back (he hoped) that it would not look as if he didn't trust him to transport them safely. It was at that point that he noticed the burning smell coming from the oven.

'The pudding!' Wayne cried out, evidently having caught the odour at the same moment. 'Didn't you turn the oven off when you got the sausages out?'

'No: you never said to,' Dean defended himself.

He immediately turned off the gas and opened the oven door. The smell was stronger now. He grabbed the oven gloves and bent down to extract the pudding. Just as he was putting it down on the working surface to examine the blackened crust he heard a crash behind him. He swung round to see Harry standing by the open dishwasher holding one plate while the other two lay smashed on the floor.

For what seemed like ages, everyone remained silent and frozen to the spot. Then Harry made a dash for the back door, leaving the remaining plate balanced precariously on top of some mugs in the dishwasher. Wayne reached out to restrain him as he passed, but he wriggled free and made his escape into the garden.

'I'd better go to him,' he said, reaching for his stick to help himself up.

'No. I'll do it. You sit back down and take it easy.'

'That's right. Rub it in! I'm useless and everything's down to you.'

'No, that's not what I meant at all. I only thought you'd had enough, with looking after the boys all day, and it was my turn. I wasn't saying … Oh, never mind! Go on then. Go and see what you can do with him.' Shaking his head in exasperation, Dean bent down to pick up the shattered plates. What a day this was turning out to be!

* * *

Tempers were also flaring in the Whittle household. Yvonne's efforts at cooking dinner had been just as unsuccessful as Wayne's, and Leo declined to try any of it.

'I'm not hungry,' he insisted.

'Nonsense!' Trevor was in no mood for truculence. 'You'll eat whatever's put on your plate.'

'But it's absolutely gross!' Leo protested, poking at the undercooked pasta and overcooked Bolognese sauce with his fork.

'It's OK, love,' Yvonne slurred. 'Just leave it if you don't want it.'

'We can't afford to let food go to waste,' his father insisted, 'even if your mother *is* a lazy slag who can't even warm up a tin of pasta sauce without burning it to a crisp!' he added, glaring towards his wife.

Yvonne looked back vacantly as if she were unaware that this remark was aimed at her.

'Go on!' Trevor growled. 'Both of you! Eat up. The way everything's shaping up this could be the last meal you get for a long time.'

'What do you mean?' asked Yvonne, staring at him in bewilderment. 'I cook dinner for you both every day, don't I?'

'The way our bank account looks right now, you'll have to be cooking them out of air then. Right now, I don't know where the rent money's coming from this month. Don't forget: I haven't had a single call-out since March. No call-outs, no money.'

'We've got my furlough pay still coming in.'

'Yeah, eighty percent! But eighty percent of nothing is nothing ain't it? And then you go drinking it all away with your gin and vodka and …' He reached out and took hold of Yvonne's water glass. He held it under his nose and breathed in deeply. 'Yeah, I thought so. You've got to stop all this secret drinking – not that it fools me.'

He slammed the glass down on the table and some of the colourless liquid spilled out.

'It's payday on Thursday. Everything'll be alright then.'

'No: it was payday *last* Thursday, and you've spent it all on your booze you stupid bitch!' Trevor's voice rose in anger and he formed his hands into fists under the table in his frustration. 'Can't you see? Can't you see what you're doing?'

Leo silently slipped off his chair and retreated to the garden. Trevor hesitated, then decided to let him go. He would speak to him later about his table manners and not wasting food. There were more important things to worry about right now. He got up and walked round the table to his wife. Standing behind her chair, he put his arms around her.

'What's happened to you, sugar dumpling? You never used to be like this all the time. I used to boast about your cooking. Your jerk chicken was famous with all the cabbies. Honestly: I used to think I was married to the best cook ever!'

'What's happened? You need to ask me what's happened? Don't you feel nothing? How d'you expect me to think about cooking when my boy's dead and cold in his grave and his killers is walking free?'

'Oh sugarplum!' Trevor hugged her closer. 'I know it's hard. It's hard for me too. I wanted to smash that policeman's stupid face in when he came round to tell us about it – too late, of course! They couldn't take the trouble to let us know before it was all over the news, could they?'

'Constable Hughes's son was killed too,' Yvonne murmured weakly without turning her head. 'And Chrissie Hughes has been very good, coming round and explaining things to me.'

'Oh yes! His son was killed. Everyone knows about that! That's all anyone talks about. Nobody cares about Harry. He was only a black boy, not a white police officer! He doesn't count.'

10. CARING

Peter hummed gently as he arranged the pineapple rings on the baking parchment. He was alone in the kitchen. Bernie was out doing their weekly grocery shop and Jonah was doing something on his computer in his private sitting room. He reached for the pot of glacé cherries and started putting one into the centre of each ring. Satisfied with his design, he went to the fridge and got out margarine and eggs to make the sponge to pour on top.

Pineapple upside-down cake! That was a blast from the past. It used to be a treat in the Children's Home where he grew up. It would appear for tea on Sunday afternoons. He could picture it now: all the children dressed up in their best clothes, fresh from Sunday School. He remembered once a fight had broken out over a claim that someone's cherry had mysteriously ended up on somebody else's plate!

He plugged in the food mixer and began creaming together the margarine and sugar. They were lucky! They had a large house and the best part of an acre of garden. The difficulty at this time of year was finding time to keep it from

117

turning into a complete wilderness – sorry, wildlife habitat! He smiled. Yes, whatever Jonah might say about the tedium of being prevented from working, they were very far from becoming bored and needing to binge on box set videos to keep themselves occupied.

For a start, there were all the videoconferences with Lucy in Liverpool and Hannah in Leeds. They were in touch with family members in other parts of the country far more now than they had ever been before Lockdown. Then there was all the queuing. In the old days (five weeks ago) he would go to the supermarket while Jonah and Bernie were at work and expect to be back and unpacked within a couple of hours – even if he had the grandkids with him to "help"! Now, Bernie went out twice each week: once for their own needs and again for Stan and Sylvia. She had got into the habit of announcing her departure with the ominous words: *I'm just going outside and may be some time.*

He emptied the bag of self-raising flour on to the scales and went to the larder for another one. He ran his hand along the shelves. There were more empty spaces than usual. He noticed that they were almost out of bread flour – but then they hadn't been able to get any yeast for several weeks so that hardly mattered – and there was only one bag of plain flour left. No self-raising at all! But he could make do with plain and add a bit of baking powder.

He finished weighing the flour and was just about to add it to the cake mixture when the back door opened and Bernie staggered in carrying a bag in each hand. She put them down on the table and went back for more. Peter called out a greeting, but she had already gone, so he turned back to the cake. He poured the flour into a sieve and held it over the mixing bowl shaking it vigorously and occasionally tapping it on the side with his other hand.

'Still no bread flour or yeast.' Bernie was back. She put a third bag down on the floor and closed the door behind her. 'Sylvia will be disappointed. Ever since we gave her the bread machine, she's been making it fresh for them every other day. I've got a loaf for her instead. I'll drop it off there tomorrow.'

She started unpacking the bags on the table, bustling round the room putting items away in cupboards and on shelves. Squeezing past Peter to get to the freezer, she joggled his hand and sent flour cascading over the working surface.

'Careful!' he shouted. 'Can't you leave all that until I've got the cake in the oven?'

'No. I've got frozen stuff. It can't wait.'

'Well go round the other way then and keep out from under my feet. And when you've got the stuff in the freezer, leave the rest until I've finished. I won't be long.'

Peter turned back to his baking. He finished sifting the flour into the mixing bowl and then did his best to scoop up what he had spilt into his hand and added it to the mixture. Then he reached for the electric mixer to stir it in.

'The queues were horrendous,' Bernie shouted out above the noise. 'It went right round the car park. I'm only glad it wasn't raining.'

Peter poured the cake mixture over the pineapple rings and spread it out with a knife. He picked up the tray to put it in the oven, but his way was blocked by Bernie, who was standing on a chair to put away a bag of rice in one of the wall cupboards.

'Sorry!' she called down when she noticed him waiting. 'I won't be much longer. I just want to get the bags empty so I can put them back in the car. I forgot to take them with me last week and it's such a nuisance having the things all lying around loose in there.'

'I'll only be another five minutes,' Peter protested, 'and then *I'll* put the things away if you like.'

'Don't be silly.' Bernie stepped down and pushed the chair back under the table. She stood back against it and gestured to Peter to go past. 'There you are! I didn't hold you up for long, did I?'

Peter put the cake in the oven and set the timer on his phone to remind him when to take it out again. Bernie was back up on the chair putting more items in the wall cupboard, so he walked round the other side of the table to get back to where he had been working. He put the bowl in the sink, reflecting that normally he would have had two youngsters eager to scrape out the mixture and lick the spoon, and then began wiping down the work surface.

'I couldn't get the grapes Jonah asked for,' Bernie continued. 'I missed them on the way round and then I couldn't go back for them because of the one way system. And there's still no hand sanitiser. No soap either, so we'll have to make do with shower gel. Oh! And I couldn't find any stewing steak, so I got you mince instead.'

'You didn't think of trying the butcher's on London Road?' Peter asked irritably, reflecting that minced beef was not really a substitute for steak – not when he had a specific recipe in mind. 'They'd be sure to have had it – and it's better than the supermarket stuff too.'

'I don't have time to drive all over the place and queue up at different shops,' Bernie grumbled. 'Just the supermarket is plenty for me. You know I've never liked shopping at the best of times.'

'Then wouldn't it be better for us to go back to me doing *our* shopping?' suggested Peter, 'Seeing as you've got Sylvia's to do as well. And then, if something isn't available, I can change what I'm planning to cook. Now I've got to think of something to do with that mince.'

'You could always freeze it for another time. Why do you always have to have the menu planned out for days in advance?'

'So that I know what to put on the shopping list,' Peter muttered.

'Anyway,' Bernie insisted, 'we agreed: *I* do the shopping because I'm less at risk from the coronavirus, and you stay at home to keep safe. You're only a whisker away from being in the over-seventy group! Besides, now that Jonah's been furloughed, I'm at home all day, the same as you, so it's only fair if I pitch in with the chores.'

'It'd be less stressful for me if you let me do it, instead of getting in the way and complaining about the queues,' Peter grumbled. 'I used to do it all *and* look after the kids so-'

He broke off at the sound of a loud crash from the direction of Jonah's room. Bernie dropped the tin of corned beef, which she had just picked up, on to the table with a clatter. They both raced out into the hall to find out what had happened.

'Jonah! What on earth is going on?' Bernie exclaimed, slamming the study door back against the wall in her haste to reach him.

His wheelchair – with Jonah still in it – was lying on its side on the floor. It was an incredibly stable design, capable of negotiating kerbs and uneven pavements. How could Jonah, with his limited ability to move, have managed to make it tip over?

'Never mind that,' he replied testily. 'Just get me back up again, can't you?'

Bernie and Peter stepped forward and together righted the wheelchair. Peter settled Jonah back into it and then Bernie bent down and started feeling him all over to check that he hadn't sustained any injuries. No obvious broken bones, only a few bruises on his right arm, which had taken the main force of the fall. She straightened up and stood over Jonah with her arms folded across her chest, looking down on him with an expression of grim determination.

'Now,' she said sternly, 'tell me how you did it.'

Maintaining a stubborn silence, Jonah ignored her question and began fiddling with the keypad on the arm of his chair, checking that the computer attachment was still working. Bernie took hold of his hand in hers and, gently but firmly, moved it off the pad.

'Stop that and answer my question. We need to know how on earth you managed to capsize a chair that has passed goodness knows how many safety tests. What was it you were doing for goodness sake?'

'I wanted to open the window,' Jonah muttered reluctantly. 'It's too hot in here.'

'Why didn't you call for help?' Peter asked wearily. 'I was only in the kitchen.'

'I was trying not to be a nuisance.'

'Oh Jonah!' Bernie sighed. 'I've never heard anything more ridiculous. Did it not occur to you what a nuisance it would have been for us if you'd done yourself a serious injury and needed to go to A and E? In the middle of a pandemic, too! Now, tell me how you did it, so we can stop you doing it again.'

'It was already open a crack,' Jonah explained reluctantly. 'So all I needed to do was to push it a bit further. You'd left that long-handled feather duster lying on the shelf over there, so I got it in my mouth-'

'You what!' Peter exclaimed. 'Do you have any idea how dangerous that was?'

'And then I used it to push the window,' Jonah continued, 'but it was stiffer than I thought and the chair kept rolling backwards, so I turned it side-on and put the brake on, and then when I pushed … I must be stronger than I thought I was.'

'You're certainly stupider than you think you are,' Bernie told him. She sighed again. 'Honestly! It's like having an unruly toddler to look after. Why can't you behave yourself for once!'

* * *

'Dinner's ready!' Gavin heard Chrissie calling in the hall. He got up slowly – a strange lethargy seemed to hit him as soon as he got home from work these days – and switched off the television. He had no idea what he had been watching; it had just been background noise to keep his mind off the quarrel with Chrissie.

Then he realised that he had still not changed out of his police uniform. He hurriedly took off his stab-resistant vest with its radio and body camera, and dropped it over the back of the armchair that he had been sitting on. The rest would have to wait; he did not want Chrissie to think that he had ignored her summons.

When he entered the kitchen she was standing by the table ladling goulash on to three plates. She looked calmer than before, but perhaps a little red around the eyes. He washed his hands at the sink and then sat down to eat.

'This smells good,' he remarked, watching his wife's face intently to gauge her reaction to the compliment. She smiled back.

'I'm sorry, Gav – about shouting at you, I mean. I didn't mean to … well, it's been a bit of a day, I'm afraid!' She put the ladle down in the casserole dish and sat down opposite him. 'Tell me about your Chinese student. Was she alright?'

'I think so. We called an ambulance and the paramedics checked her over and then Sergeant Appleton took her back to her lodgings. That's when he spoke to her friends and found out what it was all about.' He turned his head and looked through the open door into the hall. 'I wonder where Craig is. It's not like him to be late for dinner.'

'Perhaps he didn't hear me call,' suggested Chrissie. 'Do you mind going up to check? I'm not sure he'd be pleased to see me just at present.'

Nodding, Gavin got up and headed out into the hall and up the stairs. Craig's door was firmly shut. Gavin stood and listened. There was no sound from inside the room. He tapped on the door with his knuckles and listened again. Still nothing. He called out, 'dinner's ready, Craig. Chrissie's waiting for us!'

Then he remembered the noise in the hall earlier – the click that sounded like the door closing or perhaps something coming through the letterbox. There had been no package on the mat when he came past on the way upstairs. It must have been someone going out and pulling the door closed quietly behind them.

He turned the knob and opened the door a crack. 'Craig? Are you there?'

The room was deserted. Gavin stepped inside and looked round at the tidy bed, the empty shelves, the shining clean desk. Then he strode across to the wardrobe and threw open the door. There was Kenny's jacket hanging next to a white shirt and a navy parka, also originally belonging to Kenny. On the floor beneath, a pair of highly polished black leather shoes glinted in the evening sunshine falling through the window.

'What's up?'

Gavin turned to see Chrissie standing behind him.

'His rucksack's gone,' he told her, 'and his sleeping bag, and I think all the clothes he brought with him.'

'So he's left us?'

Chrissie's legs appeared to give way under her and she collapsed down on to the edge of the bed.

'It's all my fault! I drove him away. I didn't mean to upset him, but I should have realised …'

'Realised what? What do you mean?'

'I was smothering him. I only wanted to help him reach his full potential. I pushed him to go for the supervisor's job when he didn't want to. I gave him Kenny's bike and Kenny's suit; and he thought I was trying to turn him into a new Kenny. I should've seen! I should've let him be himself. I should-'

'No.' Gavin sat down next to Chrissie and put his arm round her. He pulled her towards him and kissed the line of grey hair showing between the creamy blond. 'Don't be silly. You were only trying to help. Craig'll see that when he stops to think.'

'But he thinks I was just *using* him to make me feel better about Kenny. I'm sure he does! And it's not like that at all. I just wanted him to do well for himself.'

'Of course you did; and Craig will see that too. I'm sure he will.'

'But he's gone!' Chrissie sobbed. 'He was upset about something that happened at work today, and I just made it worse, and now he's given up and gone back out on to the streets.'

Gavin hugged her closer. 'Look! He can't have got far yet. I'll go out right now and find him and bring him back.'

A few minutes later, now back in full police uniform, he was outside the back door lacing up his boots. What had made Craig go off like this? Couldn't he see how much it would upset Chrissie?

He went to the garage and got out his bike. Craig's bike was still there, so he must be on foot. That at least meant that it should be easy to overtake him – except that he didn't know which way he had gone. He mulled this over in his mind as he pushed the bike down the side of the house.

In the old days, before he came to live with them, Craig had slept rough except during the very worst winter weather when he gravitated to one of the night shelters provided by various voluntary organisations and churches. He would need to find a place to doss down where there would be some protection against the elements. Although the weather had been exceptionally dry and sunny this spring, the temperature would soon start dropping once the sun went down and April was a notoriously unpredictable month for rain.

The chances were he'd head for the city centre, where there were any number of nooks and crannies among the ancient buildings where he could hide away, safe from prying eyes and biting winds. At times of stress, people usually went in search of the familiar. Most likely he would be heading for the sheltered corner where the boundary of St Luke's College met the wall of the Holy Cross dining hall or the porch of St Giles Church or … But was that too great an assumption? Craig had been trained to survive in all sorts of terrain. He did not need – especially during this mild spell

– to hide away in corners, down in the city where there would be police patrolling and college security staff on the lookout. What if his priority was to get away from what he perceived as the overbearing attentions of Gavin and his wife? He might decide instead to head the other way: across the by-pass and out into the Oxfordshire countryside.

Gavin halted, still holding his bike, and stood for a moment, hesitating on the drive. Where should he try first? He sighed and then swung his leg over the saddle. No point hanging around here trying to second-guess Craig's thought processes. The only thing to do was to tour the streets around their home, working gradually outwards in all directions in the hope that, with the advantage of the extra speed afforded by his bicycle, he would overtake Craig before he went to ground anywhere.

As he pedalled along the familiar roads of his neighbourhood, constantly looking to right and left in the hope of catching sight of his friend, Gavin reflected that it was a pity that everyone appeared to be following government Lockdown advice to the letter. There were no teenagers congregating on street corners, no commuters hurrying back from their jobs in London, no young couples dressed up in their finery heading for an evening out.

He hailed a lone dog-walker coming the other way and asked her if she'd seen a youngish man in a camouflage suit with a rucksack on his back. She shook her head. Gavin thanked her and hurried on. If Craig had come this way it must have been some time ago or the woman would have passed him. At least the rucksack made him distinctive and likely to be noticed. But then, with so few people about, everyone was noteworthy.

About twenty minutes later, a pair of joggers also denied any knowledge of the runaway. Gavin looked down thoughtfully at his watch. It must be an hour and a half now since Craig left the house. Depending on how much time had passed between his leaving and Chrissie calling them for dinner, it could have been more. If he had been walking at his usual purposeful pace, he could be several miles away by now. Searching for him was like looking for a needle in the proverbial haystack – except that it was a moving needle and an ever-expanding haystack!

He climbed wearily back on his bicycle and set off again, pedalling slowly and pondering equally slowly in his mind. His original plan of scouring the neighbourhood wasn't going to work. Craig must be well away from the immediate vicinity by now. He must adopt a new strategy. If Craig had decided to take off across the countryside, there was nothing that Gavin could do to find him. That would require tracking dogs or helicopters or at very least personnel familiar with the territory.

He headed along Iffley Road towards the town centre. If there was any chance of finding Craig now, it would be through visiting his old haunts. He changed to a higher gear and pedalled faster. If only he could be sure that this was the right thing to do! He repeated to himself the words of an old colleague, long retired now, from Missing Persons: "Always look in the most likely places first." Well, in the case of Craig Manson, he knew all the most likely places for him to have been in the days before he had come to stay with them. He would start there.

The centre of Oxford was eerily quiet. At this time in the evening the streets should have been thronged with people going to, or returning from, the many restaurants and pubs. There should be groups of students standing in the street: earnestly discussing their latest essay subject, confidently setting the world to rights, or laughing as they swapped jokes and gossip. Now, Gavin cycled the length of the High and only passed two pedestrians. As they approached one another, walking in opposite directions, one of them stepped out into the street in order to maintain the two metre distance advised by the government.

But then, who could there be out on the streets of Oxford in April 2020? The students had already gone home for the Easter vacation by the time Lockdown was imposed, and they had remained there studying online. Academic staff of the university were working from home. Cleaners and housekeeping staff were furloughed. Almost all shops and businesses were closed. And everyone had been told: Stay at Home; Protect the NHS; Save Lives.

As he passed the high honey-coloured stone walls surrounding Lichfield College the smell of roast lamb (presumably their kitchen still had to cater for a few live-in staff and overseas students who had not been able to go home) reminded Gavin that he had not eaten since his sandwich lunch at noon. Craig must also be hungry by now. What would he do for food? All the cafés and pubs were closed, and takeaways had to be ordered in advance, online or by telephone, so probably supermarkets would be his only option.

Gavin did the rounds of grocery stores, asking everywhere if staff had seen a man answering Craig's description. No luck! Perhaps he hadn't headed for the city centre after all. It was beginning to get dark now. He would be wanting to find somewhere to spend the night. This was probably the right time to check all his favourite spots – and other choice locations which would be vacant, now that the Council had rounded up rough sleepers and put them up in some of the empty hotels for the duration.

* * *

In the small dining room of a terraced house in East Oxford, Stan Corbridge got up and went over to switch on the light. Then, leaning heavily on his stick because his arthritis was playing up, he returned to the table and lowered himself slowly back into his seat. He looked towards the computer screen, fumbling with the mouse, trying to get the pointer to move to the right place to start the recording – again! Ah! That was it. He was "live". It was disconcerting to see his own face staring out from the screen. He glanced down at his notes and began speaking, hesitantly at first, because he was not used to talking to an unseen audience, and then with increasing confidence.

'A few minutes ago we heard the familiar story of the Good Samaritan, who was the only person who, on encountering an injured man on the road, did not cross over to the other side to avoid him. I was reminded of those words the other day when I was weeding the bed in my front garden. Two people came along on the other side of the street. They were coming from opposite directions. When they started to get closer, one of them crossed over to the other side of the road – my side – so that they could pass without getting too close. And it struck me that this is often how we can act as Good Samaritans in these strange times: not by approaching people to offer help, but by keeping at a distance to avoid spreading infection.'

The door opened behind him and Sylvia stepped into the room, stopping abruptly as she saw herself on the screen, 'Sorry! I thought you'd finished.'

She backed out and the door closed again. Sighing, Stan stopped the recording and prepared to start again. It was nice of them to invite him to give the sermon at the next online morning service, but had they realised just how inexperienced he was with all this new-fangled gadgetry? He deleted the recording, rehearsed his first paragraph again in his head, took a deep breath and clicked "record" once again.

* * *

Stan was not the only one struggling with spiritual matters that evening. Kneeling at the altar of St Cyprian's church in Headington, Father Damien was saying solitary evening prayers for his parish and the wider community. It had been a long and arduous day and he was finding it hard to concentrate. He gazed upwards, fixing his eyes on the "Christus Rex" (a crucifix portraying the risen Christ clothed in royal robes and yet still with arms outstretched on a cross) that hung high up on the wall behind the altar. He did not dare to bow his head and close his eyes for fear of dropping off to sleep.

What a day! It had started, even before he was out of bed, with an urgent call to attend the hospital. A young Polish woman was about to give birth and there was concern that the baby might not live. She was begging for a priest to come to baptise the child as soon as it entered the world.

It was a still birth, but Damien had said the words – in Latin, in case the mother's English was limited – and poured the holy water and prayed silently that God would forgive him for the deception that he was playing on her. Was it so bad, when he was convinced in his own mind that, baptised or not, her baby girl would be admitted to heaven as readily as any of the saints, to give her assurance that this was so by performing a ritual that by rights could only be effective if done before death? After all, Pope Benedict himself had ruled that there was reasonable hope that children dying without baptism would be brought to eternal happiness, regardless of the church's teaching on original sin.

Then there was the child's father to comfort. He had been excluded from the birth by hospital COVID-19 restrictions and the need to care for their older child – a little boy of three. A hospital car park was not the best setting for breaking the news to a young father that his much-anticipated baby daughter had not survived the hazards of birth. Damien felt helpless, standing two metres away from the young man who gazed back with hopelessness in his eyes clutching the hand of his little son, who looked up with an expression of fear and incomprehension. What was wrong? Why was Daddy crying?

By comparison, the morning's first funeral had been easy. The deceased was an elderly man who had lived a full life and died peacefully in his bed after a short illness. His two sons and their wives were able to attend, and an old family friend spoke warmly of a life well-lived. No invitation to refreshments afterwards, of course, but at least these mourners were none of them going back to empty houses to grieve alone.

Unlike the many elderly members of his congregation whom he had spent the afternoon calling on the telephone, checking that they were alright and offering to run errands for them. So many of his flock seemed to be widowed and with families living far away. So many of the regulars whom he used to encounter praying before the Blessed Sacrament were now confined to lonely homes with no human contact. Mrs O'Keefe seemed rather down, he thought, mentally adding her to his list for daily prayers and more frequent telephone calls. How long ago was it now that she had lost her husband – two years? Or maybe three?

He concluded his prayers and clambered slowly to his feet. He must be getting old: his joints never used to protest like this whenever he spent time on his knees! He crossed himself and bowed towards the tabernacle containing the Blessed Sacrament. Then he reached for the candle snuffer. Even that small movement was an effort. He put out the candle on the right and turned to address its companion on the left-hand side of the altar. Somehow he fumbled it and the candlestick fell over. Hot wax sprayed on to his hand and over the altar hanging. Then, to his dismay, a line of flame appeared along the intricate embroidery. Looking round wildly for something with which to extinguish it, he snatched up his breviary and slammed it down on the flames, beating them frantically until they disappeared.

He surveyed the damage. This particular altar frontal had been a gift from one of his most long-standing and faithful parishioners, Deidre Carr. He knew that she had spent hours embroidering it. She would be devastated that he had spoiled it.

Suddenly overcome with weariness, he slumped down on the ornately-carved wooden chair in the sanctuary, usually reserved for visiting dignitaries such as the bishop, and put his head in his hands. What was he going to do?

How was he going to explain to Deirdre what had happened? Could the damage be repaired? He suddenly felt very much alone. He was used to having people come to him for help and advice – which he provided as best he could, sometimes very inadequately he knew – but who was there for him to confide in? He could not burden his flock with his own worries and uncertainties. They expected him to provide comfort in their fear and sorrow, not to come asking them for advice about dealing with his own doubts and blunders. His fellow priests all had their own parishes to worry about. The bishop was far too busy and important to be troubled with this sort of dilemma, at once insignificant and momentous (for Deirdre at least).

He reached into his pocket and pulled out his mobile phone. He flicked through his contacts and selected Peter. He was the only person in whom he felt he could confide – sympathetic and understanding of his situation, but not quite a member of his congregation. Or at least, not a cradle Catholic who would expect a priest to be strong and decisive, full of confidence and certainty. Peter had come late to faith after a strange, but powerful, encounter with Our Lady, which Damien had to admit he did not fully understand and for which he felt a degree of envy. The ringing tone sounded, echoing strangely in the empty church.

Then he changed his mind and stopped the call. No, it would be too much of an imposition to involve Peter. He had his own family to worry about. What right had Damien to expect him to spend time listening to the angst of a priest who couldn't even snuff a candle out without destroying a unique artefact?

* * *

'Did you find him?' Chrissie asked eagerly the moment Gavin stepped over the threshold into the kitchen, carefully leaving his boots outside. She had been watching out for him from the front window and had hurried through the house to be there to greet him as soon as he had put his bike away.

Gavin shook his head. 'No.' Then, seeing her face fall, he added, 'but don't you worry. It's warm weather and dry with it. He won't come to any harm out there overnight, and in the morning I'll report him as a missing person and we'll soon have him found.'

'I thought Missing Persons wouldn't do anything unless there's reason to think he's been the victim of a crime.'

'Or in danger of coming to harm,' Gavin nodded. 'Not normally, no, but at the moment technically he *is* committing a crime by being out there at all. We're all supposed to be staying at home, remember? And all the rough sleepers have been rounded up and put in hotels.'

'Do you mean you're going to try to get him arrested?'

'We don't arrest people unless we have to: Engage, Explain, Encourage, remember? We only move on to *Enforce* if those three don't get people to do what they're supposed to.' Dropping his gaze, Gavin became aware of something in his hand. 'Oh yes! I need to change the batteries in this. It was getting so dim by the time I got back I was beginning to think I'd have to arrest myself for riding without lights!'

He gave a half-hearted smile at his own witticism as he held up the bicycle lamp that he had brought in with him. Chrissie took it from his hand.

'No, I'll do that. You look all-in. Sit down. Have you had anything to eat?' Taking him by the arm she steered him towards the table and pulled out one of the chairs. 'I kept your dinner warm in the slow cooker. Wait there and I'll get it for you, and then I'll find some fresh batteries.'

Gavin subsided on to the chair and sat with his elbows on the table and his chin resting on his hands. The table was still set with places for both him and Craig, but he noticed that Chrissie's setting was gone. She brought over a steaming plate of goulash and put it down in front of him.

'I had mine. It was something to do. And I thought Craig might … I thought he'd be more comfortable eating his if I wasn't there.' Chrissie turned her face away abruptly. 'I – I'd better find those batteries for you.'

She busied herself rummaging in drawers while Gavin sat staring down at his plate. He was hungry, no doubt about that, but he was also dog-tired and he wasn't sure whether eating or sleeping was the more important priority. He forced himself to pick up the knife and fork. Chrissie would be upset if he didn't at least make some effort to eat the food that she had prepared.

'There you are!' She held up the bicycle lamp and switched it on and off to demonstrate that it now worked, before putting it down on the table. Then she pulled out the chair opposite her husband and sat down.

Gavin ate in silence. Every mouthful was an effort and he felt that conversation would be just too much. Chrissie didn't seem inclined to talk either. She just sat there, with her hands clutched together on the table in front of her, watching him. Her face looked tired and drawn – and anxious.

'It's all my fault,' she said at last in a flat, strangely unemotional voice. 'I was too controlling. I pushed him too hard to make something of himself.'

'Rubbish!' Gavin dropped his knife and put out his hand to take hold of hers. 'You were only trying to help him. It's not your fault if he couldn't see that.'

'Oh but he could! I'm sure of that. That's what he's afraid of. He can't stand the idea that someone cares about him.'

* * *

Oh no! Father Damien groaned inwardly as he recognised the strident ringing tone coming from the bedroom where he had left his phone while he showered before bed. Not another call-out? Would it matter very much if he ignored the summons? After all, if it had come a few minutes earlier he would have been under the shower and could not possibly have heard the ringing. Whatever it was could surely wait until morning. Or else they would find someone else. He was not indispensable. It was arrogant to believe that he was.

But what if it was a cry for help that could not wait? A dying parishioner needing absolution before they could rest in peace? What if he were the last, rather than the first, person that whoever it was had tried? Perhaps they had rung while he was in the shower and were now desperately trying again to get through to him. What if his failing to answer the phone resulted in the caller taking their own life or suffering violence from someone in their own home? What if …?

He hurried across the landing and snatched up the phone. It was Peter. What could he want at this time of night?

'Father? I'm sorry, I only just noticed the missed call. Were you trying to get hold of me?'

'Peter!' Damien slumped down on the edge of the bed. 'I'm sorry to have bothered you. I know you like to go to bed early. I was going to ask your advice about something, but it's not important.'

'Well I'm here now. What was it about?'

'No, no. It's really not important. I don't know why I rang you. It's not as if-'

'Go on. I won't get any sleep now, trying to guess what it was that was important enough to interrupt your evening prayers and now suddenly doesn't matter.'

'I didn't realise you knew my routine so well,' Damien smiled. Then he sighed. 'OK. I was feeling bad about spoiling Deirdre's altar frontal – the white one with the red and gold embroidery on it. She made it in memory of her husband who passed away at Easter five years ago. I know it took her ages to make it – all stitched by hand. We always use it between Easter and Pentecost.'

'This is Deirdre as in the cakes and scones?' Peter had often been called upon to help Damien to consume the home-baked gifts that Deirdre was in the habit of showering on her parish priest.

'That's right. She's so amazingly generous, both to the church and to me personally. She put her very soul into that frontal and I feel really bad about not looking after it better.'

'What happened? How bad is the damage?'

'I knocked over a candle and part of the embroidery caught fire. I put it out pretty quickly, but there's a whole section of it ruined, right in the front where everyone can see it. I'm going to have to tell her and apologise.'

'Maybe it won't look so bad in the morning, in the daylight,' Peter suggested.

'Or maybe it'll look worse!'

'I don't really know what to say – except stop beating yourself up about it. Accidents happen. Deirdre will understand that.'

'I suppose so.' Damien hesitated, strangely reluctant to stop his mental self-flagellation. 'I'll give her a ring-'

'But not until tomorrow,' Peter jumped in quickly, 'after you've seen it in daylight, and late enough that she'll be up. I know it's tempting to want to get it over with but far better to sleep on it. Things always look better in the morning – even if they're not!'

'Yes. You're right, of course. Anyway, I won't keep you. It's been good to talk. Keep well.'

11. NIGHT TERRORS

'I was thinking,' Dean said as they lay together in bed, 'it's not fair me leaving you at home with the boys all day every day. It's tough on you, and the boys would probably rather have a change sometimes too. I think we ought to spread the load a bit.'

'I thought you said the mail-order business needed you to go in every day.'

'Well, I do think it needs one of us to keep an eye on what's happening, but it doesn't have to be me all the time. We could take it in turns.'

'But you said-'

'I know what I said, but now I think I was wrong, OK? Just hear me out, won't you? I could take you in the car and drop you off at the Science Park. The boys would enjoy the ride – anything to get out of the house. And then, when you're finished for the day, I can come back and pick you up again. Or you could get the bus back. I know we're supposed to avoid public transport, but the buses haven't stopped running, so they must expect some people to still need them.'

'OK. Thanks.' Wayne put his arm round his husband and pulled him closer. 'You'll have to bring me up to speed with how you've got things organised over there. And what about call-outs?' he added suddenly, 'like Ray Bentham? I wouldn't be able to do those on the bus.'

'Send one of the technicians; or if it really does need one of us, *I'll* do it.'

'With the boys?' Wayne asked sceptically.

'Yes, why not? They can stay in the car while I do whatever it is I have to. Look, I'm trying to make things better for you, if you'd rather stay at home every day just say so!'

Dean pulled away and slid further down under the bedclothes.

'No. I'm sorry. I was only … And you're right: it will be better for the boys to have you looking after them sometimes. I can tell they're fed up with just me all the time. I'm really not sure I'm cut out for this parenting thing. I keep having to stop myself from shouting at them – especially Carl. I don't know what's got into him. He seems to be deliberately trying to wind me up all the time.'

'Just bored with being at home all day, I expect. So it's settled then? I'll bring you up to speed with everything and then we can start alternating who goes in and who stays at home.'

'Yeah, OK.' Wayne did not sound as pleased as Dean had hoped. After all, he was putting himself out to help his husband. He might have shown a bit more gratitude. He rolled over and closed his eyes.

'Maybe it was a mistake taking on the boys,' Wayne said unexpectedly. 'With me having had my accident and everything. I'm pretty useless with them at the best of times. Harry's always wanting to be outside playing football and I can't give him any sort of game, and Carl's … well Carl just doesn't seem to want to know. Whatever I do is wrong according to him!'

'Don't say that!' Dean, suddenly alert, rolled back and put his arm around Wayne's chest. 'How can you possibly wish we didn't have the boys? And you're a great dad. You're much more patient with them than I am. And remember what their social worker said about how much they've come on since they've been living here. She said it was a good sign that they were starting to push the boundaries. It showed they weren't scared all the time the way they used to be with their birth family. Please don't talk like that, it makes me feel-'

'Daddy Wayne! Daddy Dean!' He broke off at the sound of a high-pitched voice calling from the doorway. 'I can't sleep! Can I come in bed with you?'

'Now Harry, I thought we had an agreement: once you're in bed you stay in your room until we call you for breakfast,' Wayne held out his arm over the side of the bed and Harry ran across the room for a hug. 'I'll take you back and tuck you in and I'm sure you'll soon get off to sleep if you just close your eyes.'

He rolled out of bed and led his son by the hand out of the room. Dean lay back and waited. He heard the pad-pad of bare feet on the landing: small pattering steps from Harry and uneven heavier ones from Wayne. Then a pause and a murmur of voices and then footsteps returning.

'His bed's wet,' Wayne explained, lifting up the duvet to allow Harry to climb into the big double bed. 'The sheets need changing.'

'I'll do it,' Dean groaned. 'You get back into bed. You've already had a hard day; it's my turn now.'

'You mean, you'll do it quicker,' Wayne grumbled.

'Yes, well maybe I do!' Dean was beginning to get impatient with Wayne's determination to be offended by every effort he made to lessen his burdens. 'Does it really matter? If it means we all get back to bed sooner, what's the problem? It's not a competition. You're not any less of a man just because you've got a limp and a dodgy arm! It just means that sometimes – and only sometimes – it's better for everyone to let me do things.'

Dean collected a fresh sheet and duvet cover from the airing cupboard and then crept into the boys' bedroom as quietly as he could. Exaggerated heavy breathing from Carl's bed indicated that he was awake but pretending not to be. Dean decided to ignore him. He stripped Harry's bed and straightened the plastic under-sheet. Then he stretched the fitted sheet over the corners of the mattress and smoothed it out.

'What's going on?' Carl growled from across the room. 'How'm I supposed to sleep with you and Daddy Wayne coming in and out all night?'

'Sorry! I'm just changing Harry's sheets. I won't be long.'

'Has he wet the bed *again*?' Carl spoke in tones of deepest derision. 'He's such a baby!'

'He can't help it. I expect you were same at his age.'

'No way!'

Dean turned his attention to the duvet. The cover was damp but he judged that the quilt inside was useable. He pulled off the cover and hurled it into the corner of the room with the sheet.

'Hurry up, can't you?' Carl demanded from across the room. 'I'm trying to get to sleep over here!'

'Not long now!' Dean called back from inside the duvet cover. He could never get the hang of how to insert the duvet without getting it folded up as he did so and then having to burrow in after it. He was now attempting to push the corners of the quilt into the corners of the cover. 'There! All done!'

He straightened up and looked Carl in the eye. The boy stared back defiantly. His behaviour had definitely deteriorated since Lockdown started. Being shut in all day was clearly having an effect on his mental well-being. But no good saying anything about it. Just act normal.

'Now, I'm going to get Harry and there's to be no teasing him about wetting the bed. Do you understand?'

Carl nodded sulkily.

'And you're both to close your eyes and go to sleep right away, OK?'

He went back to the master bedroom, where he found Harry snuggled up next to Wayne, with his head on his shoulder and one arm laid across his chest. A gay man in bed with a young boy. What would the tabloid press make of such a scene? More grist to the mill of those people who objected to the idea of gay couples adopting children. Should they be more careful to avoid this sort of situation? He could remember vividly getting into bed with his own mother and father when he was small, after waking with nightmares. Would that be frowned upon these days for fear that it might be a sign of an inappropriate relationship with one of his parents?

Wayne looked up as he approached. 'Harry's been worrying that we might get coronavirus and die. I've told him we're not old enough to be at risk.'

'Absolutely' Dean agreed. He went over and gently prised the boy off his other father. 'Don't you worry, Harry. We're all being careful. Neither of us is going to get the virus and if we did we'd both be fine. Now, come along! Your bed's all ready for you. Back you go now.'

* * *

Eddie and Crystal were also lying in bed debating how better to share childcare responsibilities in the absence of external help.

'I could ask to go on nights more often,' Crystal suggested. 'Then I'd be around to keep an eye on the kids while you're working.'

'But when would you get any sleep?' Eddie objected.

'I'd be OK. I can get my head down for a few hours after you finish work and before my shift starts. And the kids will be OK if I give them something to do while I have a nap during the day.'

'Don't be so sure! I don't feel I can take my eyes off them for a minute. But in any case, there isn't time for you to have a proper sleep if you're going to wait until I've finished work.'

'But if you can't take your eyes off the kids, how are you getting any work done anyway?'

'Mostly before they get up and after they go to bed. That's why you don't see much of me in the evenings.'

'But that's exactly what I'm talking about. It was all very well when we thought this was only going to last for three weeks. Now that it's looking like it's going to be long term, we need to work out something that'll work better. We can't afford to have you lose your job.'

'There's no chance of that at the moment,' Eddie reassured her. 'We're snowed under with work. All sorts of people have suddenly realised that they need our services now that everything has to be done online. Just so long as I keep delivering the goods it'll all be OK. The only real problem is when I need to do a conference call with my line manager, because she expects to do that during the day.'

'We could ask for places for the kids at the hospital nursery,' Crystal suggested, still determined to relieve her husband of what she was sure must be a burden. 'I'm a key worker, so we're allowed to.'

'Too risky. I'd be afraid they'd pick up coronavirus from the other kids. Some of their parents could be working on COVID wards. And they keep talking about black people being more seriously affected. I don't want you being put at any more risk than you already are with working in the hospital. Tell you what,' he added, seeing his wife's dissatisfied expression. 'How about you trying to get more late shifts? If I get up at six, I can get all my work finished before you need to go in. I can tell my manager that I'm fine to do calls with her, so long as they're in the mornings. And you'll be back by midnight and you can get a proper night's sleep before the kids wake up.'

'I suppose so.'

'And you could start turning down some of the overtime that they keep asking you to do.'

'I don't like to,' Crystal sighed. 'I keep thinking: if *I* don't do it, how are they going to staff the wards? And then what'll happen to the patients?'

'They'll be even more short-staffed if you drive yourself into the ground working too hard.' Eddie decided that it was time he asserted himself and told Crystal how he felt about her work. 'I'm really worried about you. I keep thinking: what if you catch COVID? And in between thinking that, I worry that you're overdoing it, walking there and back every day and then on your feet all the time, not even getting a lunch break sometimes.'

Crystal turned to him and kissed him. 'Don't you worry. I'm tough. I'll be fine.'

* * *

One person who did not have any difficulty falling asleep that night was Gavin. After his exertions, followed by a heavy meal, his problem lay more in keeping himself awake for long enough to brush his teeth and change into his pyjamas. Chrissie tried not to disturb him as she tossed and turned, unable to quieten her mind and drift off.

Where had Craig gone? Why had she been so insensitive as to drive him away? She rehearsed in her mind all sorts of alternative things she could have said when he told her about the incident at work: carefully chosen words that would have been encouraging and not patronising. And she planned out what she would say when – if – he came home. Did he think of their house as *home*?

No point worrying about all that. Gav was right. There was nothing they could do until the morning – nothing *she* could do, full stop. She'd done the damage, but Gavin

143

would have to clear it up. Better to concentrate on what she was going to do tomorrow. She still hadn't got round to asking Gav to talk to DCI Porter about judging the bear-naming competition. Would he agree to do it? He'd probably think it was a silly idea – perhaps it was.

It was her turn to work from home tomorrow. Another teacher would be looking after those members of her class who were still attending school. That meant video meetings with those who were at home – or telephone calls if the technology let them down or they still did not have the necessary equipment. She had never taught that way before. How would the children react? Would she be able to communicate with them when all they could see of her was her head and shoulders on a screen? Would they have managed to download the work she'd set them from that strange *cloud* thing? Where was the cloud, anyway?

She turned over again and in doing so pulled the duvet off Gavin's feet. The sudden draught of cooler air woke him and he pulled back on the duvet. Chrissie got out of bed and went round to straighten it up.

'Worrying about Craig?' Gavin asked as she got back in.

'Yes,' she admitted, 'and the kids. The work I was marking last night was nowhere near as good as I know they're capable of. Some of them are really struggling. I'm going to be doing video calls with them tomorrow and I was trying to work out how to help them.'

'You'll do it,' Gavin assured her. 'It'll all be fine. You're good at your job. Everyone knows that.'

'But I'm good at doing my job the way I'm used to,' Chrissie objected. 'I'm used to being able to take hold of their hand and guide the pencil, or to sit down next to them and show them what I'm asking them to do. And with the ones who aren't good verbally, how am I going to explain things if they can't see what I'm doing with my hands?'

'I thought that was the point of it being a video call?'

'Well yes, but I've been experimenting, and I never seem to be able to get all of me in the picture properly. Either I'm too close to the camera or else I'm afraid of being too far away from the mike.'

'I'm sure it'll all be fine,' Gavin repeated.

'Yes. I'm sorry. I didn't mean to keep you awake.' Chrissie flopped back on the pillow and pulled the duvet up round her husband's shoulders. 'Go back to sleep. I'm just being silly.'

'No you're not.' Gavin put his arm round her and hugged her to him. 'You're just being conscientious.'

'I've set them a little project to do,' Chrissie told him. If she didn't ask him about DCI Porter now, she'd never get round to it. 'I've asked them to research names for that police teddy bear that someone left for Kenny, and then pick one and give a little talk on why they chose it.'

Gavin grunted encouragingly, wondering what was coming next.

'I was thinking of giving a prize for the best talk and I was wondering … do you think that DCI Porter would be willing to judge them for me and then present the prize?'

'I don't see why not … but why …?'

'He's such a good role model for the kids, and they'd feel more important if it was someone from outside the school telling them how well they've done. Would you ask him for me? I don't really know him that well.'

'I'm not sure I do either. I could ask Peter Johns to sound him out if you like.'

'Would you? That would be great!'

* * *

'Daddy!' It was years since anyone had called him that. Peter looked round to see where the voice had come from. There was nobody to be seen. He was in a long corridor. The walls were lined with white tiles, with a row of dark green ones at about waist height. He somehow knew that it was a hospital, but it wasn't the John Radcliffe where Crystal worked. How had he got here?

'Daddy!' the voice called again. It was coming from a door, far away at the end of the corridor. He knew now that it was Hannah. That must be why he didn't recognise this place. It must be in Leeds, where she lived with her husband and children. But how had he got there? He hurried forward, but the door seemed to recede as he went, so that it was just as far away as ever.

A woman in theatre scrubs appeared from nowhere and thrust what looked like a scene of crime suit at him. 'You'll have to wear this if you're going in,' she said brusquely.

He tried to obey, but before he could get his legs into the suit, another woman pounced on him from the other side brandishing a respirator mask of the sort that he'd seen fire fighters using years ago when he'd been a uniformed constable. 'Put this on. We can't have you going in without a mask.'

He seemed to be surrounded by people intent on forcing him into protective clothing. His heart raced as he tried to follow their instructions. All the time, he could hear Hannah calling to him and another voice – a child's voice, Ricky's perhaps – reciting *keep apart two metres, keep apart two metres*. How could he keep apart when they were all crowding in on him?

Then suddenly they were all gone and he was standing at the end of the corridor looking in through the glass window in the door of a hospital room. There was a bed with all sorts of equipment around it, and there was Hannah, lying there with an oxygen mask over her face. He put out his hand to open the door, but a nurse leapt out from somewhere on the right and barred his way.

'You can't go in without gloves on.'

'But we've run out of gloves!' he heard himself protest.

'You can't go in without gloves,' the nurse repeated.

'Daddy! Daddy!'

'I've got to go in. She's my daughter.'

'She can't really be your daughter,' came a voice from behind him. 'She's black.'

'She *is* mine, and she needs me!'

'Only if you're wearing gloves,' the nurse said implacably.

'But we can't get any.'

'Then you can't go in.'

'Daddy! Daddy!'

Peter woke up with a start. He lay there waiting for his heart to slow down to its normal pace and trying to adjust his thoughts to reality. He must check with Bernie in the morning whether she had managed to order any more disposable gloves. And he ought to ring Hannah to make sure they were still all OK. It was a while since they'd been in touch.

'Are you alright?' His jerking limbs as he came out of his nightmare must have woken Bernie.

'Yes. Just a bad dream. I'm sorry I disturbed you.'

'Want to talk about it?'

'Not particularly. It was just a silly thing about Hannah being in ICU and they wouldn't let me in to see her because I didn't have any gloves to put on. Did you manage to order any?'

'Yes, for an arm and a leg! And some at the usual price with estimated delivery in two months.'

'I must ring Hannah. I haven't spoken to her for over a week.'

'Why not fix up another Zoom call with her. Then the kids can join in too. But you're right, we've started to get out of the habit. We used to do videoconferences with everyone almost every day when Lockdown started, but lately we've all been too busy with other things I suppose.'

'Leeds seems such a long way away. What if something did happen to her?'

'Or to Lucy up in Liverpool,' Bernie agreed sombrely.

* * *

Father Damien emerged from a deep slumber to the ringing of the telephone in the hall of the presbytery. In his stupor it took him some time for the sound to register. How long had it been going on? He reached for the alarm clock and peered at its face in the dark: two thirty-four. It must be urgent for someone to call at that hour.

With a struggle, he forced himself to get up. His slippers seemed to have vanished, so he padded downstairs in his bare feet.

'St Cyprian's presbytery.'

'Father? I'm so sorry to bother you, but I'm that worried about Jim. He's coughing fit to crack his ribs and going a sort of blue colour in his face.' It was Hilda, one of the oldest members of his flock. She was a widow and lived with her son, James, a retired bank clerk, also widowed. He must be in his seventies now, which made Hilda ninety at least.

'Has the doctor seen him?'

'Jim spoke to someone on the telephone yesterday – not our own doctor, some sort of stand-in – but they wouldn't come out. They just told him to keep warm and drink plenty of water.'

'Have you tried ringing 111? It sounds as if he may need to go into hospital. You need to ring them and they'll tell you if you ought to call an ambulance.'

'He doesn't want to go to hospital. He says, if he's going to die, he'd rather die at home.'

Damien sighed. He remembered now that Jim's wife had died on the operating table after some supposedly routine procedure had gone terribly wrong. He had been intensely distressed at not having been with her at her passing and there having been no priest there to hear her confession and give her a final communion.

'Do you mean that you *have* rung them and they said to call 999?' he asked wearily.

There was a long pause.

'Hilda?' the priest asked anxiously. 'Are you still there?'

'Yes … I was wondering … Could you come round and anoint him for healing and … just in case …?'

'I shouldn't really. There are rules.'

'I know. I shouldn't have asked. I'm sorry.'

'No, no,' Damien broke in quickly. 'Of course I'll come. Just give me a few minutes to get dressed and sort out some PPE and I'll be right over. Just tell me truthfully: what *did* they say when you rang 111?'

'Just what you said. They said to call for an ambulance to take him to hospital. But I don't like to when Jim says he won't go.'

'OK Hilda.' Damien thought fast. 'You ring for the ambulance and then tell Jim that I'm on my way over to hear his confession and anoint him for healing. And if the ambulance gets there first, tell him I'll see him in the hospital in the morning.'

'Thank you! Oh thank you!' Hilda's gratitude was almost more than Damien could bear.

'That's what I'm here for. Now promise me you'll ring for that ambulance right away.'

He put down the phone and stood for a moment trying to gather his thoughts. What had he meant when he told Hilda that he would bring PPE? What did he have access to in the way of protective equipment? Just a surgical mask – not sufficient to prevent him breathing in virus-laden droplets from Jim's breath – and goggles for his eyes, and a box of latex gloves. Totally inadequate, but they would just have to do. Now where had he put the holy oils and the portable communion set?

As he drove through the deserted streets he had sudden misgivings at what he was doing. Had he been wrong to give in to his natural impulse to soothe Hilda's anxiety by promising to go out to visit her son? If Jim had COVID-19 – and all the signs were he did – then after coming into contact with him, Damien would need to self-isolate for fourteen days. That would mean finding another priest to officiate at the funeral that he was due to take on Thursday and pulling out of his chaplaincy duties at the hospital for a fortnight. Could he really justify knowingly imposing additional work on his colleagues and potentially more anguish on the bereaved family and the patients at the hospital, simply in order to convince one obstinate old man to follow medical advice, and to quieten the mind of his anxious mother?

It was a relief to see the ambulance already there outside the house when he arrived. He sat in the car watching as two paramedics in full PPE wheeled a trolley out of the front door and brought it round to the back of the ambulance. He could see Hilda framed in the doorway, looking out and waving to her son as they bent over him, preparing to lift him into the ambulance. Damien got out of the car and hurried over to what he judged was two metres away from the trolley.

'Jim!' he called out. 'It's Father Damien! I can't come with you just now, but I'll see you in the morning.'

The paramedics turned and stared at him. He smiled at them and then realised that they wouldn't be able to see his expression under his face mask and goggles.

'I'm his priest,' he explained. 'Would it be OK for me to come a bit closer to speak to him?'

'We need to get off right away.'

'Better keep back. We're assuming he's COVID positive.'

'I know. I just want to be sure he's seen me. He's … I'm sorry. It's difficult to explain.'

Then miraculously, or so it seemed to Damien, Jim raised his right hand and crossed himself.

'That's right Jim!' Damien called out. 'Put yourself in God's hands. And trust the doctors to look after you. I'll be there to see you tomorrow, and I'll see that your mother's OK too. Don't worry. Everything's going to be OK.'

He raised his own hand in blessing and made an exaggeratedly large sign of the cross, which he hoped Jim would be able to see and recognise. Then the stretcher disappeared inside the ambulance and one of the paramedics climbed in after it. The other folded up the trolley and handed it up to his colleague. Then he closed the door and went round to the driver's side of the ambulance.

Moments later, Damien was left standing alone on the pavement, watching the rear lights retreating into the darkness. He looked towards the house. Hilda was still there, standing in the doorway. He took off his face mask and eye shield and went a little closer. He stood at the gate and called to her.

'He's in good hands now. You go to bed now and look after yourself. I'll ring you in the morning after I've seen him.'

Hilda nodded, but did not move. With the light behind her he couldn't see her face. Damien raised his hand again and said a blessing over her. Then at last she turned to go. He watched until the door closed before returning to his car.

As he drove back, his mind was in a whirl. Fortunately he was on chaplaincy duty tomorrow, so there should be no difficulty about getting to see Jim. Thank goodness that the hospital now had adequate supplies of PPE! What to do about Hilda was more difficult. She would now have to stay in strict quarantine for two weeks. He must check that she had regular food supplies organised. Would she be able to cope in the house on her own? He had no idea how much assistance she usually got from her son in carrying out normal day-to-day activities.

The car gave a jolt as it hit the kerb. He must have dropped off for a moment. He braced his arms against the steering wheel and fixed his eyes firmly on the road ahead as he drove the remaining few hundred yards back to the presbytery. He felt suddenly very alone. He loved being a priest, and he had never wavered in his conviction that it was his vocation, but right now being the person to whom people turned for support felt more like a burden than a privilege. There was no one in whom he could confide. No one to whom he could vent his frustration at being prevented from doing all the usual things: visiting his flock in their homes, officiating at public mass, taking hold of Jim's hand as he was loaded into the ambulance.

He locked the car and trudged wearily across the small car park to the door of the presbytery. It was an effort to lift his hand to put the key into the lock and turn it, but he managed it somehow and almost fell into the house. He fumbled for the light switch, and then gave up and felt his way along the wall to his study. He would just write down a list of all the things he needed to do tomorrow before going back to bed …

* * *

'Stella? Is that you?'

Stella, in the act of creeping downstairs, turned to see her grandmother peering over the bannister rail on the landing.

'Sorry Gran,' she called back softly. 'I didn't mean to wake you. I was just going down to get a drink of water.'

'I'll make us both some tea.' Celeste's face disappeared for a moment as she hastened along the landing to join Stella on the stairs. 'That'll be better than water to help us both get back off to sleep.'

'Honestly Gran, you don't need to.'

'Don't argue. I'm awake now and I want some tea. Now are you going to stand there arguing all night or are you going to come down and help me?'

Stella grinned and gave a little sigh. 'Alright Gran.'

She could see that her grandmother was determined that they would have a "little talk" together, and for once, she felt almost pleased at the prospect. At least it would be better than running and re-running all her anxieties over in her mind again and again.

'Now tell me all about it.' Celeste commanded, putting down a steaming cup of tea in front of Stella.

'About what?' Stella played for time, unsure how to begin.

'Whatever it is that's keeping you awake at night. This isn't the first time I've heard you creeping around in the early hours. There's something worrying you. I can tell.'

'Well, it's not really anything in particular. It's just … I'm just not sure any longer that I can do it.'

'Do what?'

'I don't think I'm going to be any good as a police officer.'

'And why's that then? Has anyone said anything to you? Have you been in trouble with your boss?'

'No. It's not that. It's just … Well, the other day I had a panic attack just because of a fast car going past when I wasn't expecting it.'

'And?'

'That was it.'

'That was it?' Celeste repeated. 'You mean, nothing happened? Nobody was hurt? What did PC Hughes say about it?'

'He wasn't there. It was before we started our shift. I was outside his house waiting for him to be ready to go. But don't you see? Suppose it happened in the middle of an incident. Police officers are supposed to stay calm and cope with anything. I should've got the number of the car, instead of diving for cover in the hedge.'

'I'd say that rather depends how close it came to hitting you.'

'But that's just it. It wasn't anywhere near hitting me. It just came roaring past and gave me a shock, that's all. And I panicked because it reminded me of when Kenny was killed.'

'And because of this one incident you've decided you aren't going to be any good as a police officer?'

'No. It's not just that. I just don't seem to be able to … Take the other day, for example. I was out with PC Hughes, just on foot patrol, looking out for people who were breaking the Lockdown regulations. We saw a group of youths hanging around down one of the side streets. So I went to have a word with them. I explained that they shouldn't be there and told them to go home, but they just laughed at me and carried on as if I wasn't there. And then Gavin came up and he hardly had to say anything at all before they all went off in different directions. People just don't take me seriously!'

'You're young. It'll take time,' Celeste tried to reassure her. 'What did PC Hughes say about it?'

'The same as you,' Stella admitted.

'There you are then!'

'But I think there's more to it than that. I think I'm not the sort of person people ever do take seriously.'

'Nonsense! Peter thinks very highly of you. He's always telling me how pleased he is that you went into the police.'

'Peter thinks highly of everyone. And he's mainly pleased because he wants more black officers. Gavin's – I mean PC Hughes – is a bit like him. He's always just saying how well I'm doing, instead of telling me what I need to do to get better.'

'Maybe that's because you're doing alright.'

'Or because he knows I can't do any better.'

'Oh Stella!' Celeste sighed. 'Sometimes I think you need a good shaking! You've just told me that everyone thinks you're doing alright. If they thought you needed to pull your socks up, they'd tell you. Can't you just believe them? Look: I'll be honest. I didn't want you to be a police officer. I was afraid you'd get hurt. And when Kenny was killed, I was all set to put my foot down and tell you that you had to quit. And then Peter came to me telling me what a good officer you were shaping up to be and how much the police force needed people like you and how much you wanted to stick with it, and I promised him I wouldn't stand in your way. And now, just because a few silly boys think they look big defying the rookie cop, you're all set to throw in the towel. I'm disappointed in you, Stella, really I am!'

'It's not just that!' Stella protested. 'That was just a *for instance*. There've been loads of other times. In fact, I can't think of a single time I got things right!'

'I can't believe that.'

'Just take Kenny, for example.'

Celeste sat back in her seat with a knowing look on her face. Ah! Now here came the real reason for her granddaughter's crisis of confidence.

'If I hadn't been there, he might still be alive.'

'How do you make that out?'

'He let me make the arrest. I couldn't get the handcuffs on. It took ages. If he'd done it himself, he'd probably have got away off the road before the car came.'

'That's not what the coroner said – or the police enquiry. You were commended for trying to save him. The report said you did everything you could.'

'But it wasn't good enough. I couldn't remember what to do. If it had been someone else-'

'They'd have done just the same,' Celeste said firmly. 'Remember what his mum said at the inquest. She said how glad she was he wasn't alone when he died. And PC Hughes wouldn't have agreed to be your mentor if he thought you were responsible for his son dying, would he?'

'I know, it's just … I can't help thinking …'

* * *

Craig pressed himself closer into the crevice in the wall, trying to make himself as inconspicuous as he could. He could hear footsteps. They must be searching the building. He drew his jacket up over his head, hoping that he would be missed in the dark.

Then there was a blinding flash and a huge bang. That must have been an explosion somewhere close. The footsteps hurried away, heading for cover. There was an eerie silence for a few seconds before the wailing started. The mortar bomb had hit a building with people in it. He could hear the screams of children and the distraught cries of mothers. Then they were drowned out by another explosion, even closer this time.

Where were the other men from his section? He shouted out to them, but there was no reply. He hoped that they had found somewhere to shelter from the bombardment. There was nothing they could do until it stopped. They didn't have the weapons to retaliate – even if they could have located the source of the mortar fire. The Taliban were up there in the hills somewhere. And they – and the people of this village – were sitting targets. All they could do was to try to survive until the enemy ran out of ammunition.

In the lull that followed he heard footsteps again. Were they still after him, even under fire from their own side? He felt a hand on his shoulder and a voice speaking in surprisingly good English.

'You can't sleep out here, sir.'

In a flash Craig was awake and fighting to free himself from his sleeping-bag.

'It's alright,' Constable Timpson told him calmly. 'No need to panic. Let me help you.' He crouched down and unzipped the sleeping-bag. 'Now, tell me where you live and I'll give you a lift home.'

Craig stared up in silence, trying to make sense of what was happening.

'If you could just give me your name, sir?' Timpson persisted.

'Manson – Corporal Craig Manson.'

'And your addre- hang about! Did you say Craig Manson? Aren't you the guy that Gavin Hughes took in? What are you doing back out on the streets? You're never telling me Gavin chucked you out?'

'No,' Craig mumbled. 'I just … I like it better out here sometimes, OK?'

'No, I'm afraid it's not OK. We've cleared the streets because of the pandemic. All rough sleepers have been found places to stay. Now, shall I take you back to Gavin's place or would you rather sleep in a police cell while Social Services finds you a room somewhere?'

Craig began stuffing his sleeping bag into his rucksack, 'OK,' he growled. 'It'd better be Gavin's place, I suppose.'

It was starting to get light by the time they arrived back at the house in Arundel Road. Craig was conscious of PC Timpson's eyes on him as he let himself in through the front door. He crept upstairs, trying not to disturb Gavin and Chrissie. Peering out through the landing window he could see the squad car still parked outside. Evidently the constable did not trust him not to run off again as soon as he was gone. How long would he wait? Until morning? Surely not!

'Hello Craig. Welcome back!'

He turned to see Gavin standing there in his pyjamas.

'Ben Timpson rang to let us know he'd brought you home,' he explained. 'Chrissie's dying to see you, but I told her it'd better wait 'til morning.' He came closer and put his arm on Craig's shoulder, bringing his mouth close to his ear. 'She's been worried sick about you, you know. Go easy on her. She doesn't mean to be … Look, I know what's it's like for you guys, but … Well, just cut her a bit of slack, OK?'

Over breakfast the next morning, Chrissie did her best to play down her anguish at Craig's departure and her delight at his safe return. She resisted the strong urge to hug him when he appeared in the kitchen, contenting herself with gesturing to him to sit down and pouring him a cup of tea.

'Thanks.' He took a seat opposite her and sat for a few moments staring down at the table cloth. Then he looked up. 'I'm sorry about going off like that. Gavin told me you were worried.'

'That's alright!' Chrissie could have cried with relief. 'I'm sorry I made you feel … I know I can be a bit overbearing at times. I just … Well, I am so glad you're back!'

'Yes, well …'

'All's well that ends well,' Gavin said heartily, bringing over slices of toast for both of them. 'That's all that matters.'

They all made an effort to talk normally and act as if nothing had happened. It was only when Craig got to his feet and declared his intention of setting off for work that Chrissie gave way to her feelings and suggested that he needed a day off.

'I can call your work and tell them you're not well,' she offered. 'If I'm a bit vague about it they'll probably assume you were taken ill yesterday afternoon and that's why you went home early.'

'No.' Craig shook his head. 'Thanks for the offer, but I'd better go and face the music.'

'But you look all-in,' Chrissie argued. 'You can't have got much sleep last night. Wouldn't it be better to have a rest day and then go in fresh tomorrow and show them how good you are at the job?'

'If I'm going back at all, I'd better do it right away,' Craig insisted.

'He's right, Chrissie,' Gavin backed him up. 'No point putting it off.'

12. MISSING

'There you are!' Dean stood up from his task of tying Harry's shoelaces and patted his son on the shoulder. 'Now sit down and have your breakfast. We need to all be ready to take Daddy Wayne to work today.'

Smiling happily, Harry climbed on to a chair and reached for the box of coco pops. He was looking forward to the kick-about in the garden, which Dean had promised they could have after he finished his school work. He liked Daddy Wayne a lot, but it would be nice to have Daddy Dean at home instead sometimes, and more importantly, the decision that they'd made three days ago to take it in turns seemed to have made them both less edgy.

'Talking of all being ready,' Wayne said, pouring milk from a four-pint bottle into Harry's bowl, 'where's Carl got to? I haven't seen him today. Is he still in bed?'

'No,' Harry answered, shaking his head. 'He wasn't there when I woke up. He must've got up really, really early.'

'So, where is he then?' asked Wayne. 'Have you seen him, Dean?'

'No. I assumed he was still in his room. I'd better go and look for him.'

Dean hurried upstairs. Sure enough, Carl's bed was empty and the clothes that Wayne had laid out the previous evening, ready for the morning, were gone. He must be up and dressed, but where had he got to? The bathroom was empty; so was the tiny spare bedroom, which they used for storage. There was no small boy hiding in the airing cupboard or in either of the wardrobes.

'He's not upstairs,' Dean reported a few minutes later, 'or in the lounge. I'll check outside. Maybe he's in the garden.'

'What about the dining room?' Wayne called after him. 'I'll have a look there.'

He hauled himself to his feet and limped out of the kitchen. It always took a while to get his bad leg moving properly when he got up in the morning. The dining room was deserted. The boys were barred from going in unaccompanied – a rule that they were enforcing all the more strictly now that it was set up as a home office with their two laptop computers and piles of papers relating to the business lying on the table. However, that might have made it all the more attractive to Carl in his recent defiant mood.

Wayne bent down to look under the table: nobody lurking there – or in the dark corner next to the sideboard. He gave the room a final sweep with his eye and then made his way back to the kitchen. Harry had finished his cereal and was engaged in fitting the empty bowl into the dishwasher.

'Good boy, Harry! Now, can you think for me: did Carl say anything about getting up early to do anything this morning?'

'No.' Harry shook his head vehemently.

'He's not outside!' Dean declared, coming back in. 'I just can't think where he can have gone!'

* * *

'His bike's gone!' Wayne announced, coming in from a second sweep of the garden.

'And there's a packet of biscuits missing from the tin,' Dean told him. 'He must've gone off somewhere. I'd better go and look for him. I'll get my bike. While I'm gone, can you and Harry have a look and see if you can find any clues as to where he's heading?'

He pushed past his husband and headed out of the door. Wayne turned to address Harry.

'Now Harry, tell me honestly, did Carl say anything to you about going off on his own anywhere?'

'No.' Harry shook his head vigorously. 'Will he be OK?'

'Yes,' Wayne assured him with more conviction than he felt. 'I expect he's just playing games with us, trying to wind us up. He'll probably be back in a few minutes looking for his breakfast.'

'He won't need breakfast,' Harry pointed out. 'He's got the biscuits.'

'Knowing Carl, those won't last long. Now, will you come upstairs with me and have a look round the bedroom to see if he's taken anything else with him?'

'His phone's gone,' Harry informed him. 'He left it charging when we went to bed and it's not there now. I saw when I was getting up.'

'His phone! Of course! Why didn't we think of that before?' Wayne took out his own phone and called Carl's number. It went straight through to voicemail. He must have turned it off. Wayne left a message and then sent a text as well: *Where are you? Please ring us as soon as you get this.* Then, after a moment's thought, he sent another: *You're not in any trouble. We just want to know where you are.*

'Thanks Harry. Now let's see what we can find out from his room, shall we?'

It wasn't until they reached the top of the stairs that Wayne remembered the location tracking app that they had installed on both of the boys' phones. He had been sceptical about it when Dean suggested it. After all, the boys were too young to be allowed out on their own. But Dean had insisted that it would be useful if ever they got separated. In any case, he argued, the boys would not always be too young to make their own way to places, and if they had the app installed now, they would be used to it before they were old enough to resent the idea that their parents could monitor their movements.

Wayne sat down on Harry's bed and looked down at the screen of his own phone, trying to remember how the location app worked. At last he had it! He peered down at the tiny map on the screen. It looked as if Carl must be quite close. He zoomed in to see the exact spot. Yes! It was in Chichester Road, only a few streets away. He turned to Harry. 'Why would Carl be in Chichester Road?'

Harry shrugged. 'Probably gone to see Ollie.'

Of course! Oliver French was one of Carl's best mates. They were in the same class at school and his parents went to the church where Dean played the organ on Sundays. He must ring Dean to tell him, before he wasted a lot of time touring the neighbourhood.

'I'm sorry, Natalie,' Dean said a few minutes later, when Mrs French opened the door to him. He backed away down the path in order to maintain social distancing while they talked. 'I know it's rather early to be calling round, but I think Carl must be here. At least, that's what the tracker on his phone says.'

'Ah!' Natalie nodded. 'So, it *is* his. Ollie said he thought he recognised the case. Hang on!' she went back into the house returning a few moments later with a mobile phone in her hand. 'We found this lying on the floor when we came down this morning. It must've been pushed through the letterbox during the night. We didn't know it was Carl's.'

'So, he's not here?' Dean looked at her in bewilderment. 'Only his phone?'

'That's right. I'm sorry. I gather he's missing?'

'Yes. We haven't seen him since last night. We thought he must have come round to see Oliver.'

'I'll ask him, but I don't think he knows anything about it. He was as surprised as any of us when we found the phone.' Natalie turned round and called out up the stairs, 'Ollie! Come down here a minute. I need to talk to you.'

'What's up?' A tall, dark-skinned figured loomed behind Natalie. Standing in the doorway, Vincent French looked even larger and more imposing than he did on the rare occasions when he managed to rouse himself early enough on Sunday morning to accompany his wife and children to church. His work in the kitchen of one of most up-market hotels in Oxford kept him out late at night, with Saturday being one of his busiest days, and he was often dead to the world until noon. Dean had always found it easy to picture him there, the typical irascible chef, running his domain with an iron fist. Of course, now everything was different. Had he been furloughed? Or would he have simply lost his job?

'Dean's looking for Carl,' his wife explained. 'This is his phone.'

'I don't understand. What does Ollie know about this?'

'Nothing!' came a voice from behind them. Oliver French wriggled through between his parents. His skin was pale like his mother's, but his tight black curls and deep brown eyes gave away his Afro-Caribbean heritage. 'I haven't seen Carl for ages!'

'When exactly?' demanded his father. 'You've been talking to him on Whatsapp, right?'

'Yeah, but he never said anything about giving me his phone.'

'Did he say anything at all that might tell us where he is?' Dean asked, taking a step towards the boy and then hastily retreating again.

Oliver shook his head.

'What was it you talked about last?' Dean pressed him.

'Dunno!' the boy shrugged. 'Football mainly.'

'He didn't say anything about wanting to run away?'

'No.' Oliver looked up at his mother. 'Is he OK? I mean … He hasn't been kidnapped or anything, has he?'

'No, of course not,' Natalie said quickly. 'He's just being naughty. I expect he's bored with being at home all day.'

'He's got his bike with him,' Dean added. 'I don't think a kidnapper would take that.'

'Well, you'd better have this.' Natalie held out the phone.

'Thanks.' Dean stepped forward and took it with his arm at full stretch to avoid coming too close. 'I'd better get back now. Wayne's waiting. You will let me know if you see him, won't you?'

'Yes, of course,' Natalie assured him. 'And please, will you let us know when you find him?'

Dean mounted his bike again and pedalled furiously back home. Where could Carl be? Why had he gone off like this? And why had he got rid of his phone?

'Where is he?' demanded Wayne the moment he turned in at the front gate.

He and Harry were in the front garden waiting for Dean's return.

'He wasn't there. He must've dropped his phone through their letterbox and gone off again. I've got it here, look!'

'So, where's Carl?' wailed Harry, bursting into tears and throwing himself at Wayne. 'You said you'd found him!' he sobbed, pummelling his father with his small fists. 'You said Daddy Dean was bringing him back. You *promised*!'

'I'm sorry, Harry.' Dean propped up his bike against the wall and bent down to hug his son. 'We thought we *had* found him, but we were wrong. Now, let's all go inside and we can decide what to do next.'

'I know what *I'm* doing next,' Wayne declared 'I'm phoning the police. His school bag's gone, and some of his clothes.'

* * *

Gavin and Stella were just setting out for another day on foot patrol when the call came through on the police radio. A child had gone missing from Lewes Road and someone was needed to attend at once. He immediately confirmed that they were the nearest officers available and set off at a brisk pace. Stella had to run to keep up.

'That's Dean's address,' she panted as she trotted along. 'It must be one of their boys.'

'I know.'

'How can *anyone* go missing when they're not allowed out of the house?'

'Easy enough if they want to run away,' Gavin grunted, remembering their recent scare with Craig. 'Nobody about to see where they've gone.'

They turned into Lewes Road and immediately spotted Dean standing on the pavement looking out for them. Gavin quickened his pace even more and Stella broke into a run. Dean started walking towards them.

'It looks as if Carl's done a runner,' he panted as soon as he was within speaking distance. 'He must have slipped out in the night while we were all asleep.'

'OK. Let's just try to keep calm,' Gavin responded, putting out his hand towards Dean's shoulder and then letting it drop back to his side when he remembered social distancing. 'Let's go somewhere a bit more private and you can tell us all about it.'

Gavin and Stella stood in the back garden while Wayne and Dean, seated on a bench with Harry curled up on Wayne's lap, described what they knew about Carl's disappearance. When they had finished, Gavin pursed his lips in thought.

'Hmm,' he murmured. 'I think I'd better go round and speak to this boy, Ollie did you say his name was? Stella: you stay here and wait for CID. They should be here soon. A missing child is always a priority – although usually it turns out to be nothing,' he added hastily, seeing the two fathers' eyes widening in alarm, while Harry buried his face in Wayne's shoulder.

Although Gavin's build more closely resembled that of a heavyweight boxer than a sprinter, he had a good turn of speed when he needed to get somewhere in a hurry. It was not many minutes before he was standing back waiting for an answer to the vigorous knocking that he had inflicted upon the French family's front door.

'Oh!' Natalie said when she saw him there. 'Is this about Carl?'

'Yes, that's right. Can I come in? Or maybe we could talk in the garden: I need to speak to Oliver.'

'Yes – yes of course. Come through – or – shall I go round and open the side gate?'

'Maybe that would be best,' Gavin agreed. 'I'm sorry to put you to this trouble, but when a child goes missing …'

'Oh yes! Absolutely. We want to do whatever we can!' Natalie closed the door, reappearing a few minutes later through a gate at the side of the house. It was the left-hand end of a terrace of four. 'Come on through. Ollie's all ready for you.'

Gavin followed her through the gate and then closed it firmly behind him. Oliver was sitting on the grass, nervously plucking up daisies and dropping them in a heap in front of him. Gavin waved away the folding chair that Vincent offered him, choosing instead to get down on the grass where he could look the boy in the eye.

'Now Oliver, we need you to tell us as much as you can about what Carl was thinking about over the last few days. I gather you and he were in touch most days.'

Oliver nodded.

'I try to restrict the amount of screen time that the kids have,' Natalie put in, 'but I let Ollie use my phone once a day for a Whatsapp meeting with Carl.'

'You'll have to fill me in on that,' Gavin said, directing his words at Oliver. 'I don't know much about that sort of thing. What does that mean exactly?'

Oliver did not reply, so his mother spoke for him. 'It's just a video call – like Skype – I set it up for them and then leave them to chat for about ten minutes and then take the phone back.'

'So, you don't have a phone of your own?' Gavin asked Oliver, trying to persuade him to answer for himself. He shook his head.

'We don't let the kids have phones until they go to secondary school,' Vincent told him. 'We don't let them out on their own until then, so they don't need one.'

'Very sensible,' Gavin nodded. Then he turned back to Oliver. 'Now Ollie – is it OK for me to call you Ollie? – I need you to think hard about what you and Carl have been talking about over the last week or so. We need to try to work out why he's run away from home. Was there anything bothering him at all, do you know?'

Oliver shook his head. 'He was just pissed off with being shut in all day, same as everyone.'

'And there wasn't anything in particular that he wanted to do?' Gavin persisted. 'Nowhere special that he wanted to go to once Lockdown ends?'

Oliver gave another shake of the head. 'Well, he did say he couldn't see why we couldn't play football in the park,' he said at last.

'I see,' Gavin nodded. 'And did he seem worried about anything at all?'

'No. Nothing.'

'OK. Now, about his phone. Do you have any idea why he pushed it through your door?'

'He knew I wanted one. All our friends have got one!' Oliver flashed a defiant look at his parents. 'But he never said I could have his.'

'OK. You're doing great. Now, I'd like you to think back even further, to before school closed. It's quite unusual isn't it to have two dads? Did any of the other kids ever tease Carl about that?'

'No. Most of them thought it was cool.'

'Are you sure? Carl never told you about anyone saying anything nasty about it?'

'No.' Oliver shook his head vigorously.

'And Carl? Do you know how he felt about it?'

'He said it was awesome. He was in a kids' home before and he said that sucked.'

'So, he wouldn't be trying to get back there?'

'No way!'

'OK. Thank you. I'd better be going now. A plain clothes office may want to ask you some questions later, so it wouldn't do any harm for you to have another think about what Carl talked to you about, in case he said anything that would give them a clue about where he's gone. OK?'

'OK.' Oliver nodded.

Natalie French followed Gavin out through the gate. 'Will you find him?' she asked anxiously when they reached the front garden.

'Most runaways turn up within a few hours,' Gavin told her, hoping that this was true. 'The chances are he'll head for home when he starts feeling hungry. Now tell me: did you see or hear anything when the phone came through the door? You said it was in the night, but could it have been early this morning?'

'I'm afraid I can't help with that. It was just lying there when I came downstairs at about half past eight. Vince and the kids didn't see anything either. I'm sorry.'

'Never mind. I don't suppose it matters.'

Gavin walked down the path to the road. He waited until he heard the gate click shut as Natalie returned to the back garden, and then turned in at the next-door house and knocked on the door. This time he did not step back to wait for it to open. Instead he stood on the step, poised for action, holding his helmet under one arm.

The door opened and Trevor Whittle looked out. He immediately made to slam it shut again, but Gavin was too quick for him and had his foot in the way.

'Mr Whittle, I really am very sorry to disturb you, but I need your help.'

Trevor glared back through the crack in the door created by Gavin's foot. 'Go on then!'

'A young boy's gone missing and we think he was in this street sometime early this morning. Did you see or hear anything? He was on a bike and we think he went next door and posted something through their letterbox.'

'Why don't you ask them then?'

'I've just been there. That's how we know he's been here, but they couldn't tell me what time. I was wondering if you – or maybe Leo …?'

'A boy? How old?'

'Eight – getting on for nine. You've probably seen him around. He's friends with Oliver French. His name's Carl.'

'Carl? Yes, I think I know him. And he's gone missing? How?'

'He just wasn't there when his family got up this morning. It looks like he's run away, but we don't know why or where.'

'I'm sorry.' Trevor opened the door just a little further. 'We sleep at the back. I wouldn't know what's going on in the street.'

'And Leo?' Gavin persisted gently. 'His room is at the front, isn't it? Could you get him, please? It really is important that we find out how long ago it was that Carl was here.'

'OK.' Trevor stepped back and beckoned Gavin inside. 'I suppose you'd better come in. He's in the lounge – on the left.'

Leo was sitting on the sofa with a bowl of breakfast cereal on his lap and a mobile phone on the coffee table in front of him. He looked up when his father entered.

'PC Hughes wants to talk to you,' Trevor told him.

Gavin stood in the doorway, trying to keep his distance. 'A boy's gone missing,' he explained. 'We think he came round here earlier this morning and dropped a package through next door – for Oliver.'

'So?'

'I was just wondering if you might have seen him. Did you happen to glance out of the window at all? It would have been some time before eight-thirty.'

'There *was* a little kid on a bike. I saw it lying on the pavement and then he came and picked it up.'

'When?' demanded Gavin and Trevor together.

Leo shrugged. 'Just after Dad came and banged on my door to get up.'

'The alarm's set for eight,' Trevor explained. 'So that must've been about five or ten past.'

'So, this boy was outside at, maybe quarter past eight?' queried Gavin, looking towards Leo.

'I suppose,' he shrugged.

'Can you describe him – or the bike?'

'Just a little kid – about Ollie's age, I guess. White, skinny with a blue helmet on.'

'Thanks. That sounds like him. You've really been very helpful. Thank you.' Gavin got up to go. 'And did you happen to see which way he went?'

'Up the road,' Leo replied, pointing.

'So, he could have been heading into the city?'

'Yeah. I suppose.'

'Good. Well, thanks again. I'll leave you in peace now.'

Trevor followed Gavin out.

'Will you find him?'

'We'll do our darnedest.' Gavin turned round and looked Trevor in the eye. 'Children are always a priority for us.'

'*Some* children,' Trevor said pointedly.

'I am really sorry about Harry,' Gavin said earnestly. 'And I'm so sorry about the men who killed him being let out on bail. I couldn't believe it either when I heard about it, but there *were* reasons.'

'I don't care what the reasons were! Nothing they say can make any difference. It's all just excuses.'

'I realise it must seem like that, and believe me I do understand how you feel-'

'Yes, yes,' Trevor broke in, 'I know they killed your son too, and I'm sorry about that. What gets me …' He sighed and shook his head. Gavin noticed that his eyes were glistening with tears. 'What gets to me is the way the TV reports and the papers all keep saying "the killers of PC Kenneth Hughes" and never even mention Harry.'

'I know.' Gavin threw caution to the winds and put his arm around Trevor's shoulders. 'I wish they'd just stop reporting it, to be honest. There's nothing anyone can do about the situation and it just makes it worse seeing Kenny's face all over everywhere.'

He drew back and walked a few more paces down the drive. 'I know it's hard, but there really is a reason why they needed to give them bail. My lawyer says that they're not allowed within two miles of either of our houses, and I know that there are police officers going round to check up on them twice a day. It's not much but …' He sighed. 'We *are* doing our best. I know it isn't good enough. It never is. Now, I'd better get back to Carl's parents. They'll be hoping for news.'

'What did *he* want?'

Trevor turned to see Yvonne standing on the stairs, staring towards the closed front door. There were coffee stains on the towelling dressing gown that covered her pyjamas. Her two slippers were from different pairs. Her hair stood out round her head in a bushy black mass. Her eyes looked only half awake.

'There's a boy gone missing from home,' Trevor told her. 'One of Ollie French's friends – Carl; I think I've seen him around.'

'Oh.' Yvonne descended the rest of the stairs and headed towards the kitchen. Her husband followed her down the hall.

'It must be terrible for the boy's parents,' he said. 'Remember how we felt when Harry was missing.'

Yvonne stopped and turned. She stared at him vacantly. 'Yes,' she said softly. 'Yes, I remember.' She shook her head in bewilderment. 'I can remember … but … I can't *feel* anything. Do you get what I'm saying? I can't feel *anything*. I think I must be going mad. Nothing makes any sense anymore.'

13. SEARCHING

Meanwhile, Stella was standing rather awkwardly in the middle of the lawn facing Wayne and Dean. She racked her brains for something to say.

'He'll probably come back by himself in an hour or two and he'll be wondering what all the fuss is about,' she said at last.

'What if he's lost?' snuffled Harry, raising his head from Wayne's chest and staring red-eyed towards the young police officer. 'He hasn't got his phone. Daddy Dean gave him the phone so he wouldn't ever get lost again.'

'That's right,' Dean sighed. 'I took the boys down to stay with my parents last summer. They'd never been on a farm before, and Carl wandered off and then couldn't find his way back. That's when I gave him the phone and showed him how we'd always be able to find him if he had it with him.'

'So, he knew about the tracker?' Stella asked.

'Yes, of course. It wasn't so we could spy on him, just so we'd be able to find him.'

Stella reflected that this suggested that he might well have got rid of the phone in order not to be found, but she decided that this was not a thought to be voiced out loud.

'Well, we've got the whole of Thames Valley Police on the lookout for him now,' she said as confidently as she could. 'So, he's bound to turn up soon.'

There was a long silence. Nobody could think of anything more to say.

'I expect they'll put out a call in the media for the public to look out for him too,' Stella said when it reached the stage that she felt compelled to re-start the conversation.

'But we can't have his name or his picture in the papers,' Dean said at once.

'Why not?' Stella was puzzled.

'His birth family mustn't know where he's living,' Wayne explained.

'Oh!' Stella was taken aback. 'Then maybe they could just say "a boy of eight is missing" and ask people to report if they see a boy on a bike out on his own.'

'I suppose we'd better tell Harvey,' Wayne murmured reluctantly.

'Harvey?'

'Our Social Worker,' Dean explained. 'All families with looked-after kids have one.' He turned to Wayne. 'Give it a few more hours. No point bothering him when Carl might still just walk in the door when he decides it's time for lunch!'

'That's right,' Stella agreed. 'And it'll be better to wait for CID to get here. They'll have a plan for finding him.'

'OK.'

They all lapsed into silence again. Stella felt very helpless and stupid not being able to keep up the conversation. She should have been comforting the anxious family, not standing there like a tongue-tied schoolchild!

'Gran loved listening to those hymns you recorded,' she said to Dean eventually. 'I had to show her how to use

YouTube on her phone and now she listens to all the church services and things.'

'I'm glad she liked them.' Dean forced a smile. 'I suppose it must be hard for her on her own in the house all day, with you out at work.'

'Well, she's not alone because Danny's on furlough, but yes, she's fed up with not being allowed out. I think it's probably worse for Danny though. Most of the things he likes doing aren't allowed anymore.'

The silence that followed was broken by a loud banging on the gate. A woman brandishing a police warrant card appeared round the side of the house. She smiled and nodded at Stella and then turned to address the little group on the bench.

'Mr Major? Mr O'Brien?'

They nodded and Dean got to his feet.

'I don't know if you remember me. I'm Detective Chief Inspector Anna Davenport, and this is Detective Sergeant Andrew Lepage,' she announced, glancing towards a tall, wiry man in his thirties, dark-skinned and with frizzy black hair that he had inherited from his absentee Nigerian father. 'We're here to help find your little boy.'

'Yes, of course we remember. You helped to find the driver who was responsible for Wayne's accident.' Dean absent-mindedly put out his arm to shake hands and then hastily withdrew it again. 'I suppose you need to ask us some questions?'

'Yes, but first we need to have a look at his room and then make a thorough search of this house. I know you'll already have done that, but it's amazing how often kids turn up when we have a go.'

'But we know he's gone off on his bike,' Wayne objected. 'It's not in the shed.'

'He could have gone out and then crept back in and be hiding because he's frightened you'll be cross with him,' Anna said patiently. 'Don't worry, we're not wasting time. I've already got every officer out there alerted to keep an eye out for him. So, if he *is* roaming the streets, we'll soon pick him up. Do you have a recent photograph I could circulate?'

'Ye-es,' Wayne hesitated.

'We can give you one,' Dean continued for him, 'but you mustn't put it out into the public domain. His birth family aren't allowed to know where he lives.'

'Oh! Yes, I understand. Right! Now, perhaps one of you could show DS Lepage to his room to have a look there, while I go over the house checking he's not hiding?'

Andy looked towards Harry. 'Perhaps you could show me?' he suggested. 'And maybe you could tell me about Carl: what sorts of things he likes doing and that sort of thing.'

Harry stared up at Andy. Then he nodded and slipped off Wayne's lap. 'This way,' he said heading for the back door.

Anna watched them go and then turned back to Wayne and Dean. 'OK, now let's not waste any time. Can I leave one of you to do a really thorough search of the garden? Check all the places he could be hiding – including all the nooks and crannies that seem too small or too difficult to get to. You'd be surprised how tiny a child can make himself if he's intent on keeping away from the grown-ups'

'I'll do that,' Wayne volunteered, getting up. 'I'll start with the shed. There's a jumble of stuff at the back that we didn't think to look in earlier.'

'Good.' Anna looked towards Dean. 'Let's get cracking. We need to search the house from top to bottom. I'll just sanitise my hands and put on some PPE before I go inside your home.'

Dean waited in the kitchen while Anna put on a face mask and gloves. Whom was she protecting – herself or them? They kept saying that ordinary face masks didn't safeguard the wearer, so presumably she was trying to avoid passing the virus on to them. How likely was it that she was a carrier? Probably this was all just a show to reassure them that the police weren't taking any risks with the safety of the public. Or maybe it was to convince them of the need to stick to the social distancing rules.

Anna came inside and started opening cupboards and peering into corners. 'While we're doing this, why don't you tell me more about Carl? What sorts of things does he like doing?'

'Both boys are mad about football,' Dean told her. 'In normal times, we go out to the park after school most days for a kick-about. They're both fed up with having to make do with the garden. That's why the lawn's worn so thin.'

'Did he take a ball with him, do you know?'

'I haven't noticed one missing, but we do have a few.'

'Never mind. I'll get a couple of uniformed officers over to the park to check it out. Can you think of any other favourite haunts that he might have gone to?'

'I don't think so. He likes swimming, but the pool's closed.'

'What about friends? Can you give me a list of the names and addresses of anyone he hangs out with?'

'I can give you the names of some of his mates from school, but he doesn't exactly "hang out" with anyone. He's too young for us to let him out on his own. If he goes to play at a friend's house, we take him there and then either the friend's parents bring him back or we go to collect him.'

'Yes, of course. I just meant kids that he might have wanted to go to see.' Anna emerged from the cupboard under the stairs and stood in the hall looking around her. 'OK. I think I've exhausted the possibilities down here. While I check upstairs, do you think you could write me out that list?'

'Yes, of course.'

Dean went into the dining room to find a pen and some paper. He sat down and tried to think of all the people that Carl knew whom he might have wanted to visit. Ollie French was the prime suspect, but they'd already ruled him out. Why had Carl left his mobile phone at Ollie's house? Was it just to get rid of it to prevent them from tracking him? If so, why not just leave it at home? Surely Ollie must know more than he was letting on.

He wrote down the names of three more boys in Carl's class at school whose houses he had visited. He couldn't remember all the addresses, so what was the chance that Carl would have remembered how to get to them? Who else could there be? Carl and Harry had only been living here for just over a year. They didn't know all that many people in Oxford.

Andy stood in the middle of the bedroom, looking round. 'Can you tell me which bed Carl sleeps in?'

'That one,' Harry answered, pointing. 'And I sleep over there.'

'I see. You like Harry Potter then?' Andy commented noticing the poster over Harry's bed.

Harry nodded.

'So do I,' Andy confided. 'When I was your age, I sometimes used to wish I could make a magic spell that would stop the grown-ups being able to find me. Now, I'd rather be able to use magic to find people who are hiding from me! But I'm not a magician, so I've got to do it the hard way and look for them. Do you think you can help me?'

Harry nodded again.

'Good.' Andy got out a torch from his pocket and switched it on. 'I'm going to start by looking under the beds. Would you like to look with me?'

He lay down on his front and shone the torch under Carl's bed. Harry got down next to him and peered under too. Their search yielded a single roller skate, two shrivelled conkers and a very dusty tennis ball. The space beneath Harry's bed was similarly devoid of life – and of clues.

Andy turned to the wardrobe next. 'Let's see if Carl has been trying to get through to Narnia, shall we?' He parted the few clothes that were hanging on the rail and made a show of tapping the back of the cupboard as if checking that there was no secret door through which Carl could have escaped.

'No,' he murmured, turning back to Harry. 'I think we can safely say he's not hiding in here.'

His eye hit on a laptop computer lying on a desk next to Carl's bed.

'Is this Carl's?'

'It's both of us's,' Harry told him. 'It's for our homework.'

'Does Carl use it for anything else at all? Does he go on Facebook with it or – or …?' Andy tried to remember what the latest new social media platforms were. 'Or does he send messages to his friends?'

'No.' Harry shook his head. 'This is just for homework. He uses his phone to talk to people.'

Andy sat down on Harry's bed and gazed across at Carl's side of the room. The wall over his bed was covered with football posters. 'Aston Villa?' he asked, seeing the distinctive claret and blue strip.

'Yes,' Harry nodded. 'They're our team. Granddad says he had a trial with them a long time ago, but they didn't take him, so he went to work in an office instead.'

'Granddad?'

'We don't see him very much. He isn't allowed to come here in case Nanna finds us. We only have *supervised contact* with him.' Harry pronounced the difficult words carefully. 'Harvey tells him where to come, and we go there to see him.'

'I see. So, did you live with your Granddad before you came here?'

'Only when I was a baby.' Harry shook his head. 'I don't remember it. Carl does, a bit. He says he hates Mummy and Nanna, but Granddad was always nice. That's why we have *supervised contact* with Granddad, but he has to keep it secret from Mummy and Nanna.'

Andy turned over this information in his mind. As the much-loved only child of a single mother, he struggled to imagine what life could have been like for Carl in a family where the only adult that he could trust was his grandfather.

'So, where did you and Carl live before you came here?'

'We moved about a lot. They kept putting us with different foster mums, but Carl hated them all, so we went back to the Home.'

'And you've been living here with Dean and Wayne for how long?'

'I'm not sure.' Harry thought hard. 'Two Christmases,' he said eventually. 'I like it here. We're going to stay with Daddy Wayne and Daddy Dean forever.'

'Yes. I can see you're happy here. So, can you think of any reason that Carl might have run away? Did he have an argument with your ...' he hesitated, wondering how to describe the boys' adoptive parents, '...your dads, maybe?'

Harry shook his head. 'Only about doing his homework, but he always argues about that.'

'Or was he worried about anything?'

Harry said nothing and stared down at the floor.

'Harry? *Was* there something worrying Carl?'

'He was afraid Granddad would get coronavirus,' Harry muttered reluctantly. Then louder, 'He said Granddad is so old that he would probably die.'

'And ...,' Andy hesitated, wary of scaring the boy into clamming up again by questioning him too hard, 'and do you think he could have tried to go to your Granddad – to check he was OK?'

'How?' Harry's eyes opened wide. 'We don't know where he lives.'

'Yes, of course. OK. Well, I think we've finished here. Thank you for showing me your room. You've been a big help. Let's go down and find DCI Davenport again, shall we?' Andy picked up the laptop and put it under his arm. 'I'm afraid we'll have to take this away for a bit, just in case there's anything on it that tells us where Carl could have gone.'

They returned to the back garden where they found Wayne sitting on the bench talking to Anna, while Dean was wandering around with his mobile phone to his ear. Harry immediately ran over to Wayne and climbed on to his lap.

Anna explained that Dean was ringing round to all their friends, in the hope that Carl had taken refuge in one of their homes.

'I've organised for uniformed officers to do a house-to-house around the neighbourhood,' she told Andy, 'and Mel Stanton should be here any minute with PD Q. I told her we'd wait here until she comes, so that we can brief her.'

She turned back to Wayne, 'as I was saying, I've had a look at Carl's phone and I can't see anything on it that would help us, but he may have deleted his call history and any messages that would give us a clue, so I'll hand it over to our IT experts to check out, and I'll get someone to contact the service provider for a list of calls in the last month or so.'

'We'd better get IT to look at this too.' Andy held up the laptop. 'Harry tells me it's just for homework, but Carl may not have been keeping strictly to the rules.'

'We've got all the child safety filters and stuff on it,' Wayne assured them, 'and we've warned them about talking to anyone they don't know.'

'Still, better that we check it out,' Anna told him. 'I don't want to worry you and I expect you're right, but the people who want to groom children can be very devious. It'll be better if we just make sure that there's no chance that he's gone to meet someone that he's come across online.'

'You don't really think …?' Wayne's eyes opened wide in alarm.

'I try not to think until I've got the evidence to back it up. We just have to cover all bases, that's all.'

Dean ended his call and came over to them, dropping his phone into his pocket as he did so.

'That was Bernie I was speaking to just now,' he told them. 'I left her to last because I knew it'd take a while.' He grinned, in spite of his anxiety. 'Actually, I spent most of the time talking to Jonah. He says to tell you that he's on stand-by ready to help whenever you need him. In fact, it was as much as Bernie and Peter could do to stop him coming over here right away to take over!'

Anna laughed. Jonah had been her commanding officer at a critical point in her career and had encouraged her to take her inspector's exams. She knew that Jonah was powerless to intervene as he had threatened, since "coming over here" would entail cajoling Bernie or Peter to transport him, but she recognised the drive and determination that this statement represented. Even from his wheelchair, DCI Jonah Porter was a force to be reckoned with!

'He says to make sure you do a thorough search of the house, to check out all his usual haunts, and to get a team of officers out there doing house-to-house visits – oh! And how about a police tracker dog to follow where he's been?' Dean went on, still grinning.

'Well that's a relief!' Andy grinned back. 'I think we can tick all of those off and award ourselves a prize for second-guessing all of the Great Detective's first moves!'

'But to be serious,' Anna began, but she was interrupted by a call on her mobile phone. It was Gavin, reporting on what he had found out from the French and Whittle families.

'Well done! That narrows down the window when he left the house, and we now know to direct our search between Chichester Road and the city centre. Malc Appleton is bringing over a team to do house-to-house all across Rose Hill. I'll ask him to liaise with you, seeing as you know the area. And I'll send Stella over to help you. Now, I've got to go, I think that's Mel Stanton with PD Q.'

Dean hastened to open the side gate to let in PC Melanie Stanton and her German shepherd dog, Q. At first, Harry cowered back in Wayne's arms at the sight of such a large animal, but Mel soon put him at his ease by ordering Q to lie down and then showing Harry how to approach her.

'She's a big softy really,' she told him, 'except when she's chasing villains! There are lots of thieves and muggers out there who wish they'd stopped when I told them to, instead of trying to get away from Q.'

'Is she going to chase Carl?' Harry asked anxiously.

'No. She won't chase him, but she may be able to show us where he's been,' Mel explained. 'You see, dogs have noses that are much more sensitive than ours are, so they can track a scent when we wouldn't even notice it was there, let alone know what it was. We're hoping that she'll be able to pick up the scent that Carl will have left behind as he goes and follow him to wherever it is he's heading.'

'I suppose you'll need something of Carl's to show her what his scent's like,' suggested Dean.

'That's right,' agreed Mel, 'and then we'll need to start from the last place he was seen. How long ago was that?'

'We think he was in Chichester Road between eight and half past,' Anna told her. 'He was on a bike, but he got off to deliver a package through the door of one of the houses there, so there should be some decent scent traces for Q to pick up in the street outside.'

'Will she be able to track him if he's on his bike?' Wayne asked. 'Won't she need him to touch the ground to leave a trail?'

'No,' Mel laughed. 'That isn't how it works. We all give off a scent trail in the air – droplets of sweat, that sort of thing – and that's what Q follows. It may be quite hard for her, though, after a few hours, and especially if other people have been that way too.'

'At least Lockdown ought to help on that score,' Andy observed.

'Yes, well we'd better get started.' Mel turned to Dean. 'You were offering to get us something that will have his scent on it – an item of clothing maybe?'

'How about his football socks?' suggested Wayne. 'They're on the floor, just inside the kitchen door, stuffed inside his muddy trainers.'

'Perfect!' Mel declared. 'They'll be just the thing – the sweatier the better!'

A few minutes later she pulled up outside the Whittles' house in Chichester Road. She got out of her van and went round to the back for PD Q. The big dog jumped down eagerly, sensing that she was about to start work in earnest. Mel held one of Carl's socks in front of her powerful nose, giving her plenty of time to savour the smell before pocketing it and commanding Q to look for the scent trail left by its owner.

Q ran round purposefully, sniffing her surroundings. She paused for some time examining the fence that bounded the French family's garden. Mel deduced that this was probably where the boy had propped up his bike while he delivered the mobile phone through the slit in the front door. That was a good sign. It looked as if his scent was still lingering and hadn't been covered by those of more recent visitors to the spot.

A few moments later Q was off. She led the way along the road in the direction that Leo Whittle had told Gavin that Harry had taken. Mel hurried to keep up. On a street where there might be both pedestrians and vehicles, she could not risk letting out the lead to give Q her head.

After about a mile, both Q and Mel were starting to flag. The sun was climbing now and it was getting hot. Carl had the advantage of being on a bicycle and traveling in the cool of the early morning. May Morning! Mel shook her head in disbelief. This was like no May Morning that she could remember. Usually they would have been kept busy with students up at the crack of dawn to welcome the start of summer, or whatever it was they were celebrating. This year they were all – or almost all – back in their homes, studying online instead of carousing in punts on the river or standing beneath Magdalen Tower listening to the choristers singing madrigals.

When they reached Iffley Road, Q hesitated. She paced up and down, sniffing the air, evidently hunting for Carl's scent amid others. Mel was just starting to think that she had lost the trail when off she went again, heading along the pavement in the direction of Magdalen Bridge. They passed the Iffley Road Sports Centre at a trot and were soon approaching the roundabout by Magdalen College School. They had to wait for a delivery van to come out of Cowley Place on to the deserted roundabout. Then Q was off again, still heading towards the city centre. A bus passed them, empty apart from the driver. A pedestrian coming towards them stepped out into the road in order to maintain social distancing. It was busier here, but "busy" had taken on a strange new meaning in these days of Lockdown.

As they approached the Cherwell, Mel was struck by the contrast with the scene on the same day the previous year, when she had been called to assist with crowd-control as people thronged the streets and foolhardy students made the dangerous leap from the bridge into the river. There were no jostling crowds today – just a lone cyclist pedalling back from a sortie into town. Picking up groceries from one of the essential shops that were still allowed to open, perhaps, or maybe taking his daily permitted exercise.

At the middle of Magdalen Bridge, Q stopped. She began nosing around the benches at the side of the road there. Was this where the trail ended? Mel went round behind the benches and peered over the balustrade. Down below, through a line of trees, she could see an expanse of grass. This was the meadow that occupied the space between two branches of the River Cherwell. Could Carl have left the road here? If he did climb down to the meadow, what had become of his bike?

She led Q a little further along the road towards the town. The dog sniffed the pavement and the wall beneath the railings that bounded the Botanical Gardens. She briefly appeared to have picked up a scent and trotted on a few yards; then she stopped and went back to the benches in the middle of the bridge.

Mel tried refreshing Q's memory of Carl's scent by offering his sock again, but this made no difference. Q was determined that the trail ended at the benches on Magdalen Bridge. Taking her across to the other side of the road proved fruitless, as did an attempt to descend from the bridge to the meadow below. Had Carl perhaps boarded a bus somewhere near here? But, if so, where had he left his bike? More likely, the problem was the large number of people passing by here with the resultant multiplicity of scent trails confusing Q and preventing her from tracking Carl's route. It looked as if this was the end of the road for them.

* * *

After Mel and Q had left, Anna turned to Wayne and Dean again. 'Is there anything else you can tell me that might give a clue as to where Carl might have been going?'

The two fathers shook their heads, but Andy spoke up. 'Harry was telling me that his brother was worried about their granddad. I wondered if he might have been trying to get to him.'

'But he wouldn't know how!'

'It's too far!'

Wayne and Dean both spoke at once, both clearly taken aback at this suggestion.

'I think you need to tell us a bit more about this,' Anna said. 'Can I have this granddad's name and address?'

In the silence that followed this apparently innocent request, Wayne and Dean exchanged glances. Then Wayne got to his feet. 'Come along, Harry,' he said, taking the little boy by the hand. 'We'll leave Daddy Dean to talk to the police. I'd like you to come inside with me and help me to make a cake for tea.'

'A chocolate cake?' asked Harry, his face brightening up a little.

'If you like. A chocolate cake with chocolate icing on it – how about that?'

Dean waited until his husband and son had disappeared indoors and the kitchen door had closed behind them before answering Anna's question.

'The boys' granddad is their birth mother's father. He's the only member of their birth family that they have any contact with. He's in his seventies and has diabetes, so I suppose that's why Carl has been worried about him. He must have said something to Harry, I suppose, although he never mentioned it to us.'

'And what's his name and where does he live?' Anna asked again.

'His name is Douglas Willis. We aren't allowed to know his address, and he doesn't know ours. You'd have to go through Social Services if you want to find him.'

'You said it was too far for Carl to go to see him,' Anna pointed out, 'so you must have some idea.'

'All I know is that the boys were living in a children's home in Redditch before they came here, and the two supervised contacts that they've had with their granddad since they came to live with us were in Banbury. They meet on neutral territory, partly so that their birth family can't track down where they live, and partly in case anything happens that would create bad associations for the boys.'

'I think you need to tell me a bit more about their background,' Anna said thoughtfully. 'It could be that something that happened recently has triggered something from Carl's past and that's what's made him go off.'

'You really need to talk to our social worker about that. The boys' past is only shared on a need-to-know basis. I can tell you what we've been told, if you think it'll help you find him, but you must keep it confidential.'

'Understood. Go on.'

'They've been in Care since Carl was four and Harry was … just under one, I think. Before that, they lived with their mother in their grandparents' house – that's their mother's mother and her husband. That's who they call Granddad.'

'And they came to live with you last year, when they were seven and five, is that right?'

'Yes – well, they came to stay in autumn 2018, but the adoption didn't come through until last year. They weren't easy to place, because they – Carl in particular – find it hard to trust women, and it's usually women who take the lead in adopting and fostering. That's why they were matched with us. Their psychologist recommended an all-male household.'

'I see.' Anna had a sudden flashback to her own children's early life, when she was working long hours to establish herself in CID, and her husband was at home juggling childcare with his career as a self-employed architect. But these boys' mother must have done more to alienate them than simply being absent from much of their lives. 'And do you know what exactly …?'

'All I know is that Carl's medical record shows a number of occasions when he was taken to hospital after what his mother said was a fall, and Harry was suspected of having foetal alcohol syndrome, although that's not certain now. He *is* small for his age, which is one of the signs; but the learning difficulties that they thought he had are looking more and more like delayed development caused by a combination of trauma when he was young and then being moved around a lot. He does have some hearing impairment, but mainly in one ear and that's been largely fixed with a hearing aid, and … Sorry! I'm going on a bit, aren't I? Basically, my understanding is that their Mum and Nanna – which is what they call their grandmother – subjected them to neglect and possibly physical abuse as well, and Granddad was the only person that Carl saw as being on their side.'

'I see.' Anna thought for a few moments. 'And you say you don't know where they live – the boys' birth family – but does Carl know? I taught my kids to recite their address when they were quite small, in case they ever got lost when we were out.'

'I shouldn't think so. I don't get the impression that anyone was bothering that much with them.'

'And what about his birth family? Do you think they might try to get in touch with him? Might he have put something up on social media that they could have identified him by?'

'We've got all those things blocked on his phone and his computer – at least I think we have. I hope we have! We let him use email and WhatsApp because they seem safe enough. You can only talk to people if you know their email address or mobile number. It's not like Facebook where you can trawl around for people you've never even met.'

'Or could Carl have let something slip at one of these contact visits?' suggested Andy. 'If he likes his granddad so much, could he have given him his mobile number, for instance?'

'I shouldn't think so. Carl may love his granddad, but he hates his mum and grandmother with a passion. Whatever they did to him, he's a long way away from forgiving them – or maybe it just hurts too much to allow himself to care about them. I don't know. Anyway, I'm sure he wouldn't risk them getting hold of a way of contacting him.'

'But if his granddad promised to keep it a secret?' persisted Andy.

'I still don't think so.' Dean shook his head. 'Like I said, I don't know the full story, but the way I've pieced things together, I reckon Doug's a battered husband. From the little that Carl has ever said about it, Nanna rules the roost and Mum always backs her up against Granddad. And that fits with everything our social worker has told us too.'

'And what about the boys' father?' Anna asked. 'Does he come into this setup at all?'

'The name on their birth certificates is John Foster,' Dean told her. 'But neither of the boys remembers him at all. As far as I'm aware, nobody knows where he is.'

'OK,' Anna said, 'I think I'd better get on to social services to find out what they know about Carl's birth family. Andy! I'd like you to check out the railway station and the buses. If Carl *is* by any chance trying to get to his granddad, he's going to need transport. It's a long shot, but it's all we've got at the moment.' She turned to Dean. 'Do you think you could talk to Harry, and try to find out all he knows about where his granddad might be living? I know he's too young to remember, but Carl may have talked to him about it. A description of the house or anything might help. Don't press too hard. Just try to bring the conversation round and encourage him to chatter.'

'OK. I'll do my best,' Dean answered dubiously.

'The other thing I think we ought to do is a public appeal for information,' Anna went on.

'But no names or photographs,' Dean cut in at once. 'Nothing that his birth family could recognise.'

'That's OK,' Anna assured him. 'We'll just say "an eight-year-old-boy missing from the Rose Hill area, and we can put out a photograph of the bike, if you have one, or one like it if not.'

'Yes, I can get the one we took on his birthday. We can crop it so that you can only see the bike and the bottom half of his body holding it. And please: keep our names out of it too. We got quite a bit of hate mail when the boys first moved in. There are a lot of people out there who don't think couples like us ought to be allowed to adopt.'

* * *

When Andy arrived at the railway station, he was surprised to see PC Gavin Hughes standing there, holding his bicycle, talking to a member of station staff. Stella stepped forward to explain.

'Gavin – PC Hughes – thought it was worth trying the station because it's a place that homeless people often go to find somewhere they can sit down without drawing attention. He says runaway kids especially do it a lot.'

Gavin gestured to Andy to join him. 'This is Mr Pearson. He works in the booking office. He thinks he may have seen Carl trying to buy a ticket from the automatic ticket machines earlier this morning.' He turned to Pearson. 'If you wouldn't mind telling Detective Sergeant Lepage what you saw?'

'Things have been really quiet since Lockdown,' the booking clerk began, sounding rather nervous. 'So it was a bit unusual to see a youngster out on his own. I was in the ticket office and there was no one wanting tickets, so I had a clear view of the machines. This boy came in and started looking around at them. He must've been about eight or nine I should think – young enough that he ought to have had an adult with him, anyway. Then he got out some money from the pocket of his jeans. It looked like ten-pound and twenty-pound notes. That made it seem even more strange, so I came round to have a word with him, but as soon as he saw me, he scarpered.'

'Did you see where he went?' Andy asked eagerly.

'I followed him out of the ticket hall, but he'd gone by the time I got there.'

'Right.' Andy looked up at the camera attached to the ceiling of the booking hall. Now we need to see your CCTV footage for that time to check that he really was our runaway.'

A few minutes later, Andy was staring at a fuzzy picture time-stamped 09.23. The boy in the picture certainly answered the description of Carl Foster. 'What do you think, Gav?' he asked. 'You've met him, haven't you?'

'Yes. That's him alright.'

They watched as the boy took out a sheaf of notes from his pocket and then turned back to the ticket machine and bent over it looking for the right buttons to press to select his destination. Then his head suddenly jerked up as he became aware of Pearson approaching. The next moment he had turned and was running for the door.

'Now we should be able to catch him on the camera outside,' murmured the British Transport Police officer who was showing them the videos. 'Yes! There he is!' They watched as the figure on the screen picked up a bike and headed off past the strangely de-populated bicycle racks and disappeared out of range of the camera.

'Right. This is progress,' Andy declared. 'We've got a new starting point to search from. I'm going to get on to Mel Stanton and see if she can bring PD Q over here. They may be able to track where he went after this. The other thing we need to do is to check out all the cameras in the streets around here. There must be lots of business with security cameras that might have picked something up, and if he headed back towards the city, there'll be cameras in the shopping streets.'

'We've also found out that he's got a lot of money with him,' Stella pointed out nervously, unsure whether it was her place to contribute ideas to the discussion. 'Where can he have got it all from?'

'Most likely pinched it from one of his dads,' Gavin said with the voice of experience. 'I'll give them a ring. They'll be glad to hear we're making progress anyway.'

They stood outside on the station forecourt while Gavin and Andy made their phone calls. Stella looked round anxiously, hoping to spot a clue that might lead them to the boy, but unsure what that might be.

'Wayne checked his wallet when I told them about the money,' Gavin reported. 'He says about fifty pounds is missing. He'd left it in the pocket of his coat, hanging on a hook in the hall. Carl must have raided it for cash to buy his train ticket.'

'Right!' Andy hardly seemed to be listening. 'Mel and Q are on Magdalen Bridge. She says the trail went cold there. They're going to come over here now, but they're on foot, obviously, so it'll be a while. Can you wait for her here and show her where he was last seen? I want to go to the bus station. After he had no luck with the trains, he could have tried to get a bus. If only we knew where it was he was trying to get to!'

He got back into his car and headed off for the Gloucester Green bus station. Gavin and Stella watched him go.

'What now?' asked Stella.

'We wait, like Andy said. It'll take Mel a good twenty minutes to get here from Magdalen Bridge.'

'I was thinking – about that money Carl took?'

'Yes?'

'Well, I'd say that might make him a bit … well, reluctant to go home, in case he got into trouble for it. I know my brother Danny always used to go into hiding when he knew he'd done something that would make our gran cross.'

'Yes,' Gavin agreed. 'You've got something there.'

'Is there any way we could communicate with him? Tell him somehow that he won't be in trouble?'

'Not unless he gets in touch. A radio or TV appeal wouldn't do any good, because he wouldn't see it.'

'And there's not much chance of him making contact,' Stella nodded glumly, 'because he hasn't got a phone with him. He probably doesn't even know how to use a public phone box – even if he could find one that was working!'

Just as Mel and PD Q arrived at the station, Andy called. 'I've seen CCTV of Carl at the bus station,' he told them. 'He was looking at the National Express timetable, which suggests that he must be wanting to go further than the local buses would take him. All their services are suspended, so he seems to have given up and headed off along George Street. Can you bring Q over here to see if she can track him from there?'

The three police officers – four counting Police Dog Q – made their way to Gloucester Green at a brisk pace. When they got there, Mel refreshed Q's memory with another whiff of Carl's sock. The big dog immediately began searching for signs that the boy had been there. For what seemed like a long time she appeared to be wandering round at random, sniffing here and there, sometimes starting off in one direction and then doubling back on herself. Eventually she appeared to become more focused. She set off purposefully out of the bus station towards George Street. That looked promising, since this was the direction that Andy had seen Carl going on the CCTV images.

The others held back as Mel followed Q along the road. They passed the closed Odeon cinema and the History Faculty building. On the corner of Gloucester Street, Q hesitated before continuing on, past closed shops and restaurants to the junction with Magdalen Street and The Broad. Which way now? She made a tentative assay down Corn Market. That looked encouraging. Perhaps Carl was heading home, now that he had exhausted all possible means of transport. But, no! Q stopped and turned. She examined the junction again. This time, she set off north, past St Mary Magdalen's Church and on into St Giles. She stood undecided at the point where the road branched, finally plumping for Banbury Road.

'Good girl!' encouraged Mel. 'Track on!'

They passed St Giles' Church and the Old Parsonage Hotel. Then Q stopped again. No amount of cajoling by Mel could persuade her to go any further.

'What does that mean?' asked Stella. 'Did something happen to him here? Did he get in a car or something?'

'Not necessarily,' answered Mel. 'All it means is that Q can't separate his scent from all the others there are around. Maybe there've been a lot of people passing by here since Carl came along. I can try taking her up and down the road a bit to see if she can pick it up again, but it looks as if there's just too much going on here scent-wise. It's always difficult in built-up areas; tracking is much easier in open country where there aren't so many people.

14. WAITING

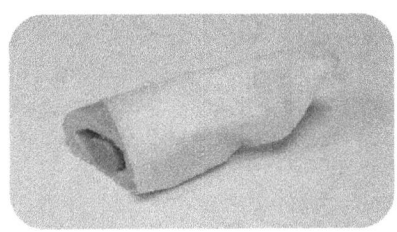

A little later that day, Chrissie's concern was with another runaway. How had Craig got on at work? Would his boss have accepted his explanation of his behaviour the day before? Or were his worries that he would be dismissed well-founded? She attempted to put these thoughts out of her mind as she tried to eat her lunch while ringing round to the parents of children who were not in school to check that they were coping with home-schooling.

She glanced up as frequently as possible, monitoring activity in her classroom (the dining hall had been closed to prevent children from different classes mixing) where the three members of her class who were in school that day were eating their sandwiches, supervised by Robyn, her remaining classroom assistant. Alfie seemed to be having trouble with opening a packet of cheese and onion crisps and Robyn was busy mopping up the table where Yasmina had knocked over her beaker of orange squash.

Chrissie sanitised her hands from the bottle on her desk before getting up and going over to Alfie's table. 'Here! Let me help you with that.' It was all very well the government talking about social distancing, but it just wasn't possible to look after children with complex needs from a distance of two metres.

He pushed the packet towards her and she opened it for him. 'Thank you Mrs Hughes.'

Chrissie went back to her desk and took another bite out of her "hikers' lunch" – a sausage cooked into a bread roll. Now, where was she up to? Oh yes! She needed to ring Rakiya's mother to check that they'd got their internet fixed. She picked up her phone but before she could select the number, it started to ring. Chrissie looked down at the screen. It was Gavin. What could he want? Surely he knew how busy she was, trying to fit everything into days that never seemed long enough?

'Hi Chrissie! Have you got a moment?'

She bit back her annoyance at being interrupted in her work. This sounded serious.

'What is it? Is it Craig?'

'No. It's … You know Wayne and Dean?'

'Wayne and Dean?' Chrissie repeated. The names sounded familiar, but she couldn't place them.

'They're friends of Peter Johns. Bernie tutored one of them when she worked at the university. They live just round the corner in Lewes Road.'

'Lewes Ro – oh yes! I remember. The gay couple. One of them was run over, wasn't he?'

'That's right. Wayne got head injuries in a hit-and-run in summer eighteen. Anyway, they adopted two little boys not long after that, and now one of them – Carl, the older one – has gone missing.'

'Missing? How?'

'Upped and left during the night. Gone off on his bike, as far as we can tell.'

'Oh the poor things! Do you remember that time Kenny wandered off during St Giles' Fair? How old was he? Seven, I think.'

'Eight,' Gavin said confidently. 'He'd just joined the Cubs. He was so proud of his new uniform that he insisted on wearing it everywhere.'

'Yes, of course! I remember now. I've never been so pleased to catch a glimpse of that bottle green sweater in my life! How old is this boy – Carl did you say? – that's gone missing?'

'Eight. That's why I was ringing – or one of the reasons. I thought you might have some ideas about how his mind will be working, and that might help us to know where to look for him. But the other thing was: he's got a younger brother, and I thought you might have some tips for his dads on how to handle him. I gather they're very close. Do you think you could pop round there after school and … no, I'm sorry, you'll be busy, won't you? I wasn't thinking. Look, just scrap all that. I'd better let you get on. Bye!'

'No. That's OK. Of course I'll call on them,' Chrissie gabbled. Gavin must have caught the annoyance in her voice when she answered the phone and be regretting having rung. 'And I'll have a think about what would make an eight-year-old run away.' She looked up at the clock on the wall. 'But, I'm sorry, I will have to go now. I've still got two more parents to ring before afternoon school starts'

Chrissie ended the call and then immediately wished she had remembered to ask Gavin if he'd heard anything from Craig during the morning. Not that it was likely that he had, but … Too late now! And she had plenty of other things that needed doing. Why were there never enough hours in the day anymore?

* * *

For Wayne and Dean, anxiously waiting for news, the hours seemed to crawl past all too slowly. They sat together on the sofa with Harry curled up between them, unable to settle to any activity, constantly checking their phones in case they had missed a call.

'Why wasn't he able to tell us he was worried about his granddad?' Dean asked for the umpteenth time. 'We could've asked Harvey to check he was OK.'

'I just wish he'd kept his phone with him,' Wayne moaned. 'Then we'd be able to let him know we don't care about the money. He's probably scared of coming back in case we're cross with him. I seem to have done nothing but tell him off this last week or two.'

'It's all my fault,' wailed Harry, catching the general mood of despair and self-flagellation. 'He *said* he wanted to go and see Granddad.'

'No Harry,' Wayne and Dean both said quickly.

'It's not your fault at all,' Wayne expanded. 'You weren't to know he'd try to go on his own like this.'

'You – you don't have any idea *where* he was thinking of going to see him?' asked Dean tentatively.

Harry shook his head.

A moment later, they all sat up straight, suddenly alert, as Dean's mobile phone began ringing. He snatched it up off the coffee table, where he had left it, handy to take any call that came through. To his disappointment it was Nick Dove, a member of their design team, who had been left in de facto charge of the company, while the two owners were occupied with their domestic worries.

'Yes?'

'Is there any news?'

'No – well not really – the police rang and said they'd got CCTV of him at the train station and the bus station, but they've lost him again now.'

'Oh! I'm sorry. Still, I suppose that means he's definitely not been abducted or anything like that, so that's something, isn't it?'

'Yes,' Dean agreed, more out of politeness than conviction.

'The thing is,' Nick said gingerly, 'I'm a bit out of my depth here. There's a consignment of cardboard boxes arrived, all packed flat, and I don't know whether I ought to have people making them up ready to put things in or to leave them to be put together as they're needed. And I've got packers saying they're running out of padded envelopes for … for whatever it is they pack in them. Could one of you come in, just for a couple of hours, to show me a few things? I'll be able to manage after that. I'm sorry. I know you must want to …'

'OK,' Dean sighed. 'Yes, of course I'll come in.'

He turned to Wayne, unsure whether he felt sorry or relieved at having an excuse to get out of the house for a while. 'Did you hear that? There's trouble at t'mill. I'll have to go in. I'll take the car so I'll be back quicker.'

Wayne and Harry stood at the front door watching him go. Then, once the car had disappeared behind the tall hedge of the next-door garden, Wayne put his hand on Harry's shoulder and guided him back inside the house.

'OK. Let's ice that cake, shall we?'

* * *

Eddie was also struggling with balancing work and family commitments. His employer had been generous in allowing him to vary his hours to fit in with Crystal's shifts, but today there was an urgent job that needed his attention and Ricky was not in a co-operative mood.

'It's not that he means to be a nuisance,' Eddie explained to his father over the phone when, in desperation, he rang Peter to ask for his help. 'It's just that he doesn't realise how distracting it is for me to have him asking questions all the time. Abbie's just gone down for her nap now, so if you could keep Ricky talking on Zoom for maybe twenty minutes, I think I can get this finished.'

'No problem! Just hand him over to me.'

Half an hour later, Eddie gave a sigh of relief as he finally finished the work that he had been trying to complete all day. What a difference it made not having his thoughts interrupted every five minutes by a four-year-old with yet another impossible-to-answer question about Life, the Universe and Everything! He could hear Ricky still chattering happily to his grandfather in the living room, while Abigail was sleeping peacefully in her cot. He was tempted to get started on the task that he had pencilled in for after the children were in bed that evening, but perhaps that would be unfair on Dad. He mustn't take advantage of his good nature and fondness for his grandchildren. He set his status to "away" on his computer before getting up and wandering through to the lounge.

'OK Ricky, say bye-bye to Granddad now and let me have a word with him.'

'Just a minute.' Ricky retreated behind the sofa with Eddie's mobile phone, on which he was enjoying his one-to-one video call with Peter. 'We're in the middle of a story. You mustn't interrupt people when they're on the phone.'

'Alright, just finish the story and then I need my phone back.' Eddie couldn't help smiling at his son's repetition of words that he had used so often to him when he had been trying to hold a telephone conversation amid his son's constant pestering for attention.

'Thanks Dad.' Eddie said when Ricky reluctantly surrendered the phone a few minutes later. 'That was a big help.'

'No problem! Always happy to be of service.'

'And are you all still OK – and Stan and Sylvia?'

'Yes. We're all fine.' Peter paused, wondering whether or not to tell Eddie about his most pressing concern at the moment.

'But?' Eddie detected the hesitation in his father's voice and realised that there was more he could say.

'You know Wayne and Dean?'

'Yes, of course.'

'And their kids – Carl and Harry?'

'Yes?'

'Carl's gone missing. He just disappeared during the night.'

'Oh! Have they called the police?'

'Yes. Anna Davenport's on the case – and Andy Lepage. You know them both, don't you?'

'Yes, of course. They were part of Jonah's team when he was looking for Abbie.'

'That's right. They're experienced officers. If anyone can find him, they will.'

'And it's not the same as with Abbie, is it? I mean, presumably he's just run off. Not like the way Abbie was snatched from her buggy.'

'Well, no, but it's just as worrying for Wayne and Dean.'

'I don't see how. They aren't his real parents, are they? They've only had him for less than two years. They can't possibly feel the same way Crystal and I did when Abbie was missing.'

'No Eddie,' Peter said firmly. 'It's *exactly* the same. In fact, in one way it's worse for Wayne and Dean. They've got a responsibility to his birth parents to look after him better than they could have done. And if time had anything to do with it – which it hasn't – you'd only had Abbie for six weeks when she disappeared.'

'Now you're just being silly. She's our own flesh and blood. That's the point. And who's to say they didn't do something to make him run away? Anyway, the chances are Carl will come home when he's hungry and everyone will wonder what all the fuss was about. Now I'd better go and see what Ricky's doing. When *he* disappears, you always know he's up to mischief!'

Peter sat for several minutes staring at the phone in his hand. He had expected more empathy from Eddie, who ought to understand the anguish of waiting for news of a missing child. And what was it he insinuating by suggesting that Carl might have good reason to want to get away from his adoptive parents? Was that what the world would think if the case ever got into the papers?

Of course, Eddie didn't know Wayne and Dean the way they did. Bernie had been one of Dean's tutors, back in the days when she was a Fellow at St Luke's College and he was an undergraduate engineering student. She had found him after his suicide attempt, when he despaired of reconciling his sexuality with his religious faith, and she had been instrumental in convincing him that he did not have to choose between God and the love of his life.

Was that what the trouble was with Eddie? Was he thinking – as his wife had actually said, getting on for two years previously when she heard about the adoption plan – that it was unnatural for a gay couple to bring up children? He *had* lived with Crystal in Jamaica for twelve years. Homosexuality was still illegal there, and the church where Crystal's father was minister preached a conservative attitude towards same-sex relationships. Did Eddie believe Carl and Harry were liable to come to harm living with Wayne and Dean? Was he even suggesting that …?

Peter got up and paced the room. It was infuriating to feel so helpless to do anything to improve the situation! He picked up the phone to ring Andy – who had been a DC under him when he was a serving police officer – for an update. Then he changed his mind. Andy would be quite busy enough without having ageing ex-coppers pestering him for news. He sat down again and keyed in the number of St Cyprian's Presbytery.

'Hello?' Father Damien's voice sounded tired.

'Hello Father. It's Peter – Peter Johns. Are you busy?'

'Aren't I always? But never too busy for you. How can I be of service?'

'I don't honestly know,' Peter sighed. 'In fact, I don't know why I'm ringing you. It's probably your duty to disapprove of the whole business.'

'That sounds intriguing. Tell me more.'

'Did I ever mention a couple of friends of ours – Wayne and Dean?'

'The names don't ring any bells.'

'No, well, they're engineers. Bernie got to know Dean when he was an undergraduate. He was organ scholar at her

college and she was in the chapel choir. The two of them –
Wayne and Dean – did a project together while they were
students, designing some gadgets for Jonah when he was
still in rehab after he was shot. And that led on to them
setting up a company making mechanical aids for other
disabled people. They designed Jonah's special wheelchair,
for example. And they've got a guy working for them on
developing a driverless car for people like Jonah, to make
them more independent. So you can see, they're doing really
good stuff.'

'Yes?' prompted Damien, as Peter fell silent.

'They're partners – and I don't just mean business
partners.'

'And?'

'A couple of years ago, they adopted two boys: Carl and
Harry. They were difficult to place because they find it hard
to trust grown-ups, but Wayne and Dean have done
wonders with them. They're much more confident and
outgoing now that they've got a stable home where they feel
secure.'

'And …?' Damien could tell that this eulogy was simply
preparing the ground for something more significant.

'But now Carl's done a bunk.'

'Run away you mean?'

'That's right. He just disappeared during the night.
Obviously Wayne and Dean are worried sick – and so is
Harry, his little brother – but … well, I'm worried for Carl
too, but I'm also worried about what people are going to
think if it becomes public knowledge. You know – a gay
couple and two young boys …'

'Aaah! And that's why you think I ought to disapprove.'

'Well, aren't you supposed to disapprove of Wayne and
Dean's "lifestyle"?'

'I'm not sure that the Roman Catholic Church is in any
position to go casting the first stone at unmarried men and
their relationships with young boys.'

'I should have known you wouldn't give a straight answer.'

'I'm modelling my technique on the answers that Our Lord gave to the Pharisees when they came to him with trick questions.'

'I'm not trying to trick you. I'm just … well, I'm not sure. It's … Well, I was thinking about when Abigail was taken from her pram. Everyone was full of sympathy for the whole family. And I was expecting that it would be the same now, but … now I'm wondering if there will be people pointing the finger and saying, "What do you expect when you let a pair of perverts adopt children?"'

'Has anyone actually said that?'

'Not in so many words, but Eddie came dangerously close – just now when I told him Carl was missing. And you'd think he, of all people, would … well, you know – understand how it feels for Wayne and Dean.'

'So, is what's really bothering you that you're frightened that your son may be a bit of a bigot? You're not responsible for your children's attitudes, you know.'

Peter did not reply, so, after a few seconds, Damien went on. 'I'll pray for them: the little boy and his … what do they call themselves, his fathers?'

'Yes. The boys call them Daddy Wayne and Daddy Dean.'

'I'll say a Mass for Carl's safe return,' Damien promised. 'And I'll put a word in for them with St James. It's his feast day today.'

'Is he the one who said, "Faith without works is dead"?'

'That's right. I think he'll be more interested in the good work your friends have been doing with the boys than in enquiring too closely into their "lifestyle" as you put it. Don't quote me on that if you happen to be talking to the bishop, though!'

'Thanks. I'm sorry to have bothered you. It's just … thinking about how they must be feeling … it brought it all back – you know: when we thought Abigail might never be found. And I feel so helpless. We aren't even allowed out to look for him!'

'It's the waiting that's hard,' Damien agreed, 'and the not being able to do the things we'd normally do to help. This …,' he hesitated, 'this coronavirus business has really tested my faith – no maybe not my faith so much as my calling, or there again …,' he sighed. 'It all used to seem so simple. People would ring me when someone was ill or dying or … and I would go round and anoint them for healing or give them communion or even just sit with them; but now … there's no touching, no sharing the bread, if someone's suspected of having COVID then not even any sitting with them unless I can manage to scrounge the full protective get-up from the hospital, which I only like to do in extremis, because I don't want to leave them short.'

'There's the phone,' Peter said, when his friend paused for breath. He hadn't expected his call to unleash this torrent of frustration and anguish. 'And your live-streamed masses. There seemed to be lots of people logged in when I watched last Sunday.'

'I know, but … take last Monday night: Hilda Flint rang. I don't know if you've met her. She doesn't make it to mass very often these days, because she's not so steady on her feet now. She was worried about her son, Jim. It sounded as if he'd got the virus and was pretty bad, so I told her to ring for an ambulance. I got there just as they were loading him into it. I couldn't do anything for either of them. I just had to let Hilda go back into that house on her own, not even knowing if she'd be able to look after herself without Jim there to help. And I daren't go in with her to see she could manage OK, in case that meant I'd have to self-isolate for a fortnight and miss a funeral I was taking. But was it really the funeral that I was worried about or just that I didn't want to get COVID myself? I really don't know, and if it was just fear, what does that say about my faith?'

'I'd say you were just being responsible. I bet you rang her in the morning to check she was OK.'

'I did, as a matter of fact,' Damien admitted. 'And she said she was managing alright, but she may have just been saying that so as not to admit she can't cope. Normally, I'd go round and I'd be able to see if things weren't right. Now, even if I did call on her, she wouldn't be allowed to invite me in.'

'It won't be like this for ever,' Peter murmured, trying desperately to think of something to say. 'You're doing everything you can.'

'But that's just it! I'm doing everything I can, but it's not enough! That's what makes me feel … that's what I mean by starting to doubt my vocation. What's the point of being a priest when you can't do the things that priests are there for – hearing confessions, sharing communion, anointing … ?'

'Getting people who need it to ring for an ambulance in the middle of the night,' Peter continued for him, 'getting out of bed to see them safely off to hospital, listening on the telephone to ex-police officers agonising over nothing-at-all! Stop beating yourself up about the things you can't do and just concentrate on the things you *can* do.'

There was a long pause.

'That's Jonah speaking, isn't it?' Damien said at last. 'That's the sort of thing he says about his disability.'

'I suppose it is,' Peter grinned. 'And there was I thinking I was being so clever and original! Oh dear! It's worse than what they say about hearing yourself say things that your parents always used to say.'

'Tell me about it!' Damien's voice sounded a little more cheerful. 'I realised the other day that I'm turning into my dad. I've found myself using any number of his favourite sayings: count your blessings, I'd rather be a live coward than a dead hero…'

'I remember when it was all fields round here?' suggested Peter. 'Young people these days have no respect?'

'You've got the idea,' Damien laughed. 'The worst was when I caught myself telling God, *it's all very well for you!*'

'I'd say that's a fair point.' Peter joined in the laughter. 'I think I might make a better fist of things of I was omniscient. It must take a lot of the guesswork out of deciding what to do for the best.'

'Thanks Peter. This little chat has done me a world of good – as my late father would have said. Now, you just take care, and I won't forget to put in a few words with Him upstairs on behalf of your young friends and their little boy.'

* * *

'Inspector Davenport? This is Harvey Summerskill. You wanted to speak to me about one of the children on my caseload?'

'Yes. Thank you for ringing. It *is* rather urgent.'

'So I gathered. I'm sorry I couldn't speak to you when you rang the office; it's against our safeguarding protocols to discuss any of our children without doing an identity check and getting senior approval first. It would be all too easy for an abusive family member to masquerade as a police officer in order to get information about the whereabouts of a child.'

'Not to mention GDPR[5] requirements,' Anna agreed. 'But now that we've got past the formalities, what I need from you is as much information about Carl's background as you can give me, in case it helps us to track down where he could have gone. In particular, his brother told us that he's been anxious about his grandfather and we think he could be trying to get to him.'

'I see – or I think I do. But what exactly do you need to know?'

'Names and addresses would be a start. I gather from his new parents that his birth mother lives with his grandfather,

---

[5] General Data Protection Regulation: an EU regulation transposed into UK law by the Data Protection Act 2018, which puts responsibilities on people and bodies that hold personal data not to share them except within strictly-defined parameters.

and that's where Carl and Harry lived too, before they were taken into Care?'

'Yes. That's right. The family has been dysfunctional since before Carl was born. Their mother, Victoria, is addicted to alcohol and cocaine. She's very dependent on her mother, who sees herself as a sort of matriarch. Annette Willis – the boys' grandmother – has anger management issues and lacks empathy. Within the family, what she says goes, or you face the consequences!'

'And her husband, Carl's granddad?'

'Doug Willis is completely under Annette's thumb and lives in fear of her. Nine out of ten cases of domestic violence involve men abusing women. This is one of those rare cases in which the woman causes serious physical harm to the man. In fact, we think Doug has suffered attacks from both his wife *and* his daughter, but he won't admit to any of it – too ashamed!'

'What about the boys' birth father? Where does he come into this?'

'John Foster? He's long gone. Victoria had a very on-off relationship with him, by all accounts. For most of their time together, she chose to live with her mother so she could keep him at arm's length. They'd split up permanently before Harry was born, but he allowed his name to be put on the birth certificate.'

'So there's no possibility that he could have tried to get the boys back?'

'No. I don't think he ever had much to do with them even when he and Victoria were an item. We did look into the possibility that he might give them a home, after we'd given up on attempts to support Victoria to take them back, but I don't think we were even able to track him down by then.'

'And Carl wouldn't have tried to find him?'

'No. Look! We've been working with the family for years: right from when Victoria was a child. Annette doesn't give anyone from outside a chance – not Social Services, not the Health Visitor, not her daughter's boyfriend, no one. I've had Carl and Harry on my books for years – pretty well since Carl was born. He doesn't remember anything about his father. He never got a look-in. Annette is determined that they don't need anyone's help, and she's trained Victoria to think that social workers are the enemy and all men are beneath contempt.'

'And getting back to the boys' grandfather – Douglas?'

'He used to try to keep the boys safe from Annette's rages and Victoria's addictions, but he's too weak to stand up to them. He has a real bond with the boys, especially Carl. After we'd worked with the family for years, trying and failing to get Annette and Victoria sorted out so that they could take the boys back, we tried to persuade him to leave Annette and make a home for them by himself, but he's too dependent on her to take the plunge. That's why, in the end, we decided that adoption was the best solution for Carl and Harry.'

'I see. Now, just suppose Carl wanted to visit his grandfather. Would he know where to go?'

'I shouldn't think so. He hasn't been back to their house for years – not since he was taken into Care. He was only four then. I don't see how he'd remember it.'

'Well, I think I'd better pay a visit, just to be certain.'

'I – I'm not sure that's a good idea. It's important Annette and Victoria don't … It could be dangerous for Doug if they find out that he's been seeing the boys. And dangerous for the boys if either of them gets wind of where they're living now.'

'We won't tell them that. We don't even need to let them know we're based in Oxford. Thames Valley covers such a wide area that they won't have a clue whether the boys are in Banbury or Bracknell.'

'I don't know,' the Social Worker said slowly. 'I'll have to ask my supervisor.'

'And meanwhile, there's an eight-year old boy lost somewhere between Oxford and wherever it is that his birth family live, and we don't have any idea where that might be or how feasible it would be for him to get there,' Anna observed coldly. 'Moreover, for all you know, it could be that his mother or grandmother have already made contact with him somehow and persuaded him to come to them by threatening to harm his granddad. You could be sending him into the hands of these violent women that you and your colleagues – not to mention the Family Court – deem unfit to care for him!'

'If you put it that way … I suppose I can at least tell you that it's Leamington that you need to be looking at.'

'Leamington Spa?'

'Yes. That's where they live.'

Anna looked towards Andy. 'There are regular trains from Oxford,' he told her.

'So that could be where he was trying to get to when he went to the station. How about buses?'

'There's a National Express coach service, but it's not running at the moment.'

'I can't see how Carl could have known about any of that,' Harvey interrupted. 'He's only an eight-year-old.'

'But we do know that he tried to buy a ticket from an automatic machine in Oxford station,' Anna told him. 'Unfortunately, we don't know where he wanted to go. I really must insist on speaking to his birth family. If you can't give us the address, perhaps you could take us there and introduce us?'

'We're not supposed to meet anyone except in emergencies.'

'This *is* an emergency!' Anna heard her voice rising in frustration, but she forced herself to speak calmly. 'A boy's safety is at stake. You *must* either give us the address or arrange for us to meet the family some other way – and it *has* to be today.'

'Alright,' Harvey agreed reluctantly. 'Have you got a pen?'

Within a matter of minutes, Anna was on the road in Andy's car, heading up the M40, bound for Leamington. The road was almost empty and it would have been tempting to put his foot down, disregarding the speed limit, but he kept within the law despite mounting frustration as the minutes ticked away. Why couldn't Summerskill have handed over the address right away? All that business of "you must be careful how you handle these people" and "you don't want Doug Willis's blood on your hands, do you?"! What about Carl Foster? That's what he would like to know. And Summerskill was supposed to be Carl's protector!

Despite the grand title, Royal Leamington Spa was not inhabited exclusively by well-heeled middle-class families on good incomes. As they drove along the street where Carl's birth family lived, they saw signs of deprivation in the peeling paint on front doors and the rotting wood of window-frames. These houses were almost certainly privately-rented properties with landlords who were not pro-active in making repairs and improvements, or else their owner-occupiers had fallen on hard times and had no cash spare for maintenance of the roof over their heads.

'Twenty-four, twenty-six,' counted Anna. ''That must be it! There! On the left. Go past and pull in a bit further on, so they don't see us coming.'

As they passed the house, they saw that this one was in a better state of repair than the neighbouring properties. The front door looked newly-painted and the brickwork around it had been recently re-pointed. The small front garden was tidy and the low wall that surrounded it still had its Victorian railings standing up along its top. A grey-haired man in blue overalls was bending down to paint the wrought iron gate that barred the way from the pavement to the tiled path leading to the front door.

'That must be Douglas Willis,' Anna murmured. 'That's a bit of luck! We should be able to talk to him without his dragon of a wife even knowing.'

They had to drive on some distance before Andy could find a safe place to park. The road was full of vehicles, because so few people were going out to work. As they walked back along the deserted pavement, Andy asked the question that had been nagging at him ever since Anna's conversation with the social worker.

'Do you really think a grown man could be living in fear of his wife and daughter?'

'Why not?'

'You'd think he'd be able to stand up to them, wouldn't you?'

'That depends. Maybe he's a five-stone weakling and they're both Amazons. Or maybe they don't attack him with their bare hands. There are plenty of dangerous weapons around the house that a woman might use: kitchen knives, hot irons, rolling pins …'

'But then, why wouldn't he leave?'

'Probably the same reasons women don't leave their abusive partners: nowhere else to go, frightened that they'll come after them, they love them and they think they'll change. There are all sorts of reasons, and for a man, there's the added problem that they probably won't be believed if they tell anyone.'

'Take care there! Them railings is wet paint,' the man in the overalls called out to them as they approached.

'You're doing a good job there,' Anna replied, looking down at the grey undercoat on the railings. 'Would you be Mr Douglas Willis?'

'Who's asking?'

Anna held up her warrant card. 'DCI Anna Davenport, and this is DS Andrew Lepage. We need to have a word with a Mr Willis, who lives at this address, and since nobody is supposed to be leaving their homes at present, I assume that's who you must be, but can you just confirm it?'

'Yes. That's me,' the man nodded, straightening up to look Anna in the eye. 'But what's all this about?'

'It's about your grandson, Carl,' Anna told him. 'He's missing from home and his brother thinks he may be trying to get to you. He's frightened you might get coronavirus. Has he been in touch with you at all?'

'Carl's run away? How'd they let him do that?' The man's eyes opened wide and he stared at Anna in disbelief. 'They said he'd be safe. That's why they took him away.'

'His adoptive parents care for him very much,' Anna hastened to assure him, 'but they can't keep him locked up. He crept out of the house while they were asleep last night and, as I said, his brother thinks it's because he was worried about you. So now I'm asking you again: has he been in contact with you at all?'

'No. It's not allowed. All I get is: twice a year, round about the boys' birthdays, Social Services ring and tell me where to come and I get a couple of hours with them. That's all. I'm not allowed to know where they live and they're not allowed to know my number.'

'Carl used to live here with you, didn't he? Do you think he'd remember this house? Would he be able to find it?'

'He was only three when they took him away. How would he remember?'

'Doug!'

Anna looked up and saw a tall woman in a cotton print dress standing in the open doorway staring out at them. Willis swung round instantly and hurried up the path to speak to her.

'These here are police officers. They've come about Carl. He's run away and they want to know if he's come here.'

'OK Doug, I'll deal with them.' She pushed past him, getting a smear of grey paint on her dress as she did so, from the brush that he held in his hand. 'Now look what you've done! Can't you be more careful with that stuff?'

She strode down the path and took up an aggressive stance a foot or so short of the gate.

'What's this Doug's telling me about you lot allowing Carl to run away?'

'Are you Mrs Annette Willis?' Anna asked calmly.

'That's my business. Answer my question.'

'I can't discuss Mr Willis's grandson with anyone outside of the family. So now, please answer my question. Are you Mrs Annette Willis?'

'Yes, I am, and I want to know what's been happening to my grandson to make him run away. You've got no business snatching kids away from their mothers and sticking them in places that don't look after them properly!' She turned to her husband, who was still standing by the front door holding the dripping paintbrush in his hand. 'Don't just stand there like a half-wit. Go and get Vicky out here! She's got a right to hear what's been happening to her kids.'

Douglas disappeared inside the house and Annette turned her attention back to Anna and Andy.

'Come on! Spit it out! What's happened to Carl and Harry?'

'Nothing has happened to Harry,' Anna told her. 'He's completely safe with his new family, but very upset that his brother had gone missing. He told us that Carl was worried about your husband. He has diabetes, is that right?'

Annette nodded. 'Not that it's any business of yours.'

'I agree, but apparently it was preying on Carl's mind, because of the news reports about people with diabetes dying from COVID-19. That's why we think he may have tried to contact your husband or to come here to see him.'

'Come here! That's rich! When you lot've been keeping him away from here for the past five years! The last time he was allowed home for a visit was when he was five. He'd just started school and he was showing off his new uniform. Only he pushed Harry down the stairs, and the social worker blamed Vicky and that's when they started harping on about adoption.'

Another woman came out into the garden. Anna knew from the social services records that Victoria Willis (or did she call herself Foster?) was thirty-eight, but she looked far older. She could have been Annette's sister rather than her daughter. She swayed slightly as she stepped down from the house and put out one arm to steady herself.

'What's this about Carl?' she asked, her eyes darting from Anna to Andy and then down to a packet of cigarettes in her left hand. She took one out and fumbled it into her mouth.

'I'm sorry to have to tell you that your son has gone missing,' Anna informed her. 'We think he may be trying to get here. Has he been in touch with you at all?'

There was a long pause while Victoria searched in her pockets for a lighter. Anna began to wonder whether she had heard the question. Eventually, with shaking hands, she managed to ignite the cigarette. She drew in a deep breath and then exhaled smoke through pursed lips. Finally she looked towards Anna again.

'No,' she said and then promptly took another drag on her cigarette.

'I told you. He's not allowed,' Annette insisted. 'And he wouldn't know how, if he wanted to. Bleeding Social Services! Now, if you don't mind, we've got better things to do with our time than stand around chatting to a load of cops who don't know how to do their jobs. Come on, Vicky!'

She took hold of her daughter's arm and steered her back in through the front door.

'And you can come in and all,' she added grabbing Douglas with her other hand.

'I'd better just finish undercoating the gate,' he pleaded. 'Then I can get myself cleaned up and I won't get paint in the house.'

'OK.' Annette released his arm. 'Just don't go gabbing to the cops about things that don't concern them. Stick to painting, OK?'

'We'll be going then,' Anna said. 'Thank you for your help.'

As they walked away, Andy could sense Annette's eyes on them. He glanced back and saw her standing on the step, waiting to check that they were really going. Then, a few seconds later, he heard the front door close. Evidently she was satisfied that they were not planning to question her husband any further.

They walked back to the car in silence. Andy got into the driving seat and pulled on his seat belt. He turned on the ignition and was about to put it into gear when there was a tapping on the passenger window. Anna wound it down to speak to Douglas Willis, who was standing nervously on the pavement.

'Please,' he begged, 'you will let us know when you find Carl?'

'Yes. I'll see to it that someone tells you,' Anna promised. 'Do you have a number we can ring you on?'

'No. Better not. Annette always answers the phone, and she – she might not take kindly to having the police ringing the house.'

'You don't have a mobile?'

'No. Annette doesn't hold with them – well only just the one for her to take when she goes out, so she can ring for me to pick her up. She doesn't drive, you see. It's different for me. I don't need one, and it's all an expense, isn't it?'

'OK. Well, in that case, how do you suggest we get in touch to tell you when we find Carl?'

'I hadn't thought of that.' Douglas stood in silent perplexity. 'I don't suppose you could come round again, could you? Chances are I'll be outside most days. I've got the railings to finish and the garden always needs weeding at this time of year.'

'OK. We'll do our best,' Anna told him. 'And if Carl does manage to contact you, let me know, won't you?' She handed him her card, which he put away carefully in the pocket of his overalls. Then he turned abruptly and hurried back to resume his painting.

'I reckon the house is in such good nick because he likes to do jobs outside to get away from his missus,' Andy observed as they drove back past the house, where Douglas was painstakingly applying more grey undercoat to the gate, 'and I bet he takes his time over them and all!'

He drove on through almost empty streets to join the motorway again. As they approached Junction 12 (the B4451 to Gaydon) Anna's phone rang. It was Jennifer Moorehouse, a civilian member of staff. 'I thought you'd be interested to know: Carl's browser history shows that, during the last few days, he searched for times of buses and trains to Banbury.'

'Banbury?' repeated Anna. 'Why would he want to go there?'

* * *

Why indeed? That was exactly what Carl was asking himself as he headed north towards Kidlington. His bicycle was not running as well as it had been and pedalling had become much harder. The road seemed suddenly to have become very rough too. Every turn of the wheel seemed to jolt the saddle under him in a very uncomfortable manner. He was on a service road that ran parallel to the main Oxford to Banbury road through the large village of Kidlington. Looking round, he saw a Sainsbury's supermarket across the main road. Ahead and on his left there was a row of small shops. His destination was somewhere even further on – but how far? He had never cycled even as far as this in one day before, and it had suddenly become such hard work!

Eventually, he decided that there must be something wrong. He got off and looked down at the bike. It wasn't long before he spotted the problem. The back tyre was flat! He must have a puncture. What could he do now? Why had he abandoned his phone? If he'd kept it, he could have rung Daddy Wayne and Daddy Dean and they would have come to get him – if they still wanted him, now that he'd stolen that money from Daddy Wayne!

To his left, the row of shops had ended and there was a small park-like area of grass, with flower beds, trees and a bench. A glass-fronted noticeboard headed *Kidlington Parish Council* displayed notices about local events. Carl propped his bike up against one of the trees, slipped his schoolbag off his shoulders and sat down on the bench.

He got out the packet of biscuits and bottle of water that he had brought with him as provisions for the journey. Only two biscuits left! He would eat one now and save one for later. It must be lunchtime – probably later than that even – it could be teatime! If he still had his phone he'd know what time it was. It was stupid of him to get rid of it just to stop Daddy Dean from knowing where he was. If he still had his phone, maybe Daddy Dean would be here now with the car to take him and his bike back home!

But then, he would have failed in his mission. He might as well not have bothered setting out at all! He finished the last biscuit and tipped the final drop of water from the bottle down his throat. Whatever happened he couldn't stay here forever. But what else could he do? He didn't know where he was or how to get home. His phone would have been able to tell him. Why, oh why had he put it through Ollie's door?

Ollie? Was there any way he could contact him? *He* wouldn't be cross with him for running away or for taking the money from Daddy Wayne's wallet. Wasn't there a phone box by where he'd come into the park? He turned round in his seat and there it was. He got up and walked over to it. The heavy door was difficult to open, but he got inside at last. Now, how did you work one of these? It said *coins and cards*, but he didn't have any coins. He only had the notes that he'd stolen from Daddy Wayne.

As he came back out of the kiosk, a blue double-decker bus approached along the main road, travelling fast in the absence of any other traffic. It slowed to a standstill at the bus stop and a solitary passenger stepped down. It was a woman dressed in the orange-and-white uniform of Sainsbury's supermarket. She walked briskly along the pavement to the pedestrian crossing to start her shift at the store.

Carl stared as the bus moved off again. Perhaps he could get a bus back to Ollie's house! He carefully crossed the service road and approached the bus stop, feeling a little more hopeful now.

The array of bus timetables on the board next to the shelter was confusing. There seemed to be so many different routes and numbers! Then a name jumped out at him: Banbury!

15. HOPING

Crystal was working an early shift that day, which meant that she arrived home before four in the afternoon. The two children raced to greet her as soon as they heard her key in the lock.

'Granddad did a story with me!' Ricky told her. 'I was very good. Daddy got lots of work done.'

'Well done!' Crystal smiled down at him. 'Now can you both just keep being good while I change out of my uniform? I won't be long.'

She went into the bedroom and closed the door. After a long day at the hospital followed by the walk home, she wanted a few minutes of respite before facing the onslaught of her children's irrepressible energy.

Eddie, sitting on the bed with his laptop, looked up from the computer as she came in. 'Another bad day?' he enquired, seeing her drawn features.

'Not really,' she smiled back, sitting down heavily next to him and bending down to unlace her shoes. 'I'm just a bit tired that's all. Everything takes longer with all these new COVID-19 protocols. I just need a breather and then I'll start thinking about what we're going to eat this evening. How's your day been? Ricky tells me he's been good, but then he also said you'd had to call on Peter's help, so I don't know whether to believe him!'

'Oh, they haven't been that bad,' Eddie laughed. 'I just had to have some time to get a job done for work. That's why I rang Dad. He was great. He managed to keep Ricky talking for nearly half an hour.'

Crystal got up and started taking off her uniform tunic.

'Dad had some news for us while he was on,' Eddie continued. 'You know Wayne and Dean?'

'The young man who was knocked down in a hit-and-run the summer before last, and his …?' Crystal hesitated. She always felt uncomfortable speaking about relationships that seemed so foreign to everything she knew.

'That's right. You remember they adopted two little boys?'

'Yes?'

Crystal opened the wardrobe and took out a dress.

'Well, one of them – the older one, Carl – has run away. The police are out looking for him.'

Crystal froze in the act of putting the dress over her head. Then she pulled it down and stared at Eddie.

'Why? What did they do to him? What will happen to the other boy?'

'Nothing as far as I know. Dad was all *it's like when Abbie was snatched from her pram*. He was talking like it was the same as … well as it would have been for us if Ricky had run off.'

'I don't know what to think,' Crystal said, reaching behind her head to button up the dress. 'I always thought it was strange allowing two men to adopt children. It's not natural and it must confuse the kids, growing up with two dads instead of a mum and a dad.'

'I suppose Dad sees it differently because he didn't have a mum and dad of his own. The only adult he ever talks about from when he was a kid is his Housefather at the Children's Home. He seems to have made a big impression on him.'

'It's good for boys to have a male role model,' Crystal nodded, bending down to remove her uniform trousers from beneath her dress, 'but I think they need a mum too. If they grow up thinking that it's just as natural for two men to … If they live with two men who sleep together, how're they going to learn that the normal thing is a man and a woman? Surely they must be more likely to become homosexual themselves?'

'Dad would say that it's been scientifically proven that gay people are born that way.'

'I don't see how that can be.' Crystal hunted under the bed for her slippers. 'Kids don't even think about that sort of thing until they're teenagers. It seems much more likely it's all down to things that happen to them when they're growing up. If I was those boys' mother, I wouldn't like to think they were living in a house with two men who might … I'm not saying they'd do anything intentionally to harm them, but it's well-known that homosexuals are often attracted to boys, isn't it? They might not be able to stop themselves.'

'You'd better not let Dad hear you saying that. I could tell it never crossed his mind the boy could have had a good reason to run away.'

'So *you* think that too? I was afraid you thought I was being silly.'

'I don't know!' Eddie sighed and shook his head. 'I really don't know what to think. 'I mean: we've met them and they seemed completely normal. You'd never have known they were any different from me and Dad. They aren't all mincing and effeminate or anything like that. Wayne used to be a prop forward in his college rugby team: you can't get much more macho than that!'

'Yes, I know.' Crystal stood up and started towards the door. 'I know they both seem so nice; and they're doing really good work with the stuff they make for disabled people, but … I just can't believe it's right them having two young boys living with them like that.'

* * *

As Gavin headed home from his day at work, he took a diversion along Lewes Road and called in on Wayne and Dean. Both fathers were at home again now. Wayne invited Gavin into the back garden where Dean was acting as goal-keeper while Harry practised penalty shots into a goal painted on the back wall of the house. They stopped their game when Dean saw Gavin appearing round the corner.

Wayne bent down to speak to his son. 'Daddy Dean and I need to have a grown up talk with PC Hughes now. Do you think you could find something to do indoors by yourself, just for five minutes?'

Harry hesitated for a moment, then nodded. 'You *will* tell me if they find Carl, won't you?'

'Yes, of course; we'll tell you everything,' Wayne promiscd.

'Is there any news?' demanded Dean, the moment the kitchen door closed behind Harry.

'Not much,' Gavin admitted. 'He seems to have headed up Banbury Road on his bike, but we lost him after that. I'm really sorry.'

'Lost him?' shouted Wayne. Then mindful of the open windows in neighbouring houses on that warm day, he lowered his voice. 'How can you have lost him? An eight-year-old boy out alone on a bike and the police can't manage to follow him up Banbury Road and pick him up!'

'It's not as simple as that,' Gavin explained patiently. 'We didn't get there until a couple of hours after him. We did send patrol cars up as far as the ring road looking for him, but he may have gone off down a side road or … I know it sounds like just making excuses, but a boy on a bike could cover a lot of ground in two hours and we don't know where he was aiming for.'

'Is that it then?' asked Wayne. 'Have we lost him? I mean, if he's out there, why haven't you found him? Do you think someone else has picked him up? You know – someone on the lookout for young boys?'

'Tell us honestly,' Dean pressed him, when Gavin did not answer. 'What chance is there of finding him now?'

'As far as we can tell, he's still on his own,' Gavin told them. 'There's no sign that he's under any duress from anyone. It's mild weather and it's stayed dry, so he's not likely to suffer from exposure. It's just a matter of finding where he's gone. I do think there's a very good chance we'll find him in not too long.'

'Do you really think so?' Wayne persisted. 'You're not just saying that?'

'I don't know what we'll do if he doesn't turn up,' Dean added. 'I suppose people will say they're only adopted, but to us they're our boys – just like-'

He broke off suddenly, remembering that Gavin's only child had been killed less than five months previously.

'Just like my Kenny,' Gavin finished for him.

'Yes,' Dean mumbled. 'I'm sorry, I didn't mean to …'

'That's alright. And if it helps, I do understand what you mean about not appreciating how much … When Chrissie and I got married, we couldn't afford to start a family right away. So we started fostering. It was Chrissie's way of having children in the house without so much expense. We took in kids short-term in emergencies – when their parents had to go into hospital and that sort of thing. It's surprising how attached you can get to them even in only a week or two.'

'But you gave them back,' Wayne said. 'You always knew you were giving them back. We thought that Carl and Harry were here for keeps! What if they say we're not fit parents, because Carl ran away?'

'That's right,' Dean put in. 'That's the thing. If anything happens to Carl, they might take Harry away from us too. I don't think I could bear it.'

'It wasn't easy sometimes, giving them back.' Gavin stared into the distance as he remembered. 'There were these two in particular … later on.' He sighed. 'When Chrissie fell pregnant, we told Social Services that we wouldn't take any more kids. But then she had a miscarriage – and then another – and we began to think we'd never have children of our own. And they were so short of places that they asked us if we'd take these twins – just babies, almost new-born – whose mother had been sectioned[6]. They said it'd probably only be for a few weeks, but it turned out to be over two years. Now, it really was hard giving them back!'

'I'm surprised, after two years, they didn't think it was better for them to stay with you permanently,' observed Wayne.

'But by then, their mum was out of hospital and ready to look after them,' Gavin told him. 'It wouldn't have been fair on her for us to keep them – especially when we'd got Kenny by then. It would have been nice though,' he added wistfully. 'We always wanted a string of kids, and Chrissie couldn't have any more after Kenny.'

'Oh! I'm sorry,' Wayne and Dean said together.

'Oh well! Maybe it was for the best,' Gavin shrugged. 'It was hard work having two-year-old twins and a baby with almost constant colic. I dare say we did a better job of bringing up Kenny without the half-dozen younger siblings that Chrissie would have liked! And she didn't want to be stay-at-home mum, because she loved her job too much, so … It's all a matter of getting a balance, I suppose. Jobs are important too.'

'Yes!' Dean agreed with feeling. 'Running a business used to seem like fun, but just now it's something we could

---

[6] Detained in hospital under the provisions of the Mental Health Act 1983, as stated in section 2 or 3 of the Act.

do without. You don't happen to know anyone who's an expert in managing a mail-order warehouse, do you?'

'No, I'm afraid not.' Gavin turned to go. 'Well, I'd better be going. I expect young Harry will be wanting you, and … well, I'd better be going.'

'You will let us know if there's any news of Carl, won't you?' Wayne called after him anxiously.

'Yes, of course, but it'll most likely be DCI Davenport or DS Lepage who'll know about it first. Don't worry: when they find him, you'll be the first to know.'

'And tell them to make sure he knows he's not in any trouble,' Dean added, 'and we've made his favourite strawberry trifle for when he comes home.'

Gavin pushed his bicycle back out to the road and headed home. It had been a frustrating day, with nothing to show for his efforts at the end of it. Stella had been disheartened too, he could tell. And Wayne was right, with every police officer in Oxford primed to keep a lookout for the runaway, how was it that he had evaded their notice for so long? Why had no passer-by spotted him out on his own and questioned what he was doing there? Was it possible that some paedophile had happened upon him and "befriended" him? Would the next news be of an early-morning dog-walker reporting the finding of a child's body in a shallow grave?

Turning in at the drive, he saw Craig standing at the side gate, struggling to open it while holding his bike. They walked along the path to the garage together.

'Job going OK?' Gavin enquired, trying to sound casual. He knew that Craig was on probation after the incident earlier in the week. Even the smallest hint that he was trouble might lose him his job.

'Yeah,' Craig muttered. 'It'd be better if we had a supervisor who knew the first thing about supervising, but I expect that's just me being bitter and twisted after not getting the job.'

'I expect he'll get better after he's been doing it for a while.'

'Yeah, maybe. Like I said, it's probably just me. Maybe I should look for something else.'

'No harm in looking,' Gavin agreed cautiously.

'But maybe I'm no good for any job. I'm sure that's what Declan thinks!' Craig thrust the bicycle into the garage, sending it clattering against the lawnmower.

'If Declan thinks that, then Declan is wrong,' Gavin declared, 'but I don't suppose for a minute that he does. Look! Everyone feels like that sometimes – useless, I mean. Only just now, I was thinking what a failure I've been today! There's an eight-year-old boy run off on his bike, and I've been chasing after him all day and not seen hide nor hair of him! I've just come from his parents' house now. He's been gone since before breakfast this morning, and all I could say to them was, we've got officers out looking for him and he's bound to turn up soon.'

'What boy?' Craig demanded at once. 'Where? Why did he run away?'

'His name's Carl,' Gavin told him. 'He lives just round the corner, in Lewes Road. He's adopted. His parents – his new parents, I mean – think he may be trying to find his birth family – or rather his grandfather, who seems to be the only one of them that he cares about – but everyone agrees that he wouldn't know where to go, because they're only allowed to meet under supervision and never at the grandfather's home.'

'Lewes Road?' Craig exclaimed, picking up the bike again and pushing past Gavin to get it out of the garage. 'Why isn't the whole neighbourhood out looking for him?'

'Two reasons: first, we know he got as far as the railway station, because he was picked up on CCTV cameras there, and there's evidence he was headed up the Banbury road sometime this morning, so no point hunting around here; and second, we can't have crowds of people out on the streets when there's a pandemic on.'

'Are you saying it's more important keeping people indoors because of the virus than finding an eight-year-old boy who's going to be sleeping on the streets if we don't find him soon? What if he's been kidnapped?'

'No evidence of that on the CCTV.'

'Well, if he's out there on his own, it won't be long before someone picks him up – and I'm not talking about model citizens wanting to rescue a lost boy and turn him in to the police! Those streets out there are dangerous places to be if you're a kid. I know! I've lived on them!'

'I know too, but things are different now. They've cleared the streets.' Gavin put out his arm and rested his hand on Craig's shoulder, but Craig shook it off.

'Well I'm going to look for him, even if no one else will! I don't care! You can report me if you like, but I'll just say I'm doing my daily exercise. I know all the hiding places. If anyone can find him, it's me'

* * *

It was not until he had chained up his bike outside St Giles Church that Craig cooled down enough to realise how hopeless his mission was. It was all very well telling Gavin that he knew all the nooks and crannies where a homeless person might shelter from the elements, but that knowledge was only any good if Carl could be assumed also to know about them. In normal times, his contacts within the homeless community would have given him a network of street people who might have been able to give him intelligence about the boy's movements that day, but they had all been housed under the *Everyone In* scheme.

Oh well! He was here now. He might as well have a look round.

He set off up Banbury Road, peering over hedges and through railings looking for likely hiding places in the grounds of the large houses that lined the road, most of them now converted into university departments or student accommodation. No sign of a boy or of a child's bicycle!

After an hour he had worked his way along the left-hand side of the road as far as the ring road. He crossed over and started down the other side, heading back towards the city centre, still systematically inspecting every conceivable hiding place along the way. He knew that his quest was pointless. If Carl was still on his bike and intent on putting as many miles as possible between himself and his home, he would have crossed the by-pass and be halfway to Banbury by now! But would an eight-year-old really have that much persistence? Wasn't it more likely that he would have turned back when he grew tired or hungry?

Craig was feeling very hungry himself. It would have been more sensible to have had dinner and then set out to hunt for the boy in the evening. What had he achieved by his reckless impetuosity? Nothing, except to upset Chrissie, whose lovingly-prepared food would be spoiled! Declan was right – he was a useless waste of space! He never got anything right.

'Hi Craig!'

He looked up from exploring an extra-bushy part of a long, tall hedge that bordered a row of low-rise flats, and saw Stella, still in her police uniform, standing behind him holding her bicycle.

'Hi Stella! Are you still on duty? I thought you worked the same shifts as Gavin?'

'No. I just thought I'd have another look for Carl – a little boy who's gone missing from home. Did Gavin tell you about him?'

'Yes. That's what I'm doing too.' Craig straightened up and stood looking down on Stella. 'Not that there's much chance of finding him. I just wanted to be doing something. You know how it is.'

'Yes. I'm the same. To be honest, it was mostly just an excuse to get out of the house. My gran was … well I got upset when I was telling her about Carl. I don't know why.

I just couldn't help it. And then *she* got upset about me being upset and … I think there must be something wrong with me. I seem to over-react to everything!'

'Like when that car went past the other day?'

Stella nodded.

'The red BMW heading straight for you and Ken-'

'It was silver,' Stella interrupted. Then she stopped and looked up at Craig. 'How did you know?'

'Been there; done that; got the tee-shirt,' Craig grinned. 'PTSD is like that. You think you've got over it and you're fine now, and then … It's nothing to be ashamed of – or so people keep telling me!'

'That's what the counsellor that they fixed me up with said too,' Stella smiled back, 'but that doesn't make it any less embarrassing when it happens. The other day, I was convinced I saw Kenny's killer walking down the street towards me, but when he got close up he looked nothing like him. Not that I saw his face in the first place – I only know what he looks like because of the pictures in the papers and seeing him at the police station after he was arrested.'

'Probably all to do with this nonsense about letting them all out on bail. Your sub-conscious playing tricks on you.'

'I suppose so, but knowing that doesn't make it any less scary – thinking I can't trust my own eyes, I mean. In my job, I'm supposed to be observant. I'd be no good as a witness if I keep seeing people who aren't there!'

'Have you told Gav about it?'

'No. I don't want to worry him. I have thought of resigning though.'

'Why would you do that?'

'I'm just not sure I can hack it as a police officer. I don't think I'm tough enough. If I was I wouldn't still be so shaken up about seeing Kenny …'

'It's not a matter of being tough. There are some things that just stick with you, that's all.'

'D'you think?'

'I *know*. And now that we've both admitted that we're completely useless, maybe we'd better give up on this hopeless search and get back home to the people that we were escaping from.'

They set off back down the road, Stella pushing her bike and Craig keeping pace alongside. There was no need to talk; they both *knew*.

16. LOST … AND FOUND

Unaccountably, Craig found himself unable to follow his own advice. The next morning he was up early and spent an hour before breakfast out on his bike, hunting vainly for the missing boy. When he came back in, he found Gavin talking excitedly on his mobile phone. He brought the call to an end when he saw Craig.

'Look, I've got to go now. Thanks for the update. I'll call in and let the parents know first thing.'

'Have they found him?' Craig asked eagerly. He could tell from Gavin's demeanour that this was progress and not the ominous news that they had all been dreading.

'Not yet, but they *have* found his bike.'

'Where?'

'Kidlington – well, just outside, I suppose – a few yards beyond the Sainsbury's roundabout.'

'So, what happened? Was he abducted from there, d'you think?'

'There's no evidence of that. It's got a flat tyre, so the chances are he just abandoned it there and carried on on foot.'

'Well then, what are we waiting for? Let's get out there and look for him! I'm kicking myself now: I got as far as the ring road last night. If only I'd gone a couple of hundred yards further, I might have found him then.'

'Hold on!' Gavin remonstrated. 'There's no need for all that.'

'All what?' asked Chrissie, catching the tail-end of their conversation as she entered the room.

'Louise Otterbourne found Carl's bike in Kidlington last night,' Gavin explained. 'I was just telling Craig that there's no point him rushing off to help look for him.'

'Gav's quite right,' Chrissie agreed. 'You sit down and eat your breakfast. No point doing anything on an empty stomach.'

'They've had a team of trained officers out there since daybreak,' Gavin added. 'I know you want to help, but really a civilian would only get in the way.'

Craig pulled out a chair with rather more force than was strictly necessary and sat down. Chrissie poured tea for him. Gavin offered a slice of toast.

'Thanks.' Craig took the toast and reached for the butter. 'So, you're off to tell his mum and dad?'

Gavin froze with his knife in the marmalade jar, poised to scoop a helping out on to his toast. He looked towards Chrissie, who also seemed to be turned to stone. Their eyes met and they exchanged a look which Craig could not decipher.

'What is it?' he demanded. 'What have I said?'

'Nothing.' Gavin was obviously trying to dismiss this faux pas that he had made, whatever it was. 'It's only … when I said Carl's parents lived in Lewes Road, I wasn't talking about his mum and dad.'

'I know. I meant his *adoptive* parents – his new mum and dad.'

'But that's just it.' Gavin seemed to be struggling to find the right words. 'Carl doesn't have a new mum and dad – he's got two dads.'

'I don't understand.' Craig looked at Gavin and then turned to Chrissie.

She nodded and smiled. 'Carl and Harry have been adopted by a gay couple,' she explained.

'They're living with a pair of poofdahs? And you wonder why he ran away?'

'Don't talk like that,' Gavin cut in with uncharacteristic sharpness. 'Wayne and Dean are just like any other couple.'

'How very politically correct!' Craig observed sarcastically.

'And they're completely devoted to their two boys,' Chrissie added. 'I went to see them yesterday afternoo-'

'I bet they are!' interrupted Craig. 'I've known a few guys like that – they lo-o-o-ve little boys!'

Gavin and Chrissie pounced on him together.

'There's no call for that,' Gavin said in his move-along-there-nothing-to-see-here police officer's voice.

'Oh do stop!' Chrissie was more emotional. 'You've never even met them. I've had lots of adopted children in my classes over the years and I can tell you, they're none of them interested in children in that way.'

'But two gay men?' Craig was still incredulous. 'How come it's allowed? I wouldn't want any kid of mine living with a couple of pervs.'

'All prospective adopters are very carefully vetted,' Chrissie told him stiffly.

'And in this case, I understand there were particular reasons why a two-dad household was chosen,' Gavin added.

Craig bit into his toast. There was clearly no point arguing any more. Gavin and Chrissie were towing the party line. The next thing he knew they'd be accusing him of homophobia! He wasn't homophobic. It was up to them what they did in private. He just didn't think it was right to put young boys living with them, that's all!

He finished his breakfast as quickly as he could and then set off for work, grateful to get out of the house. He almost collided with Stella as he pushed his bike out through the side gate. She was on her way in, ready to start another day of foot patrol with Gavin. Seeing her leap back, wide-eyed as he pushed open the gate he recognised the tell-tale signs of lack of sleep and heightened alertness to potential danger. It had been good that she'd opened up to him a bit yesterday. Should he say something now?

No! Better let her start her day without knowing that he was aware of her jumpiness. It would only start her worrying that other people might notice too – not a good start to the day for someone whose job depended on her staying calm under fire. And in any case, whatever he said would be bound to be the wrong thing. He always did say the wrong thing. He'd almost blown it with Gavin and Chrissie the other day – after all they'd done for him too! And just now? He mustn't have explained himself properly. If he'd managed to find the right words, surely they'd have understood. Or maybe he was the one who didn't understand?

Stella was standing there staring at him. She must have said something, but he hadn't taken it in.

'Gavin's just finishing his breakfast,' he told her, hoping that this was a reasonable response to whatever it had been. 'He's got some news about the lost boy.'

'Really?' Stella's face lit up. 'I've been so worried! Have they found him?'

'No, not the boy, just his bike – in Kidlington, just beyond where we were looking for him last night.'

'Oh!' Stella looked rather crestfallen. 'I was hoping … I really wanted him to have some good news. He seemed so … We're all upset about Carl going missing, but I had a feeling Gavin was taking it more to heart than … I think it's reminding him of Kenny. And, of course, he knows Wayne and Dean. Wayne was seriously injured in a road traffic accident a couple of years ago and Gavin was first on the scene. It was a hit-and-run. The first thought was that it was deliberate – a homophobic attack. I think Gavin feels sort of … I don't know … like he ought to have found Carl by now.'

Craig's heart began beating faster as he listened to this long speech. Was this an invitation to confide in Stella? His mind raced as he tried to assemble his thoughts into some sort of coherent combination of words.

'It's hard when you're used to being the fixer for other people,' he began, finding his mouth suddenly dry and his voice hoarse. He cleared his throat and went on. 'I mean, it's hard when you find out that you can't keep them safe after all. When I was out in Afghanistan, there was this village – deserted, we thought. The Taliban had retreated to the hills. I sent four of my mates into this building – more of a ruin really – to search it, just in case there was anyone left inside. It turned out it was booby-trapped. An IED went off and the whole house came down on top of them. I should have been leading from the front. I should have been the first inside, and I should have known there might be a bomb.'

Stella looked up at him. He saw her hands gripping harder onto the handlebars of her bicycle.

'That's just exactly how I feel about Kenny!'

* * *

Carl staggered out of the pile of grass cuttings in which he had spent the night. The gently decomposing vegetation had kept him warm as the temperature outside dropped down into single figures, but nevertheless his limbs felt stiff. He banged his arms across his chest to get his blood circulating and then tried some of the warm-up exercises that his football coach had taught him.

What now?

He felt cold around his middle. He pulled his hoody, which had ridden up under his armpits during the night, down to his hips. As he did so, he noticed smudgy grass stains on his white tee-shirt. It had taken Daddy Dean ages to clean that shirt after he spilled ketchup down it the other week. He'd be cross about having to do it all over again. And Daddy Wayne would be cross about the money.

He was very hungry and thirsty. It must be hours and hours since he finished the biscuits and drained his water bottle. He would have to go home. He needed food, and there was nowhere else that he could get it. He'd tried Sainsbury's, but there was a long queue and a notice saying *no children under 16*. At least that meant that he hadn't spent any of the money in the end. Maybe Daddy Wayne wouldn't be too cross about it if he gave it all back. And he could wash the tee-shirt himself. Maybe, if he kept his hoody on, he could get it clean in the bathroom without anyone knowing about the stains.

He pushed his way through the belt of trees and bushes that bordered the road. There was a line of chestnut palings preventing him from getting out on to the pavement. Last night he'd found a place where they had collapsed against a heap of dead leaves and he'd climbed over easily, but this was a different spot and he was trapped.

He started walking along inside the fence, heading towards Oxford, continually looking for a way out on to the road. It was hard going because his way was constantly being blocked by bushes and brambles, but he persevered. He had to get home!

At the sound of a car, he instinctively ducked down. He squatted amongst dense undergrowth and peered out through the palings. It wasn't just one car; it was two. And they were both police cars! He crouched even lower and pulled his hoody up over his face so that only his eyes would be visible if they looked that way. Nanna had told him that the police would come and take him away to prison if he was naughty. And he'd stolen that money! What if they were looking for him?

* * *

'We've had officers out since first light searching the area,' Gavin told Wayne and Dean, 'and they'll be starting a house-to-house, now that it's late enough that it won't cause a panic among the residents having the police knocking on their doors. The main thing is: we now know where to start looking, and he can't have got all that far now that he's on foot.'

'But what I don't get is why he hasn't been spotted already,' argued Wayne. 'A boy out on his own, when everyone's supposed to stay at home. You'd think someone would notice.'

'Carl's very good at hide-and-seek,' Harry piped up. 'I can never find him.'

'You've got a good point there,' Gavin agreed, smiling down on the little boy. 'And we do think he doesn't want to be found. That's most likely why he got rid of his phone. Now it would really help if we knew where he was trying to get to. Are you sure he didn't say anything to you that would give us a clue?'

Harry shook his head solemnly. 'No. He never said anything to me.'

'There was something I thought of in the night,' Dean said tentatively. 'I remember once, we were cycling along Banbury Road and Carl wanted to know why it was called Banbury Road. I told him that if you went far enough along it you'd get to Banbury, and-'

'-and Banbury is where we went to meet his granddad!' Wayne finished for him. 'Off course! How stupid of us! Why didn't we think of that before? There's a contact centre there where we took the boys to meet their granddad on neutral territory.'

'Where Mum and Nanna can't find us,' put in Harry.

'That's right, Harry,' Dean agreed, putting his arm round his son.

'We went on the train,' Harry continued. 'It was exciting.'

'Yes!' cried Stella excitedly. 'It all fits, doesn't it? First he tries to get a train ticket to Banbury, but he gets scared when the booking clerk comes over; so then he tries the bus station-'

'And finally, he thinks maybe he can cycle all the way,' continued Dean. 'I suppose he thought the staff at the centre would know where his granddad was.'

'But that doesn't tell us where he is now,' Wayne pointed out dejectedly. 'He can't be trying to *walk* all the way, can he?'

'Didn't they say they found his bike near a bus stop?' asked Stella. 'There are buses to Banbury that go through Kidlington.'

'That's a good point,' Gavin agreed. 'I'll get on to the SIO right away.'

He had a brief conversation with Anna and then turned back to the two fathers. 'Don't worry. Now we've got this new lead, I don't suppose it'll be long before we find him. DS Lepage is going to check out the buses right away and DCI Davenport is going over to Banbury personally to brief the police there to start looking for him. And meanwhile, PC Gilbert and I will be patrolling around here, in case he heads for home.'

'OK. Thanks,' Dean mumbled. After the rush of adrenaline when the Banbury connection suddenly fell into place, he now felt all the more despondent. Carl had been missing for more than twenty-four hours now. Was it really likely that he would return safely after all this time?

* * *

'Yeah, there was a kid asking about a ticket to Banbury yesterday.' The driver dropped his cigarette butt and ground it into the concrete with his shoe. 'Spun me some yarn about going shopping for his granddad.'

'Where was this?' PC Toby Hitchin asked eagerly.

'Garden City.'

Hitchin's face fell. This sounded less promising. 'Where's that?'

'Kidlington. By Sainsbury's. Dunno why they call it that, but that's the name of the stop.'

'Oh, right!' That must be the place his sergeant had told him about – the place where their Oxford colleagues had found the boy's bicycle. 'And did you sell him a ticket?'

'Nar!' the driver shook his head. 'It didn't look right, a boy that age out on his own, with this COVID business on. Like I said, when I asked him what he was doing out on his own, he came up with this story about going shopping for his granddad. I said, "What's wrong with Sainsbury's?" After all it was just over the road. So then he got down from the bus and run off.'

'Which way did he go?'

'Dunno. I wasn't watching.'

'OK. Now, could you have a look at this picture and tell me if you think it's him?'

The bus driver peered down at the photograph on Hitchin's phone.

'Yeah. Reckon that's him. Skinny kid in a white tee-shirt with a bag on his back.'

'Thank you. That's very helpful.'

Hitchin waited until he was outside the bus depot before punching the air in triumph. From what he'd heard about the case so far, this was the first actual sighting of the boy since he left the railway station. It confirmed that he was trying to get to Banbury, and that it was unlikely that he had succeeded ... although it was possible that he'd found another bus driver who was more easily convinced by his trumped-up story about shopping for an elderly relative ... or he might have come up with something that sounded more plausible. Suppose he had claimed that he lived in

Banbury and was trying to get the bus home …? It was worth carrying on with their painstaking search of the backstreets of Banbury. You never knew, he might even get to be the one to find the boy and bring him home!

* * *

Father Damien meanwhile was cycling slowly back down Banbury Road from Wolvercote Cemetery. It was part of his penance for spoiling Deidre's altar frontal. Her parents' grave was there and this was their wedding anniversary. Deidre always put flowers on the grave on that day, but this year … would it be a terrible imposition to ask Father Damien to do it for her, seeing as she was supposed to be shielding?

He had bought some flowers from the supermarket, hoping that they were what Deidre would have chosen, and placed them in the vase that stood in front of the headstone. Then he had taken a photograph with his phone to show her later – he wasn't sure how – and stood for a few minutes in silent prayer. Now he was on his way back to a solitary lunch at the presbytery and then the ever-lengthening to-do list.

A movement to his left caught his attention. A small figure on the pavement suddenly darted behind a bus shelter. Not quite knowing why, Damien became convinced that this was someone trying to avoid being seen. He slowed down even more as he approached the bus stop, running the past few minutes back to himself in his mind.

The boy – he was sure it was a boy – had been walking along the pavement, going in the same direction as he was. He was wearing a black hoody and had a bag on his back. He glanced back over his shoulder, giving Damien a brief glimpse of a white face … and then he had made a dash for cover.

Damien went on past the bus stop, taking care not to look towards the shelter as he did so. Then he stopped a few yards further on and pretended to be trying to fix something on his bike. He propped it up against a tree on the stretch of grass that ran between the pavement and a long, tall hedge, which bounded the grounds of a line of apartment blocks. Feigning deep concentration while flashing an occasional glance back towards the rear of the bus shelter, he monitored the boy's movements.

Carl – he was convinced that it must be Carl – remained crouching down out of sight of the road. Damien continued to peer earnestly down at his rear wheel and to fiddle with the adjustment on the brake. Carl crept out from his hiding place and started walking again, keeping close to the hedge. Damien waited as he came closer, then …

'Hello Carl!' he greeted him as he passed between the bicycle and the hedge.

Carl's eyes opened wide and his mouth dropped open too. He stared at Damien for a second and then he took off, running at full pelt along the side of the hedge. Damien ran after him. It was a long time since he had been called upon to indulge in such feats of athleticism and once again he began to feel his age. However, he was determined not to allow the boy to get away. He forced himself to accelerate and soon he was gaining on him. Carl might be younger, but Damien had the advantage in terms of length of leg.

He brought him down in a rugby tackle – something that he had not done since his school days – and they lay on the grass, both panting and eyeing one another suspiciously.

'Carl? You are Carl, aren't you?'

The boy continued to stare at Damien, saying nothing. His eyes were wide and scared.

'It really is time you went home,' Damien told him, trying to speak in a calm matter-of-fact voice. 'Everybody's worried about you: Daddy Wayne and Daddy Dean and your brother Harry and everyone.'

The boy's lower lip trembled and he looked close to tears. Damien relaxed his hold on him and helped him into a sitting position. 'Why don't I ring for one of your daddies to come and take you home?'

Carl nodded silently and wiped his nose on the sleeve of his hoody.

Damien took out his phone and called Peter. He would know how to contact Carl's parents. He could hear it ringing out. Come on Peter! Pick up!

'Hello Father, what can I do for you?'

'Peter! Thank God! I need you to-'

All of a sudden, Carl was on his feet. A moment later he was gone, racing off at top speed, following the line of the hedge back towards the centre of Oxford. Instinctively, Damien got up too. A police car sped past on the other side of the road, its blue light flashing. Was that what had spooked the boy? He took a few steps towards the road, hoping to flag down the car, but it was too late. It was obviously in a hurry to get somewhere – an accident on the by-pass, perhaps.

He became aware of Peter's anxious voice continuing on the phone.

'Father? Are you still there? What's up?'

The priest forced himself to stand still and answer Peter's questions, fighting off the desire to renew the chase at once.

'I've found Carl. I thought he was going to let me take him home, but he's just run off again. Can you get someone over here to help? We're on Banbury Road, just inside the ring road, and Carl's heading towards the city centre.'

'OK. I'll do that. Are you alright?'

'I'm fine. Now I'll have to go, I want to see if I can catch him up.'

Damien snatched up his bike, mounted it and took off in pursuit. The boy was fast and Damien had lost time with his telephone conversation, but he was gaining on Carl now. Then the boy swerved to the left and seemed to disappear into the hedge. Damien stopped and looked round. Yes! There was a gate in the hedge and someone had left it open.

It led to a path that ran between the blocks of flats and out to the road on the other side.

Damien dismounted and pushed his bike through the gate. No sign of Carl, but he could not be far away. He looked round. The area behind the flats was mostly grass, with just the occasional ornamental tree to give it a bit more character. None of those was large enough to hide behind, not even if you were a small boy. So where had he gone?

Damien pushed his bike along the path, continuing to look to right and left all the time in the hope of spotting Carl. All of a sudden a flash of movement caught his eye. The path ahead ended at a gate, which filled the space between one of the apartment blocks and a low, flat-roofed building attached to the adjacent block. And there was movement on top of that building! A small figure in black was just hauling itself over the edge of the roof. Then it was upright and running away. It stopped, hesitating at the other end of the building before disappearing from view.

Damien threw down his bicycle and ran across to the gate. Peering through it, he could see the path continuing past a line of doors – the low building must be storage rooms for each of the flats – to another grassed area and the road beyond. He rattled the gate in the hope of getting it to open, but it remained firm. Then he peered in at the window of one of the ground floor flats with the aim of attracting the attention of one of the residents, who might be able to let him through, but the room the he looked in on was deserted.

He looked at the solid brick wall that stood in his way. Could he haul himself up on to the roof in the way Carl had done? How had he managed it? There seemed to be nowhere to get any purchase to push himself up, unless the boy had managed somehow to slip his small feet into the gaps in the trellis of which the gate was constructed? It was no good, he was merely wasting time: Carl could be two streets away by now.

He walked back across the grass and retrieved his bike. He pushed it back out to the main road and propped it up against the hedge. Then he got out his phone and called Peter again.

'Don't worry,' he answered cheerfully as soon as Damien had explained the situation. 'The cavalry are on their way! Jonah's supposed to be off work, but that hasn't stopped him throwing his weight about. Just keep a lookout for- in fact, isn't that a squad car I can hear now? You'd better get ready to tell them where to go.'

Damien looked up and saw that Peter was right. A police car had stopped, its blue light still flashing, and a uniformed officer was getting out and striding across the grass to speak to him.

'Father Damien Rowland? I hear you've got news of a runaway boy?'

17. HARD CHOICES

It had been an uneventful day: no arrests, not even any fixed penalty notices for parking offences or cautions for shoplifting. Just a polite reminder about the ban on socialising when they came across two older women gossiping in the street. And then, of course, there had been the webinar setting out for them the new rules that they would have to enforce when Lockdown ended on 4th July. Gavin had a feeling that the gradual easing of restrictions was going to be more difficult to police than the simple *Stay at Home* message had been,

He and Stella strolled along Lewes Road enjoying the summer sunshine, glad that the messages coming through on their radios were all directed at other officers in different parts of the town. Not long now to the end of their shift.

Dean was in his front garden, standing halfway up a pair of stepladders, leaning out across the bay window of their dining room. When Gavin saw what he was doing, he stopped dead and stood staring. Following his gaze, Stella saw the letters AEDOS scrawled across the window in red paint. Dean had nearly finished removing the initial P with a scraper.

Gavin strode up the drive and stood two metres away from Dean, looking up at him. 'Hi there!'

Dean, absorbed in his task, jumped at the sound and caught hold of the steps to steady himself.

'Oh! Hello. Hi Stella!'

'When did this happen?' Gavin asked, pointing at the writing.

'Not sure. We only noticed it a couple of hours ago, but I had the curtains closed this morning to stop the sun shining on the computer screen, so it could have been there all day.'

'Have you reported it?'

'To the police? No.'

'You ought to.' Gavin bent down and picked up a long strip of paint from the scrapings that had fallen to the ground. He placed it between two pages of his notebook. 'Forensics will be able to tell us what sort of paint this is that they used. That may help us to pin down who did it.'

'No, don't bother. We don't want to make a fuss.' Dean turned away and began hacking at the letter A. 'At least the boys are too young to understand what it means.'

Stella stared at him in amazement. 'But we can't let whoever did this get away with it. This is hate crime!'

Dean shrugged. 'Just par for the course. There are plenty of people out there who think guys like me and Wayne shouldn't be allowed anywhere near kids, never mind having any of our own. Your house-to-house enquiries when Carl ran away, and then him being brought home in a police car, drew attention to us. I suppose someone's been putting two and two together and coming to the conclusion that he must have had a good reason to run away.'

'You mean, they think you must have been abusing him?' Stella asked. 'Don't they realise that Social Services would never have allowed him back if there was any question of that?'

'I don't suppose they bothered to think about it. In some people's minds *gay* and *paedophile* are the same thing; and not everybody trusts Social Services.'

'But that's awful!' Stella's eyes opened wide in horror.

'I'll have to report it, now that I've seen it,' Gavin told him. 'And I'd advise you not to ignore it. This sort of thing can escalate. So watch out for things being pushed through your letter box or-'

'What sort of things?' demanded Dean.

'Fireworks, dog pooh, anonymous notes …' Stella reeled off.

Dean allowed the hand holding the scraper to drop to his side as he twisted round to look down at Stella. 'Has that happened to you?'

'Well, the notes and the dog pooh – and a Muslim friend of mine had a lit firework that burned her hall carpet.'

'I'm sorry. That really shouldn't happen. I didn't realise-'

'Neither should that,' answered Stella, pointing up at the letters on the window.

'How *are* the boys?' Gavin asked to change the subject.

'They're both doing great,' Dean smiled, getting down from the steps. 'Carl's back to his old self since having a video call with his granddad. Harvey – that's our social worker – has promised to keep an eye on him and see he doesn't get coronavirus. I just hope he doesn't, but there's nothing more we can do on that score.'

'Infection rates are falling,' Gavin said reassuringly, 'and it won't be long before Carl's allowed to see his Granddad for himself.'

'If we can get him away from his wife and daughter,' Dean answered grimly. 'According to Harvey, after he heard about Carl trying to get to him, he made plans to leave them, but then he changed his mind. I can't understand it. From what Harvey says he must have a miserable life with them.'

'But if you asked him, I expect he'd tell you he still loved them,' Gavin told him. 'And his wife would swear blind she loved him too. I've seen it lots of times. I remember my sergeant when I first started out in the force saying, "Never get involved in domestics. You can't win. As soon as you try to arrest him for knocking her about, she'll be screaming at you to get out of the house, and telling you he does it because he loves her." This *coercive control* stuff that they talk about these days is a complicated business.'

'The main thing is for Carl not to be worrying about his Granddad any more, isn't it?' Stella suggested. 'He's really convinced that everything's going to be OK?'

'Yes, he seems to be,' Dean nodded, 'but the thing that's made the biggest difference is … well, you'd better see for yourself. Come round and have a look.'

Smiling broadly, he put down the scraper on the top of the stepladder and headed for the side gate.

'You take Stella round,' Gavin said, picking up the scraper. 'I'll get on with this. It's alright,' he added, seeing Dean opening his mouth to protest, 'We've already met. Better not to overwhelm her with too many new people all at once.'

'What did PC Hughes mean?' Stella asked as she followed Dean through the gate. 'Who's he talking about?'

'Come through and I'll show you,' Dean grinned back.

They rounded the corner of the house. Immediately, a ball of black-and-tan fur hurled itself at Stella's legs, barking madly. Carl raced over and took the puppy by the collar.

'Down, Star!' he said commandingly. 'Down!'

The dog strained against his grip, still looking up at Stella. She wanted to greet this new intruder on her territory, who might be an enemy that needed seeing off the premises – or might, on the other hand, be the bearer of doggy treats.

'Down!' Carl repeated firmly.

Stella stood still, watching, wondering what would happen. After a few more seconds of protest, the puppy conceded to the boy's authority and lay down on the path.

'Good girl!' Carl reached into his pocket and brought out a treat. He bent down and held it out on the palm of his hand for the dog to take. Then he patted her vigorously on the shoulder, 'Well done, Star!'

'Meet Star,' Dean said to Stella.

'She's going to be a police dog,' Carl informed her. 'Like PD Q.'

'Q found Carl when he ran away, didn't she Daddy Dean?' Harry added, running over to speak to their visitor. 'He was hiding behind some bins and nobody else knew where he was, but she sniffed him out. And then Carl came home in the police van with her. He's lucky! I've never been in a police van.'

'Star was PC Stanton's idea,' Dean explained. 'When she saw how interested the boys both were in Q, she told them about puppy socialisers.'

'That's what we are!' Harry interrupted. 'We've got to teach her to do what we say and to not get scared of things.'

'I grew up on a farm,' Dean added, 'so I'm used to having dogs around all the time.'

'Daddy Dean won a prize!' Harry said proudly. 'Didn't you, Daddy Dean?'

'I was only ten at the time,' Dean laughed. 'I won a junior sheepdog trial. I didn't really deserve it. It was my dad's dog who did all the hard work. Anyway, Mel suggested that I could apply to be a volunteer puppy socialiser. And the boys were all for the idea, so … Well, here we all are!'

'It wouldn't be feasible if we were both still going out to work every day,' Wayne put in, 'but working from home, we can keep her company, and *she*'ll keep the boys company while we're busy.'

'And we've got to get her used to going to lots of different places,' Carl chipped in. 'Mel said. So they can't make us stay in all the time anymore!'

'Well now, that isn't quite what she said,' Dean interjected. 'She just said that we'd probably need to take her out more than once a day, and that it would count as a "reasonable excuse" to leave the house, even if we'd already done our exercise.'

'Come and see her kennel,' Harry begged, pulling at Stella's sleeve and then dropping it suddenly and backing away when he remembered about social distancing.

Stella followed him over to a large wooden structure that had appeared on the patio, under the living room window. There was a sturdy mesh run attached, its door fastened open to allow the puppy to retreat inside if she chose.

'Mel and some men brought it in a van,' Harry told her. 'And me and Daddy Wayne made her name.'

He pointed at a wooden sign attached to the side of the kennel. Painted on it in rather wobbly letters was the name *Star*.

'She's called Star because she's going to be a star police dog,' Carl said proudly. 'She's already learnt lots.'

'I wanted her to try to find the people who painted that nasty word on our window,' Harry put in. 'But Daddy Dean said she wasn't old enough yet. He wouldn't ring Mel to come and get Q to do it either,' he added in a disappointed tone.

'Q has got lots more important things to do,' Dean told him. 'The paint will come off. It doesn't really matter about finding who did it.'

Gavin scraped the final part of the S off the window and stepped down heavily to the ground. Standing back on the lawn, he surveyed the window to check that he had not missed any of the paint. Then he folded the stepladder and picked it up under his arm to carry it round to the back of the house.

He heard voices in the garden as he walked down the side path. A dog barked. No, not a dog, a puppy. As he turned the corner into the back garden, he caught sight of them: Carl in the middle of the lawn playing a game with Star. He stopped dead, and then stepped back into the shadow of the house as a wave of emotion caught him unexpectedly.

That was how Kenny had been with his dog, Skipper, an exuberant beagle with a white-tipped tail always held high in the air above his black and brown back, like a flag signalling his presence in the long grass where he loved to play. Kenny had begged for a dog for his tenth birthday. Chrissie and he had argued against it: he would be lonely while they were out at work all day; Kenny would get bored with taking him for walks every day; he would shed hairs over the carpets and chew the furniture. But Kenny had continued to plead and, in the end, they had given in.

To be fair to Kenny, he'd kept his end of the bargain pretty well. There hadn't been many days when Gavin had been the one going out on a rainy night to give Skipper his daily exercise. Only one armchair had suffered seriously from the puppy's teeth; he was more interested in looking out for unattended food to steal, which he did frequently. Kenny had had hopes of joining the Dog Section one day, but his applications had been turned down. If he had been successful, he wouldn't have been in that back lane in Kidlington when Shane Butler drove his car at him and Stella and …

Gavin took out a large white handkerchief from his pocket and wiped his face. It was remarkably warm today, even for "flaming June" and his stab-resistant vest made him sweat. Then he composed himself and stepped out into the sunshine of the back garden.

'I've got it all off,' he told Dean. 'Where do you want these?'

'Give them to me, answered Wayne. 'I'll put them away.'

Gavin handed over the stepladders and Wayne carried them across the grass to the shed. Dean hurried ahead to open the door for him.

'I've taught Star to fetch,' Carl told Gavin proudly. 'Watch!'

The two police officers looked on as Carl threw a rubber ring across the grass. Star bounded after it, snatched it up in her mouth as it bounced into a rhododendron bush, and brought it back to the boy. She stood looking up at him, her tail wagging furiously.

'Good girl! Sit!' he commanded.

The puppy continued to stand there, looking round at all the watching faces. Perhaps she was put off by having such a large audience. Carl put out his hand and pressed down firmly on her rump. 'Sit!' he repeated.

Star gave in and squatted down on her haunches. Her tail continued to wag, swishing against the grass.

'Give!' Carl put out his hand and took hold of the ring. At first Star seemed reluctant to give up her trophy, but then somewhere in her doggy brain it occurred to her that if she gave the ring back, the boy might throw it for her again. She opened her mouth and let the ring go.

'Well done Star! Good girl!' Carl patted her on the head and then looked round at Gavin and Stella. 'Isn't she clever? I bet she'll be an even better police dog than Q!'

'With such a good trainer, I wouldn't be at all surprised,' Gavin agreed. Then he turned to Wayne and Dean, who had returned from putting away the ladder. 'Thank you for giving Craig a job. He seems much happier with you than at that other place.'

'No,' Dean smiled back. 'We're the ones who ought to be thanking you. Craig's completely transformed the mail-order business. He's the only one of the lot of us who's ever worked in a warehouse before and he came up with all sorts of ideas that we'd never thought of.'

'And he's got such an air of authority,' Wayne added. 'You can tell he's been in charge of people before. The packers all have tremendous respect for him.'

Gavin stood staring for several seconds. This did not sound like Craig at all. 'I'm glad he's fitted in,' he said at last. 'I was afraid … he hasn't had any flashbacks or panic attacks then?'

Wayne and Dean exchanged glances.

'Well, there was a rather funny incident.' Dean said. 'A helicopter flew over while he was outside with a couple of the guys loading the van. Craig instinctively dived for cover and it took them about ten minutes to get him out from under the van. I suspect it was more embarrassment than anything else, after the initial reflex response. But anyway, I'd briefed them all before he started, so they just took it in their stride.'

'If anything, I think it enhanced his reputation,' Wayne added. 'They all think he's a war hero now.'

'That's great!' Stella said enthusiastically. 'It's time Craig had something go right for him.'

'He's had a tough time of it,' Gavin agreed. 'It's been hard for him settling to civilian life. I'm glad your guys understood and cut him some slack. Now we'd better be getting on.' He turned to Carl again. 'Thank you for showing me how well Star's coming on. You're doing a good job there – you and Harry both,' he added seeing the younger boy looking enviously at his brother, 'but now, we really must be going.'

They carried on patrolling the streets, exchanging brief greetings as they went with those householders who were outside busily weeding their gardens, painting their front doors or doing other DIY jobs that being kept at home all day had inspired them to attempt. Stella reflected that Lockdown would have been a whole lot harder if the weather had not been unusually warm and sunny. She could not remember another year when it had hardly rained between mid-March and June. As they walked along Chichester Road, she noticed that Trevor Whittle's taxi was parked out in the street instead of in its normal place on the drive. Coming closer, she heard the sound of a basketball being bounced on the concrete.

'Good afternoon Mr Hughes!' Trevor called out as they passed. 'And Miss – I'm sorry, I don't know your name?'

'I'm Stella – Stella Gilbert.' Stella looked round in surprise at this friendly greeting. Trevor Whittle was standing there with a basketball in his hand, bouncing it absent-mindedly on the ground every so often to punctuate his words. Leo was there too, waiting patiently for his father to finish his conversation so that they could resume their shooting practice.

'Have you got a minute?' Trevor continued. 'Yvonne would like to speak to you.'

'Of course,' Gavin smiled. 'Where …?'

'I'll let her know you're here.'

Trevor threw the ball to Leo, who immediately began dribbling it round the drive in complicated patterns, which reminded Stella of the figure skating that she had sometimes watched on TV. His father danced round him on his way past and disappeared down the tunnel that led to the back of the house.

'How're things?' Gavin asked Leo.

'OK,' Leo answered without pausing in bouncing the ball, then, 'good: things are good now, thanks.'

He positioned himself in the centre of the drive and took aim at the hoop. The ball bounced off the rim and he ran to catch it, almost colliding with his mother as she emerged from the tunnel. 'Sorry Mum!'

'Just watch where you're going,' she smiled back, hurrying past with a piece of paper in her hand.

Stella stared at her as she headed towards them. She was wearing a cotton print dress under a clean white apron; her hair was neatly braided and her eyes had lost the vacant, half-asleep look that Stella was accustomed to seeing.

She walked up to Gavin, holding out the paper. 'Could you give Chrissie this? It's a recipe she asked me for. It's easier writing it down than doing it over the phone. And tell her I made those flapjacks of hers and Leo loved them.'

'Yes, of course.' Gavin took the paper and then stepped back to preserve their two metre distance. 'Chrissie told me you'd been chatting. She'll be pleased to hear that you're looking so well now.'

'Yes, well …' Yvonne dropped her eyes and started twisting the fingers of her two hands together. Then she looked up at Gavin and said earnestly, 'You must thank her for me. I'm sure she's got much more important things to do than … And tell her I really am going to stick with it this time.'

'I will,' Gavin promised.

Yes, well … I'd better let you get on then.' Yvonne turned to go and then swivelled back round again. 'That little boy you were looking for? Is he OK?'

'Yes. He's doing fine.'

'Good. I'm glad he's safe. I wouldn't want … Sorry, I'd better go. You won't forget to thank Chrissie, will you?'

'I won't.'

Stella watched as she went back up the drive and into the darkness of the passageway. She walked much faster than on previous occasions, almost with a spring in her step by comparison. It was hard to believe this was the same woman that she had seen slumped on the sofa in her pyjamas, the TV remote in one hand and a glass of gin in the other, only a few weeks ago.

'Your mum's right,' Gavin called to Leo. 'We'd better be going.'

'What did she mean?' Stella asked, as soon as they were far enough away not to be overheard. 'About sticking with it, I mean.'

'She's off the booze. According to Chrissie, she hasn't had a drink for over a fortnight.'

'Is that why she's so … different? I mean: is how she was just now what she's really like?'

'I suppose that depends what you mean. What is anyone really like?'

'I don't understand.'

'People change. The last few months have shown me that. Things change them. Things like … '

'Like seeing your friends blown up by the Taliban?' ventured Stella, carefully avoiding the more personal examples that immediately sprang to mind.

'Yes,' Gavin nodded, 'or finding your son hanging from his neck in your hall. I never knew Mrs Whittle until after Harry was killed, but piecing together things she and Leo told me, I fancy she tends to turn to drink whenever something happens that she can't cope with. So, when you ask what she's really like, I don't know what to say. Well, you've seen, haven't you? It all depends whether she's drinking or not.'

'She sounded just now like she wanted to kick the habit for good.'

'I'm sure she does, and I'm sure she means to do it, but … well I've seen lots of people try and fail, so …'

'I suppose you mean all the winos on the streets,' suggested Stella.

'Not just them. I was thinking more of some of my old mates in the force. It's an easy habit to fall into, what with the long shifts, the unsocial hours and some of the things you see.'

Stella didn't know what to say. She hoped her boss wasn't gearing up to some sort of confession. She'd never known Gavin to drink to excess. He didn't even join in with the pint down the pub at the end of the day, the way most of their colleagues did (or used to do, before COVID changed everything) preferring to get back home to Chrissie, but …? He had been under a lot of stress, what with Kenny's death and now his killers being out of jail for nobody knew how long before their trial.

'Chrissie's given her the number of Alcoholics Anonymous, but, of course, their meetings are all virtual ones now. My best hope is that Trevor will keep her going for long enough to … but then there'll be the trial coming up; that'll be another trigger point.'

'*Mr* Whittle seemed a lot nicer today too,' Stella said, trying to find something more to be optimistic about, 'and Leo seemed happier too.'

'Yes. That's the thing; it affects the whole family.' Gavin looked at his watch. 'We'd better hurry. We mustn't be late for the judging!'

* * *

'I don't know why Chrissie wants *me* to be there,' Sylvia muttered to Stan as they wrestled with the computer, trying to click on the link in the email that she had sent them. 'All I did was to make the clothes for that bear she gave me to dress.'

'I suppose she wants to thank you in front of the class,' Stan answered. 'There! That's done it. It says, *the host will let you in soon.* That's what it says when Bernie does one of these with us.'

The screen changed and they could see Chrissie in a large rectangle with Gavin sitting beside her. Above them were four smaller rectangles: in one, they could see themselves; the next held Bernie against a backdrop that they recognised as her living room; the third window displayed Jonah, with Peter just visible on his left; and finally, they saw Stella sitting on her own in what appeared to be a bedroom.

Then what seemed like dozens more windows opened, as all the children from Chrissie's class were allowed into the meeting.

'Goodness!' Stan exclaimed. 'How many are there?'

'Only ten,' Sylvia told him. 'That's what Chrissie said, anyway. It's small classes because they all have special needs.'

Eventually the screen settled down.

'She's turned us off!' Stan pointed out to Sylvia. 'Look! The microphone thingy's gone red.'

'She's *muted* everyone,' Sylvia agreed, proud to have learned the correct terminology. 'It's so that everyone doesn't have to listen to you rabbiting on! Now shush, I think she's going to start.'

'Welcome everyone to the final of our Name-that-Bear competition,' Chrissie declared when everyone was assembled in the virtual classroom. 'And let me begin by introducing you all to our panel of judges. Some of you may already have met my husband, PC Gavin Hughes. He's been walking the beat as an officer in Thames Valley Police for thirty-two years now.'

She paused while the children, and accompanying parents, gave a round of applause. Stan noticed that the microphone symbols next to each face suddenly changed from red to white.

'At the other end of the spectrum, we have PC Stella Gilbert, who only joined the force last year, but has already been making her mark as a first-rate police officer.'

The screen magically changed so that Stella's rectangle grew to become the centre of attention, while Chrissie and Gavin were relegated to a small window at the top of the screen. There was more applause.

'How did she do that?' asked Stan.

'Bernie's controlling it all from her end,' Sylvia told him. 'She's what's called the *host* of the meeting. She can mute and un-mute people and choose which window is the big one. Oh dear!' she added in a lower voice, 'I think everyone else probably heard all that.'

'And chairing our expert panel today,' Chrissie continued, 'we have celebrity cop and police hero, Detective Chief Inspector Jonah Porter!'

The windows were re-sized again and Jonah appeared, large as life, in the centre of the screen. He smiled round acknowledging the clapping and cheering coming from the excited audience. Then all the microphone icons went red again, apart from Jonah's, and he began speaking.

'Thank you very much, and thank you, Mrs Hughes, for inviting me to be part of this exciting event. We've read all your research reports and watched your videos and I'm sure that my fellow judges will agree that they were all of an extremely high standard and it was very hard to choose which should be the winner. In the end, we narrowed them down to a shortlist of five, which we're going to play to you in a minute, so that you can see what we were up against in picking a single winner. They are: ...'

He paused as a drum roll sounded across the airwaves, powered by Peter, who had found one on the internet and was now playing it on his phone for everyone to hear.

'Alfie, with *PC Fuzz*!'

Bernie unmuted the microphones to allow a round of applause to be heard. A small boy with brown hair flopping over his eyes momentarily occupied the large window on the screen.

'Rakiya, with *PC Leo*.'

More applause and a brief view of a girl in a wheelchair, who waved one arm jerkily above her head in acknowledgement.

'Elsa, with *PC Gotcha* ... Archie, with *PC Growler* ... and Clarissa, with *PC Bertie Bear*. Well done to all of them!'

Bernie allowed a final, longer, round of applause before muting everyone to enable Jonah to introduce the first video. After it finished, the three judges all said a few words about why they had chosen it for the short list.

When all the talks had been heard and all the judges' comments made, Chrissie took over proceedings again.

'And now the moment you've all been waiting for,' she declared dramatically. 'DCI Porter is going to reveal the winner!'

Another drum roll sounded and Jonah's face filled the screen. He smiled towards the camera as he waited for silence.

'And the winner is ... Rakiya Rahman with PC Leo!' Jonah waited for the resultant applause to die down (finally muted by Bernie) before continuing. 'It was a hard choice, but in the end it was a unanimous verdict. We all thought that it was a very clever idea to take the initials L-E-O, standing for Law Enforcement Officer, and make them into a name – especially a name that means "lion". All our officers try to be as brave as lions, and, as Rakiya pointed out so well in her talk, PC Kenny Hughes, whom we are remembering here, certainly was. Well done Rakiya!'

'Thank you, DCI Porter.' The focus of the meeting switched to Chrissie again. 'And now, Rakiya, I have great pleasure in presenting you with your prize, which was made by a very talented friend of mine, who is here today, Mrs Sylvia Corbridge!'

All of a sudden Sylvia could see herself staring out from the large rectangle in the centre of the screen. Stan was there too, looking over her shoulder. Was she supposed to say something? Why hadn't they warned her about this? She forced a smile and waved back, her hand appearing very large on the screen. To her great relief, her image was soon replaced by Chrissie, holding up the bear that Sylvia had dressed.

'As you can see, this bear is a female police officer,' Chrissie told them. 'You can tell that because she's wearing a bowler hat instead of a helmet. And Sylvia has made prizes for each of the runners-up as well.' She put down the bear and held up a small piece of dark fabric, stiffened with card and embroidered with the letters ER in silver, twisting it round in an effort to get the camera to focus on it. 'Police badges for you all to wear!'

'Now the question is,' Jonah broke in, 'what are you going to call *this* bear?'

'I've got a good idea.'

Everyone stared at the sound of a disembodied voice that none of them could recognise. Chrissie, still occupying the large window in the centre of the screen, turned round in her seat and seemed to be beckoning to someone to come closer. Eventually a man's face appeared next to hers.

'It's Craig!' Sylvia whispered to Stan. 'You know! That homeless man they took in after-'

'Sshhh!' Stan hissed. 'Let's hear what he's got to say.'

'I think she ought to be called Stella,' Craig said, looking very uncomfortable in front of the camera, 'because she's going to be a stellar police officer!' Then he dropped his voice and added, 'like one or two others I know.'

THANK YOU

Thank you for taking the time to read Lost in Lockdown. If you enjoyed it, please consider telling your friends or posting a short review. Word of mouth is an author's best friend and much appreciated. Thank you,

RECIPES

PETER'S CARROT & COURGETTE SOUP

Ingredients

1lb courgettes, peeled and diced

1 lb carrots, chopped

2 onions

½ teaspoon marmite (optional) or use your favourite seasoning

Small clove garlic (or use dried garlic granules)

1 vegetable stock cube

1 tablespoon tomato puree (or to taste)

1½ pints boiling water

Method

1. Put all the ingredients into a large pan and boil until the vegetables are soft.

2. Pour into a blender and blend to soup consistency.

3. Return to the pan and simmer for a further 20 minutes, adding more seasoning to taste if required.

Serve with bread rolls or "door-step" slices of bread.

WAYNE'S CHOCOLATE PUDDING

Ingredients

2 ounces margarine	3 ounces brown sugar
4 ounces self-raising flour	1 ounce cocoa
2 eggs	3 ounces dark chocolate

Method

1. Set the oven on 180°C /350°F / Gas mark 4.
2. Chop the chocolate into small pieces.
3. Cream together the margarine and brown sugar.
4. Beat in the eggs.
5. Add the flour and cocoa and mix well.
6. Add the chopped chocolate.
7. Bake for 40 minutes.
8. Serve with chocolate sauce, white sauce, custard or cream.

EDDIE'S CHILD-FRIENDLY RICE BISCUITS

Ingredients

4 ounces ground rice

3 ounces sugar

4 ounces self-raising flour

1 dessertspoon golden syrup

4 ounces butter or margarine

Method

1. Put the flour, ground rice and sugar into a bowl and rub in the butter or margarine. Alternatively mix in a food processor.

2. Add the golden syrup and mix well to form a soft dough.

3. Roll out on a floured surface.

4. Cut out using biscuit cutters and put on a baking tray.

5. Bake for 20 minutes on 180°C /350°F / Gas mark 4.

6. Cool on a wire rack.

Makes 12 large biscuits or more small ones.

CHRISSIE'S CHOCOLATE CINNAMON CAKE

Ingredients

4 ounces margarine	8 ounces self-raising flour
4 ounces sugar	2 ounces cocoa
4 eggs	1 teaspoon cinnamon

Method

1. Line a 7" round baking tin with baking parchment.
2. Set the oven to 190°C /375°F /Gas Mark 5.
3. Cream together the margarine and sugar.
4. Beat the eggs and add them to the mixture.
5. Sift the flour and cocoa into the basin.
6. Mix well.
7. Pour the mixture into the tin.
8. Bake for 30 - 40 minutes, testing by inserting a knife into the centre. If it comes out clean, the cake is done.

CHOCOLATE FUDGE PUDDING

Ingredients

Pudding

1 ounce butter

4 ounces sugar

2 eggs

3 ounces self-raising flour

2 ounces cocoa powder

½ teaspoon vanilla essence

1 tablespoon milk

Sauce

4 ounces brown sugar

2 ounces cocoa powder

½ pint boiling water

Method

1. Set oven to 190°C /375°F /Gas Mark 5.
2. Place all the pudding ingredients in a food processor and mix together.
3. Pour out into a shallow ovenproof dish.
4. Put the brown sugar and cocoa together in a jug and pour the boiling water over them. Mix until they dissolve.
5. Pour the sauce over the pudding mixture.
6. Put in the oven and bake for 40 minutes.

PETER'S PINEAPPLE UPSIDE-DOWN CAKE

Ingredients

1 tin pineapple rings in juice
4 ounces softened margarine
8 ounces self-raising flour

Glacé cherries
4 ounces sugar
2 eggs

Method

1. Line a 1-inch deep baking tray with baking parchment.
2. Using a fork, take out the pineapple rings from the tin, one at a time, and arrange them on the baking parchment, covering the bottom of the tray.
3. Place a glacé cherry in the centre of each pineapple ring. If you like, you can add more cherries in the gaps between the rings.
4. Cream together the margarine and sugar.
5. Beat in the eggs and pineapple juice.
6. Sift in the flour to make a soft cake mixture. If it's too runny add more flour.
7. Pour the mixture over the pineapple rings and spread it out evenly.
8. Bake for 40 minutes at 190°C /375°F /Gas Mark 5.
9. Check that the cake is set firm before turning it out on to a wire rack to cool.

WAYNE'S CHOCOLATE ICING

Ingredients

120g dark chocolate
1 tablespoon hazelnut chocolate spread (Nutella or supermarket own brand)

Method

1. Melt the chocolate over a pan of hot water or in the microwave.
2. Add the chocolate spread and mix thoroughly.
3. Pour over the cake.

Makes enough to ice an eight-inch round cake.

HIKERS' LUNCHES

Ingredients

14 ounces strong flour (white, wholemeal or a mixture)

1 teaspoon yeast

½ teaspoon salt

1 teaspoon sugar

2½ tablespoons vegetable oil

8 thick sausages (or 1lb sausage meat)

Method

1. Make bread dough in the usual way. A bread maker is ideal.

2. Remove the skins from the sausages (or use sausage meat).

3. Wrap each sausage in dough.

4. Leave to rise in a warm place for about half an hour.

5. Set the oven to 200°C /400°F /Gas Mark 6.

6. Bake for 20 minutes, then reduce the temperature to 180°C /350°F / Gas mark 4 for a further 20 minutes.

7. Cool on a wire rack.

STRAWBERRY TRIFLE

Ingredients

1 tin strawberries

1 sachet strawberry jelly crystals (to make 1pint)

Trifle sponges or sponge fingers

1 pint milk

2 tablespoons custard powder

1 tablespoon sugar

½ pint whipping cream

Method

1. Dissolve the jelly crystals in ½ pint boiling water.
2. Add the strawberries including any juice or syrup.
3. Arrange the sponges in the base of a large serving dish.
4. Pour over the jelly mixture, making sure that the pieces of sponge are saturated.
5. Leave in a cool place to set.
6. Make the custard using the milk, custard powder and sugar (or use tinned custard).
7. Pour the custard on to the top of the trifle and leave to cool.
8. Whip the cream and spread out over the top of the custard layer.
9. Sprinkle with sugar strands or hundreds and thousands.

CHRISSIE'S MULTIGRAIN CHOCOLATE FLAPJACKS

Ingredients

4 ounces oat flakes	6 ounces demerara sugar
2 ounces rye flakes	6 ounces butter or margarine
2 ounces barley flakes	2 ounces raisins

For the topping: 8 ounces chocolate

Method

1. Melt the butter and sugar together in a pan.
2. Remove from the heat and mix in the cereal flakes and raisins.
3. Pour into a shallow baking tin and press down firmly.
4. Bake for 30 minutes on 190°C /375°F /Gas Mark 5
5. Mark into squares with a sharp knife, then leave to cool.
6. Melt the chocolate in a bowl over a pan of boiling water or in a microwave.
7. Pour the chocolate over the flapjacks and spread out evenly.
8. After the chocolate has set, turn out and break into squares along the marked lines.

ACKNOWLEDGEMENTS

I would like to thank many Facebook friends, especially those from the *Pesky Methodist* group, for commenting on ideas for developing this book. In particular, many people suggested names for the police teddy bear, the winning entry (Leo) being supplied by Lorraine Reed from *Dr Graham Clingbine's book, author & reading group.*

I am grateful to Gillian Gilbert for reading the manuscript, giving helpful comments and pointing out typographical errors.

I am indebted to the authors of a wide range of internet resources, which have been invaluable for researching the background to this book. In particular, *Care for the Family*'s (https://www.careforthefamily.org.uk/) personal stories provided insight into the different ways in which parents may be affected by the death of a grown-up child. . Other sources include:

- Wikipedia (https://en.wikipedia.org/),

- Google Maps (www.google.co.uk/maps),

- OpenStreetMap (https://www.openstreetmap.org/),

- The Mum Educates (https://themumeducates.com),

- Behind Blue Lines (https://www.behindbluelines.co.uk/the-podcast/).

I consulted a number of publications during the writing, including:

- *KS2 English Targeted Question Book: Grammar, Punctuation & Spelling - Year 3 (CGP KS2 English)*, Coordination Group Publications Ltd (CGP) (22 May 2014), ISBN: 978-1782941316

- *Treating PTSD: A Compassion-Focused CBT Approach*, Shirley Porter, Routledge 2018, ISBN 978-1-138-30333-1

- *Understanding Victims of Interpersonal Violence: A Guide for Investigators and Prosecutors*, Veronique N Valliere, Routledge 2020, ISBN 1-4987-8048-3

DISCLAIMER

This book is a work of fiction. Any references to real people, events, establishments, organisations or locales are intended only to provide a sense of authenticity and are used fictitiously. All of the characters and events are entirely invented by the author. Any resemblances to persons living or dead are purely coincidental.

Many of the locations and institutions that feature in this book are real. Their inhabitants and employees, however, are purely fictional. In particular:

- You will search in vain for Chichester Road, Lewes Road or Arundel Road in Rose Hill;

- Lichfield, St Luke's and Holy Cross colleges are all fictitious;

- None of the police personnel are based on any officers from Thames Valley Police or any other police service.

- The school where Chrissie Hughes works is imaginary as are the staff and students.

MORE ABOUT THE CHARACTERS IN THIS BOOK

This book is the second of a trilogy of stories about Gavin and Chrissie Hughes in the aftermath of the sudden death of their son, Kenny. The first in this series, **Weed Killers**, was published in 2020.

Many of the characters feature in the fourteen **Bernie Fazakerley Mysteries**:

1. **Two Little Dickie Birds**: a murder mystery for DI Peter Johns and his Sergeant, Paul Godwin.

2. **Murder of a Martian**: Peter and Jonah solve a double murder and Peter meets Martin Reiss for the first time.

3. **Grave Offence**: Peter investigates an assault and a suspicious death, while Jonah is in rehab in the spinal injuries centre.

4. **Awayday**: a traditional detective story set among the dons of Lichfield College.

5. **Death on the Algarve:** a mystery for Bernie and her friends to tackle while on holiday in Portugal.

6. **Mystery over the Mersey**: a murder mystery set in Liverpool.

7. **Sorrowful Mystery**: Jonah investigates a child abduction and Peter embarks on a new journey of faith.

8. **In my Liverpool Home**: Bernie and her friends return to Liverpool to investigate a suspicious death in Aunty Dot's Care Home.

9. **Organ Failure**: a body is discovered under the organ in St Cyprian's Church and Jonah is called in to investigate.

10. **Rainbow Warrior**: One of their friends is injured in a hit-and-run incident and Jonah is convinced that this is attempted murder.

11. **Admission of Innocence**: Father Damien calls Peter and Jonah out of retirement to solve a murder case and prevent a miscarriage of justice.

12. **Lethal Mix**: Three of Lucy's student friends are injured in an anti-Muslim hate crime in Liverpool. Jonah, Peter and Bernie assist Merseyside Police to bring their attacker to justice.

13. **A Secret Gardener?** Bernie's friend Martin discovers a body in the Fellows' Garden of his Oxford College.

14. **Crowd of Witnesses**: Jonah decides to write his memoirs, beginning with a murder investigation from 1982.

Bernie Fazakerley also appears in three other novels:

- **Changing Scenes of Life**: Jonah Porter's life story, told through the medium of his favourite hymns.

- **Despise not your Mother**: the story of Bernie's quest to learn about her dead husband's past.

And there's a book of short stories, in which Peter narrates his side of the story:

- **My Life of Crime**: the collected memoirs of DI Peter Johns. This includes some episodes that appear in other books, but told from a new perspective, as well as some completely new stories.

You can find them all on Judy Ford's Amazon Author page:

www.amazon.co.uk/-/e/B0193I5B1M

Visit the Bernie Fazakerley Publications Facebook page here: www.facebook.com/Bernie.Fazakerley.Publications.

Follow Judy on Twitter: Twitter.com/JudyFordAuthor

GLOSSARY OF UK POLICE RANKS

Uniformed police

Chief Constable (CC) – Has overall charge of a regional police force, such as Thames Valley Police, which covers Oxford and a large surrounding area.

Deputy Chief Constable (DCC) – The senior discipline authority for each force. 2nd in command to the CC.

Assistant Chief Constable (ACC) – 4 in the Thames Valley Police Service, each responsible for a policy area.

Chief Superintendent ('Chief Super') – Head of a policing area or department.

Police Superintendent – Responsible for a local area within a police force.

Chief Inspector (CI) – Responsible for overseeing a team in a local area.

Police Inspector – Senior operational officer overseeing officers on duty 24/7.

Police Sergeant – Supervises a team of officers.

Police Constable (PC) – 'Bobby on the beat'. Likely to be the first to arrive in response to an emergency call.

Police Community Support Officer (PCSO) – A uniformed civilian member of the police service.

Crime Investigation Department (CID) – Plain clothes officers

Detective Superintendent (DS) – Responsible for crime investigation in a local area.

Detective Chief Inspector (DCI) – Responsible for overseeing a crime investigation team in a local area. May be the Senior Investigating Officer heading up a criminal investigation.

Detective Inspector (DI) – Oversees crime investigation 24/7. May be the Senior Investigating Officer heading up a criminal investigation.

Detective Sergeant (DS) – Supervises a team of CID officers.

Detective Constable (DC) – One of a team of officers investigating crimes.

These descriptions are based on information from the following sources:

[1] Mental Health Cop blog, by Inspector Michael Brown, Mental Health co-ordinator, College of Policing.
https://mentalhealthcop.wordpress.com/, accessed 31st March 2017.
[2] Thames Valley Police website,
https://www.thamesvalley.police.uk , accessed 31st March 2017.

ABOUT THE AUTHOR

Like her main character, Bernie Fazakerley, Judy Ford is an Oxford graduate and a mathematician. Unlike Bernie, Judy grew up in a middle-class family in the South London stockbroker belt. After moving to the North West and working in Liverpool, Judy fell in love with the Scouse people and created Bernie Fazakerley to reflect their unique qualities. She has worked in academia and in the NHS.

As a Methodist Local Preacher, Judy often tells her congregation, "I see my role as asking the questions and leaving you to think out your own answers." She carries this philosophy forward into her writing and she hopes that readers will find themselves challenged to think as well as being entertained.